"I'm no good for you," Ned said.

"No good for you at all. I'm a person without a future, which means I have nothing to offer you. Absolutely nothing. I'd never forgive myself if I didn't make that clear to you. I want you so damn much that every atom in me is aching. But I have to be sure you know what you're getting into."

Shelley walked across her shop to the big front window and looked out. Ned had put his cards on the table and was leaving the next move to her. Her mind twirled like a kaleidoscope from which a single pattern was emerging. If she and Ned were to be together for only a single night in her life, it would be better—infinitely better—than never being together at all.

She turned to him. Her voice was unsteady as she said, "Please...come home with me tonight."

Dear Reader,

Magic. It dazzles our senses, sometimes touches our souls. And what could be more magical than romance?

Silhouette **Special Edition** novels feature believable, compelling women and men in lifelike situations, but our authors never forget the wondrous magic of falling in love. How do these writers blend believability with enchantment? Author Sherryl Woods puts it this way:

"More. That's what Silhouette **Special Edition** is about. For a writer, this Silhouette line offers a chance to create romances with more depth and complexity, more intriguing characters, more heightened sensuality. In the pages of these wonderful love stories, more sensitive issues can be interwoven with more tenderness, more humor and more excitement. And when it all works, you have what these books are really all about—more magic!"

Joining Sherryl Woods this month to conjure up half a dozen versions of this "special" magic are Robyn Carr, Debbie Macomber, Barbara Catlin, Maggi Charles and Jennifer Mikels.

Month after month, we hope Silhouette **Special Edition** casts its spell on you, dazzling your senses *and* touching your soul. Are there any particular ingredients you like best in your "love potion"? The authors and editors of Silhouette **Special Edition** always welcome your comments.

Sincerely,

Leslie Kazanjian, Senior Editor
Silhouette Books
300 East 42nd Street
New York, N.Y. 10017

MAGGI CHARLES
A Man of Mystery

Silhouette Special Edition

Published by Silhouette Books New York

America's Publisher of Contemporary Romance

For Alexander Hudson Koehler... with a lot of love.
If you grow up to be half as wonderful
as your father is, you'll be very wonderful indeed.

SILHOUETTE BOOKS
300 East 42nd St., New York, N.Y. 10017

ISBN: 0-373-09520-1

First Silhouette Books printing April 1989

Printed in the U.S.A.

MAGGI CHARLES

has had a varied writing career, contributing to government reports, public-relations releases, newspapers and magazines. Her nonfiction topics include gourmet food, travel, antiques and history. Primarily, however, she concentrates on her true love—romance fiction and mystery novels. Born and raised in New York City, she has lived for the past twenty years on Cape Cod with her writer husband. They have two sons and two grandchildren.

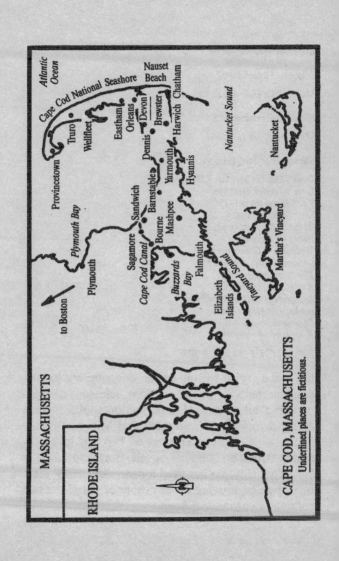

CAPE COD, MASSACHUSETTS
Underlined places are fictitious.

Chapter One

The snow began to drift down toward the middle of the afternoon, the flakes gentle at first, melting as soon as they touched concrete and asphalt. Then, abruptly, the pattern changed. Driven by a mounting wind, the white crystals started to whirl faster and faster in a frenzied ballet, swirling across the parking lot and pirouetting past storefronts and around building corners, leaving drifting, glacial trails in their wake. Pausing in the task of trimming her shop window with lengths of gold and silver tinsel, Shelley noticed that the mall was beginning to look like a Christmas-card scene.

Did the change in weather mean he wouldn't come?

Possibly, she conceded, and was startled by a sudden stab of disappointment.

Frowning slightly, she moved a box of large gold and silver satin balls closer to the window, then tried to concentrate on the task at hand as she spaced first a gold ball then a silver one between the tinsel loops. But thoughts of the man who had become such a mystery to her kept intruding.

Each late afternoon for the past three weeks—except on Thanksgiving Day and on Sundays when the shop was closed—he'd been coming to Video Vibes to rent cassettes. But she knew no more about him now than she had the first time he had walked through the door.

His taste in videos offered no clues. Rather, it only provoked her curiosity about him all the more. The variety of his film choices, alone, would have been enough to make her aware of him and curious about him even if nothing else had. Eclectic was putting it mildly! Usually, he rented two videos each weeknight—three on Saturdays—and they ran the gamut from old classics to science fiction, romance, horror, war stories, comedy, mystery, musicals, adventure, even cartoons. She doubted if he had missed a single category in the shop.

He seldom bothered with the latest releases, and Shelley assumed maybe that was because they cost more. She rented most of the cassettes for two dollars a night, but the recent releases were four, and at that there was usually a waiting list for them.

She didn't know, of course, that cost was a factor with him, but it was a logical assumption—at least, if one were to judge by his clothing. Or, she corrected herself, the little she'd seen of it. Consistently, he wore a shabby tweed overcoat that was sizes too large for him, and a battered Irish wool hat that long ago had lost its shape.

The weather had been unusually cold since Thanksgiving. Because a lot of her customers were older people who lived in nearby condominiums, Shelley was careful to keep her shop comfortably warm. But her mystery man had never so much as unbuttoned his overcoat while searching out a video, nor had he ever removed the mis-shapen hat.

She couldn't imagine anyone wearing outer clothes like his if they had the money to buy more attractive ones. On the other hand, the memory of his extracting a hundred-dollar bill from his wallet, just one bill nestled among others, remained imprinted in her mind.

Yes, he was an enigma. And regardless of his shabby appearance he was definitely attractive. Provocatively so, making Shelley wish, every time she saw him, that she could see more of him. That she had the gumption to ask him to take off his coat, his hat, and to remove the tinted glasses that obscured the color of his eyes.

He was tall, reasonably young—Shelley placed him in the mid-to late-thirties—and she liked what she could see of his face. He had good, clear-cut features. A broad forehead, straight nose, firm, strong chin. Also, despite the outdated, oversized clothes, there was a decided air of confidence about him. A quality that gave the impression of a person who was used to being in charge of things.

She liked his voice, too. Well-modulated, it had a good timbre to it. But, though she'd strained to detect the note of a regional accent that might offer a hint to where he had come from, there wasn't any. He spoke what might properly be called well-educated, standard English.

To add to the puzzle, she mused, as she judiciously hung a gold ball and then a silver one, there was the tricky matter of his name.

She'd been at the checkout desk on his first visit, when he'd approached with an assortment of videos. She'd automatically given him a form to fill out, suggesting simultaneously that he might like to join Video Vibes's club.

"We rent cassettes for approximately half price to club members," she told him. "There's a ten dollar membership fee, but if you watch many movies you'll repay the cost of it in no time at all. If you'll put down your name and address, and a phone number where we can reach you..."

When he didn't answer her she glanced up at him and was surprised to see that he was frowning. Then he said, "There wouldn't be much point to my joining your club. But...I do want to rent a VCR from you."

Surprised, thus sounding more flippant than she intended, she retorted, "Why not buy a VCR? The rental costs are high, out of necessity. We can't risk loss and damage, which means we must pay insurance on the equipment. So, again, you'd save money in the long run if you'd make the purchase. We can arrange for time payments."

"It's not that," he said. "The fact is, I don't know how long I'll be around the Cape, so there'd be no more point to my buying a VCR than there would be to my joining your club."

"I see," Shelley mumbled, after a rather uncomfortable moment. "Well," she said then, "suppose you fill out the form for our records. We'll need that information."

He nodded and Shelley stepped over to help another customer. When she turned back to him and scanned the form to see what he had written, she found he had scrawled the single name, Alexander, and nothing more.

Both irritated and perplexed, she looked up at him, her gaze meeting his tinted lenses. "I really do need more than this, you know," she informed him rather tersely.

Almost at once, her attention was drawn to his mouth. The slight smile that curved his lips—a very slight smile—

made her conscious, maybe a bit too conscious, of the perfection and fullness of his mouth. Generous, she thought absently. If there's any truth to facial analysis, one would have to say that he must be a very generous person, with a mouth like that. And . . . passionate.

The word rang silently, a small bell only she could hear.

He said, "Look, there's really no other information that would be of use to you at the moment. I doubt I'm going to be staying in the place where I'm living now, and I have no telephone." He paused. "Here," he decided, "why don't I simply give you some money as . . . security. For both the VCR and the cassettes."

As he spoke, he thrust a hand into the pocket of his shabby tweed coat and withdrew a black leather wallet. He extracted a bill, and Shelley noted with surprise that it was a hundred-dollar bill.

"Suppose you keep this as a deposit," he suggested.

From the way he was dressed, she didn't see how he could possibly afford to toss out a hundred-dollar bill as a deposit.

"Please," he said, and she caught that note of assurance in his voice. "It will be the simplest way for both of us."

"All right," Shelley said, though she still wasn't happy with the situation. And a few minutes later she signed over both a VCR and a very strange combination of videos to him.

The next day he brought back the two cassettes and spent nearly an hour picking out another two. And every afternoon since, he had followed the same procedure.

He was always pleasant. And he didn't exactly avoid encounters with her. But she noticed that if there was someone else around to check out videos he usually went to the other person. And when he had to take his cassettes to her he kept conversation to a minimum, giving her the impression that he'd learned the art of rebuffing any verbal overtures.

All of which only whetted her curiosity all the more.

Now she paused in her decorating for a moment to look outside. The snow was coming down more heavily than ever. It was almost five-thirty, and she doubted she would have many, if any, customers on such a night.

Usually she closed at six. But with Christmas only a little more than three weeks away she had decided to start staying open until nine each night, maybe even until ten. With a near blizzard raging outside, though, there didn't seem much point to hanging around tonight.

The business was new enough to her so that she was still feeling her way. She had opened her shop just after Labor Day, figuring that by the time "the season" came to Cape Cod next summer she'd be experienced enough to handle the boom.

For that matter, the off-season wasn't any longer the quiet time it used to be. Each year people came earlier and stayed later, and so business had been quite good.

No complaints, Shelley thought, as she placed the last satin ball and stood back to survey the effect. *I think I've finally found my niche.*

She had rented the big family homestead she had inherited from her grandmother and was living in a small winterized cottage on the property. She had a cat named Puffy, an excellent stereo with a good collection of records and a small circle of compatible friends and acquaintances, some of whom dated back to her high school days here on Cape Cod, some of whom had loomed on the scene more recently. Occasionally she went to Boston to a performance of the ballet, or maybe a musical or a good play. And she had friends in Boston, too, who she saw when she was in the city.

Considering the circumstances that had made up her life thus far, she told herself, as she reached for some strands of gold and silver tinsel to drape along the shelves, she'd done a reasonably good job of pulling herself together and creating a pretty full existence for herself.

Earlier, there'd been enough excitement, emotion, chaos, trauma to last her...forever. She could string nouns together like Christmas-tree lights, she thought wryly, and most of them would apply to the past she had closed a firm door upon. Now, at age twenty-eight, she wanted just what she had here and had worked very hard to get. Peace, primarily.

Peace. Her back was to the window and the door as she thought about peace and the season of the year that was supposed to exemplify it. She couldn't remember when she'd last truly enjoyed Christmas, but she was determined to enjoy it this year. She had been thinking of having some friends over to the cottage for eggnog, and maybe doing something old-fashioned such as stringing popcorn and cranberries to decorate each other's trees....

The shop door thudded shut and Shelley whirled around, both hands clutching tinsel garlands.

The man who identified himself only as Alexander was standing just inside the shop entrance, brushing snow off his shabby coat.

As she watched, he took off his glasses, reached for a handkerchief and started wiping the lenses. As he did so, his eyes met hers across the space of the few feet between them...and Shelley swallowed hard. He had gorgeous eyes. Light winter blue, fringed by a wealth of very dark lashes.

He smiled, that slight, difficult-to-read smile, and said, "I wondered if you'd still be open, considering the weather."

"I wondered if you'd come," Shelley told him, the words escaping her before she paused to think of how they might sound to him. "That's to say," she added hastily, "you've become such a . . . regular."

"So I have, I suppose," he agreed. He put the glasses back on, and she had the feeling he had shuttered a couple of very revealing windows that might have yielded some extremely interesting glimpses of himself, had he permitted her to look just a little longer. He reached in his overcoat pocket, withdrew a plastic bag and said, "I brought these cassettes back." As he spoke, he took the bag over to the counter, removed the cassettes he'd rented the day before and set them down side by side.

Shelley watched his hands, and noticed something she hadn't noticed before. He had beautifully shaped hands, with long fingers and blunt, neatly filed nails. They looked like hands capable of . . . all sorts of things. He could be a concert pianist, she mused. Or an artist.

She had an active imagination, and she had to suppress the urge to stand and wonder about his past.

She scanned the titles of the cassettes he was returning. *Image of Bruce Lee* and *What's New, Pussycat?*

Not quite as wild a range as some of the ones he'd taken out but diverse enough, Shelley thought. She wished she knew what made him tick!

She typed the name Alexander on the computer, checked off the returned cassettes and then suddenly became aware that he was watching her . . . closely.

Glancing up, she saw that he'd taken off his Irish wool hat, and his hair was thick, smooth and sandy . . . shades lighter than those dark eyelashes and finely arched brows.

Now he was unfastening the buttons of the oversized tweed overcoat and she glimpsed a gray sweater that looked as if it needed to be defuzzed. The sweater topped snug-fitting jeans that must have been washed a hundred times. And when he lifted his hand to push back a stray-ing strand of hair, a black leather belt centered with a heavy silver buckle came into view, spanning a slim waist.

Again, Shelley swallowed hard. She still couldn't see nearly as much of him as she wanted to see—the coat, even unbuttoned, remained too much of a camou-flage—but even so she was revising some initial impres-sions. She'd assumed he'd be skinny, maybe because the coat was too big for him. But now...

She met his eyes, and wished he'd take off his glasses again. As it was, he was too inscrutable.

Questions raced through her mind, most of them questions she'd gone through before, so they easily piled one upon the other. What was he doing here on the Cape at this time of the year? Not working, evidently, though that—like most of her conjectures about him—was just an assumption on her part. Where had he come from? Why did she have this crazy idea that he was escaping something?

Forcibly Shelley brought herself back to reality and asked, "Do you want to take out some other cassettes?"

He blinked as if she'd startled him—that much she *could* see behind those tinted glasses—and it struck her that he'd been woolgathering just as she had. About her?

Come on, Shelley, come on, she chided herself.

But he was watching her closely again. She could feel his eyes upon her, even without looking at him.

He said gently, "I don't want to hold you up."

"What?" She was startled out of the beginning of an-other reverie.

"I imagine you may want to close and get home. So..."

"No, no," she said hastily. "That's okay. I plan to finish up the decorating before I leave tonight. The storm's already done a job on the streets, I'd just as soon wait until the road-clearing crews start doing their thing. So go ahead and browse, if you like, while I start in on the tree."

Earlier in the day, Brian and Benny—teenaged twins who worked part-time for her—had helped her get the big balsam straight in its metal container, and then had strung the lights for her. Most of the shops had artificial trees, but Shelley had been determined to have a real one and it was a beauty. Unfortunately, though, she had neglected to ask one of the twins to put the filmy gold and silver angel up on top for her, which meant she was going to have to get out her small stepladder and do some careful balancing.

Though she thought of herself as being a reasonably tall person, Shelley was just a shade over five foot six.

Alexander—Alex? Mr. Alexander?—started moving slowly along the first row of cassettes. He always took his time picking out movies, which Shelley found rather fascinating in view of the odd mixture he inevitably selected. His choices would have been easier to understand if he merely reached out blindly and settled for whatever he grabbed first.

She went back to the storage room, got the ladder and was setting it up by the tree when her mystery man observed, "That doesn't look very stable."

She spun around to see that he was standing almost at her elbow, glancing from her to the ladder to the tree.

She smiled ruefully. "It'll do," she promised. "Anyway, it's the only ladder I have."

"Then could I help?" he offered. He shrugged slightly, and added, "I'm taller than you are."

"Well, mostly I'm concerned about the angel," Shelley admitted. "She's kind of fragile."

The angel was nestled in tissue in a square white box. Shelley withdrew it, and Alexander said, "She looks like a family heirloom."

"She is. At least, I've had her ever since I can remember."

He glanced around, spotted a sturdy chair, picked it up and carried it close to the tree. Before Shelley realized what he was about to do he flung off his overcoat, climbed onto the chair with a single step, then said, "Let me have her, okay?"

Shelley handed the angel to him, thinking as she did so that he'd made the move onto the chair with the dexterity of someone whose muscles were extremely well toned. She realized, guiltily, that she'd assumed he might be rather weak physically. Maybe just recovering from a devastating illness or recuperating from a terrible accident in which he'd been so gravely injured he'd lingered for months at the very edge of death.

Curb it! Shelley admonished herself sharply.

As it was, she was having the chance to get a very good look at him, since his back was to her as he carefully positioned the angel. And what she saw was more than enough to convince her that he was in extremely good shape. The jeans were snug enough to reveal taut hips, well-developed thighs and calves. As he reached out toward the treetop, the gray sweater became molded to his broad shoulders, and there was a sense of latent strength and coordination in the way he moved, the way he handled himself.

Suddenly he turned and glanced down, and Shelley felt as if her cheeks were catching fire. Seldom, if ever, had she stared at a man so blatantly.

"Like me to hang some of your ornaments up here on the high branches?" he asked pleasantly.

"That would be great," Shelley managed.

They began to work together on trimming the tree, saying almost nothing as they did so. Yet, the relative silence between them was remarkably companionable. Once in a while he'd mutter, "Uh-uh, not another gold one. Suppose you find something red, or maybe blue?"

After a time he dispensed with the chair and delved, himself, into the boxes of ornaments, coming up with glistening crystals, a very small, fuzzy teddy bear, a star that looked as if it had been fashioned from cinnamon glass and a gold partridge in a gold filigree pear tree.

"Do you have icicles?" he asked, when finally they'd hung all the ornaments. When Shelley produced the box of thin metallic strips, he suddenly grinned, and the result was electrifying.

"The way a person hangs these on a Christmas tree says a lot about his character," he warned.

"Oh?" she asked, more than slightly mesmerized. Without a doubt, he looked more virile and exciting than any man she'd ever seen. His sandy hair was slightly tousled, there was good color in his cheeks, and both the way he was speaking and the way he was smiling at her seemed very natural. No restraint, none of the holding back she'd always sensed before. Also, although he was slim, he was certainly not skinny. No, Shelley thought, her mouth suddenly feeling dry, he was anything but skinny.

"There are different schools, where icicle hanging is concerned," he informed her, his mellow voice tinged with a nice note of amusement. "The throw it at the branches school. The strand at a time school. The several strands at a time school. The absolutely even school. The deliberately long and short school..."

"Which are you?"

"That depends."

"Well, which are you tonight?"

"Whichever will make your tree look prettiest," he told her.

They compromised by hanging the icicles a few strands at a time. Then they turned on the twinkling, multicolored tree lights and shut off the other lights in the shop so they could get the total effect of what they'd done. In the near darkness they stood close to each other, studying their handiwork. Shelley had turned down the heat earlier, and it was rather cool in the shop. But she felt glowingly warm, and it was easy to imagine that some of the warmth enveloping her was emanating from him. Then, the most amazing experience of the night was the sudden throb of desire that hit her, a direct jab that diffused slowly, increasing her heartbeat, weakening her knees....

She heard the man at her side say softly, "It's beautiful," and she glanced at him swiftly, surprising an expression on his face that blended bleakness with what she could only think of as a yearning so intense it hurt to see it.

She said, hesitantly, "Mr. Alexander?"

He looked as if she'd stung him. "What?"

"Well, that is your name, isn't it? Or is Alexander your first name?"

"No. My first name's Edward. Most people call me Ned. And you?"

"Shelley. Shelley Mitchell."

She waited for him to say something. Even hello. When he didn't she said, "I plan to start serving eggnog in the shop when it gets a little closer to Christmas. But while I had the chance, I got the makings earlier today. The makings for the 'with' eggnog, that is?"

"The 'with' eggnog?" he asked, puzzled.

"Well, it's wise to have one bowl 'with' and one bowl 'without,'" she said.

"Ah, I see what you mean."

"I don't have the eggnog part of the eggnog yet," Shelley told him. "But I was wondering if you'd join me in a pre-Christmas drink, in celebration of trimming the tree? Maybe some bourbon and soda? Or rum?"

"Bourbon and soda would be fine."

Shelley led the way to the small room at the back of the store, which was part kitchenette and part office. She took a tray of ice cubes out of the tiny refrigerator, poured out a liberal shot of bourbon for both of them and asked him to say when, when it came to the soda.

As they sipped, she said, "We may need this to warm the cockles of our hearts once we leave here. Last time I looked, the snow wasn't letting up at all." She sighed. "I just hope my car doesn't decide to turn temperamental on me."

"Your car doesn't like cold weather?"

"No. Sometimes I think it was born in Florida, or maybe down on some Caribbean island. What about you? Are you parked nearby?"

He shook his head. "I don't have a car. At least, not just now. I did have, till a week or so ago. But ... I gave it up."

Her eyes widened. "Are you saying you're walking in this weather?"

He smiled that slight smile again. "It's not exactly Siberia out there, Shelley."

He used her name easily. She liked the sound of it on his lips. She agreed, "No, not Siberia. But maybe the North Pole? And to think it's only the beginning of December. Santa should be right at home if this keeps up."

She noticed he'd finished his drink and suggested, "Another?"

"No, thanks," he said. "One will be enough to heat me on my way."

He preceded her back into the shop. She lingered to switch off lights and to be sure that the back door, opening onto an alley at the rear of the mall, was securely locked. When she rejoined him, he'd already switched the tree lights off for her. After thanking him, she continued hesitantly, "Ned..."

"Yes?"

"May I give you a lift home?"

He shrugged into the shabby tweed coat as she watched, then picked up the Irish wool hat. Without looking at her, he said, "Thanks, that won't be necessary."

"It's not a question of being necessary," Shelley persisted. "Look, you stayed to help me with the tree or you would have been home long before now. Anyway, it's no trouble..."

"It's no trouble for me to walk, snow or no snow," he replied smoothly. "Thanks all the same, Shelley," he added, then followed her out the door.

Outside, the snowplows were at work in the parking lot and along the entrance and exit roads to the mall. Shelley stood under the roof overhang that edged the shops and walks, irresolute. Her car was around the side, in a reasonably protected place. Also, she could use the sidewalk which bordered the buildings to reach it, so she wouldn't have to get out into the weather.

She said again, "Honestly, Ned, I'd be more than happy to drop you off. If you're worried about driving with me in this kind of weather I assure you I was brought up in New England, I've been driving in snow and ice since I was a teenager."

"I really like to walk, Shelley, even in a snowstorm," he explained patiently. "But thanks again."

He turned up his coat collar and tugged the wool hat down over his head. Briefly, Shelley was diverted by another snowplow coming into the parking lot, its giant headlight arcing a blue-white beam across the wintry scene. When she turned again, Ned wasn't there. She tried to make out his outline through the white, polka-dotted night, but she couldn't. He'd vanished, almost as if he'd never been there at all.

She couldn't remember when she'd felt so desolate.

It was almost a relief to fight a few small battles, first with her recalcitrant car and then with the elements on the way home. Her snow tires saw her up her driveway, past the big house to her small cottage. Puffy, her large gray-and-white cat, greeted her at the door with a series of enthusiastic meows. Inside, she used her Cape Cod lighter to ignite the logs already placed in her fireplace. Her clothes felt cold and damp, so she changed into a thick, quilted robe, then made herself some hot chocolate and settled down with it in front of the fire, Puffy promptly curling up at her feet.

As she sipped, thoughts of Ned Alexander possessed her. Ned Alexander, who mystified her, intrigued her, exasperated her . . . and aroused her.

It wasn't until much later she remembered that he'd never gotten around to checking out his usual quota of videos tonight.

Chapter Two

During the night the power went off in most of the town and with it the heating system in the cottage. Shelley woke to a cold, cold December Saturday morning...and an icy shop, once she reached Video Vibes.

She put in a quick call to the mall manager, was assured that steps were being taken to restore the heat in the store, and was promised that within an hour or so she should be warm as toast.

Fortunately she had a small gas stove in the kitchenette, so she was able to make coffee. Mug in hand, she strolled around the shop, assessing the Christmas decorations with the thought of deciding what more, if anything, was needed.

It was as she neared the tree that she saw the wallet, half hidden by a chair. She immediately recognized the slim, black leather, English-style billfold and knew it must have fallen out of Ned Alexander's coat pocket when he'd tossed the coat aside before putting the Christmas angel in place.

Shelley picked up the wallet and stared at it curiously. It was the first thing she'd seen that belonged to her mystery man that didn't look shabby. The billfold was relatively new and expensive. And there were three letters discreetly stamped in gold in one corner. E.A.B.

So Alexander wasn't his last name, after all. Alexander was evidently his middle name.

He'd told her two-thirds of the truth, she thought ruefully, fingering the billfold, wanting to open it, yet strangely loath to do so.

Ned Alexander Question Mark could hardly have made it clearer that he was a person who valued his privacy to an unusual extent. He had even refused a ride home in a driving snowstorm because, Shelley strongly suspected, he didn't want her to know where he was living.

Why? Why should merely knowing where he was staying in this small Cape Cod town be so important? Did he think she would beat a path to his door if she discovered his place of residence? Shelley posed this question to the world at large, resenting its implication even as she voiced it. She wasn't one to barge in where she wasn't wanted.

Yet, for all of this mystery man's reserve and evident desire for isolation, there had been a wonderful warmth to the time they'd shared together trimming the tree. A genuine camaraderie. Shelley would have said he had enjoyed the small part of getting ready for Christmas every bit as much as she had.

Again she stared down at the wallet, fingering the smooth black leather. It occurred to her that if he was concerned about it he could have called her at home. At least she had given *him* her correct name, and she was listed in the local phone book.

Hadn't he missed the wallet yet? Or perhaps he didn't realize he had lost it in her shop? Might he even now be making the rounds of places he'd been yesterday trying to locate it?

If he carried any identification at all, it was probably right in her hands. Such as an address or a phone number or both. So, it only made sense to open the wallet and glance through the contents . . . didn't it?

Shelley never answered her own question, because the mall manager arrived on the scene at that particular moment with the power company representative in tow, and for the next half hour everyone's concentration focused on getting the heat back on.

Once the utilities were working, it was as if someone had blown a whistle, issuing a signal to Christmas shoppers that the roads were pretty well cleared, the mall was open for business and Christmas wasn't *that* many shopping days away. Potential customers swarmed, and a lot of them had put videos on their shopping lists. Shelley had anticipated that this might happen and luckily had found a source for cassettes of great old classic, black-and-white movies, among other treasures, which she was able to offer for an astonishingly low price while still making a profit.

Business became brisk as the day progressed. Meanwhile, Shelley took the precaution of locking the black leather wallet in her small office safe and, after that, she literally didn't have time to do any further thinking about her find.

When "Ned Alexander" came into the shop fairly early in the afternoon, she wasn't ready for him. It was a different time slot for him and when she saw him her fingers began to fumble over such simple tasks as ringing up a sale.

He waited until she rectified an error she had made on her computerized cash register, and the customer left in the wake of an exchange of "Happy holiday" greetings. Then he approached the counter, smiling the slight smile she found so enigmatic. As casually as a person could possibly pose a question, he asked, "Did I happen to leave my wallet here last night?"

Shelley tried to speak and discovered she had lost her voice. Simultaneously, she realized she was staring at him and she couldn't wrest her eyes away. He looked so different, and the difference was due to the fact he wasn't wearing the obscuring, tinted glasses.

His eyes were such a light, clear blue. The contrast with his very dark lashes was not only unusual, but surprisingly erotic. The thought played small games with Shelley's psyche. Erotic wasn't a word she used ordinarily, it was just not a part of her regular, working vocabulary. But right now it fit. So did other words such as sexy and sensual, which she ordinarily didn't deal with too much, either. It wasn't that she was repressed, or that she'd never had any relationships, or that she was turned off men. Rather, she knew very well that she was capable of being a warm and passionate woman. Capable of putting her heart on the line, without exercising any great degree of caution. As a result, she'd been burned a couple of times. Though not that severely. She liked men. Hoped, one day, that the proverbial knight in shining armor would come charging through the door at Video Vibes.

Should that happen, she was prepared to settle down and become a model wife and mother. Above all else, she would give her children the commitment and security that had been snatched from her at a very important time in her life.

She narrowed her eyes, trying to envision Ned Alexander Question Mark as a knight in shining armor, and it wasn't all that difficult.

Maybe he looked especially terrific because he'd just shaved, she decided. And because he'd also dispensed with the hat today, thus revealing that his smooth hair— as seen in daylight—had the burnished glow of antique brass about it. And, though he was still wearing the shabby, oversized tweed overcoat, the coat was open, revealing a black turtleneck that was striking on him.

"My wallet?" he repeated patiently, as the moment of silence between them stretched. "I thought maybe I'd dropped it in here last night."

Shelley located her voice. "Ah, er, yes, your wallet," she managed. "I put it in the safe."

Ned Question Mark raised a quizzical eyebrow. "Oh?" he queried politely.

"Yes. Give me a minute, and I'll get it," she told him, aware that two customers were converging and she'd need to check out their videos first.

"Take your time," Ned offered generously. "I'll pick out some movies. I forgot to take the cassettes I selected last night."

He moved off, and Shelley's eyes automatically followed him. Unfortunately it soon became mandatory to focus her attention elsewhere as business became brisker and brisker. It was a relief when Caroline Marston arrived at ten-thirty so she could get away from the checkout counter for a while.

Caroline was a plump, pretty widow, probably in her late fifties, who lived in one of the condos behind the mall. She had been working part-time for Shelley since

October, and had agreed to put in some extra hours from now until the end of the holiday season. Shelley doubted Caroline needed the money—more likely she was a little lonely and liked being around people, meeting people. *Join the club,* Shelley thought wryly, watching Caroline greet a regular customer. *A lot of us are lonely. Some hide it better than others, that's all.*

That bit of silent wisdom prompted her to think about Ned Question Mark, who was still roaming the aisles studying the video cassettes. Was he lonely? Somehow he didn't seem so. Rather, he seemed like a loner. Which was, or could be, something else entirely.

With Caroline at the front desk, Shelley made her way to the back of the store to retrieve the wallet from her safe. As she did, she passed Ned in the horror section. He turned as she approached, holding a cassette that Shelley wouldn't have put on her own VCR had she been paid to do so. There was a limit to her tolerance for horror.

"Did you have a chance to get to your safe yet?" he asked her.

Shelley had been told that her face was a dead giveaway, and she was sure it was giving her away now. "Sorry," she said. "We've been rather rushed, and I'm just on my way now to get it."

Once in her small office/kitchenette, Shelley closed the door behind her and found herself wishing that this small business with the black leather wallet had never happened. That beautiful, expensive little object aroused too many questions.

She didn't know a damned thing about Ned Question Mark, Shelley reminded herself. Except that he did a good job of placing a Christmas angel on top of a tree. And that he had a surprisingly well-toned physique for someone who went around in an old tweed overcoat sizes too big for him. And that—crazy, crazy, crazy though the mere idea was—it wouldn't be difficult at all to fall in love with him.

But she'd had enough of living in a dreamworld, she thought angrily. A long time ago she'd discovered all about the tendency for idols to develop feet made out of clay. She didn't need any more of that sort of thing. She'd adored both her father and her brother, who was nearly eight years older than she, and it still hurt to think that their feet had been pure, pure clay. Her father had pulled off frauds in his own insurance company for years, until the law finally caught up with him. Once out of business college, her brother had joined the "family firm" to become totally immersed in the same sorry scams.

Shelley sighed. Her father would probably still be serving time in a penitentiary had he not suffered a fatal heart attack just before going to trial. Her brother had been luckier, at least she supposed that's what his fate might be called. He had fled the country immediately after their father's arrest and immediately before those same authorities started on his trail. The last Shelley had heard, Stan Mitchell was still off in a far corner of the world where he managed to live like a king on the money he'd taken with him, and where there was little chance of his ever being discovered or extradited back to the States.

Shelley needed no more mysteries in her life. And she was starting to have some very odd feelings about Ned Question Mark. She began to wish she'd looked in the wallet while she had had a chance. Maybe she still had a chance....

She opened the safe with trembling fingers, withdrew the wallet, and heard Ned observe, "Ah, yes, I think that *is* mine."

Shelley whirled to see him standing on the threshold. He'd opened the office door, which always squeaked slightly, with such finesse she hadn't even heard him.

Her suspicions went into overdrive. She asked darkly, "How can you be so sure at this distance?" They were probably nine or so feet apart. "You don't have your glasses on," she reminded him.

"Contact lenses," he said briefly, touching a corner of one eye. "Sometimes I wear them, sometimes I don't," he added, with that way he had of stating without elaborating. "I believe you'll find the initials E.A.B. in gold on the wallet, in the lower right corner."

"Yes," Shelley admitted unwillingly.

"It belonged to a friend," Ned Question Mark said smoothly. "And was given to me for my birthday last year."

"Your friend had his own initials put on it?" she asked skeptically.

"No. Someone had given it to him previously for *his* birthday. But he doesn't like English-style billfolds."

Ned was coming closer as he spoke. He reached out for the wallet, his fingers grasping the smooth leather. Shelley, for reasons she couldn't possibly have explained, didn't let go. For perhaps thirty ridiculous seconds, she and Ned engaged in a small tug-of-war.

He won. And the ease with which he shook off her grip made her realize that he was strong as an ox, despite the rather diffident impression he tended to create.

"Thanks," he said, then favored Shelley with a dazzling smile.

With the exception of the single time he'd grinned when talking about putting icicles on the tree, she'd only seen that quiet, enigmatic little curve of the lips he was prone to indulge in from time to time. Now his entire face was transformed. He looked incredibly handsome, dangerously sexy, and he had so much charisma he could package and sell quantities of it and still have plenty left over.

The smile ebbed as he said, "Well, then. I've picked out two movies that I've left with your assistant. Last night, though, when I returned the previous ones I didn't owe anything extra, did I?"

"What?" Shelley asked weakly. Then said hastily, "No. Actually, I owe you for helping me with the tree. Just take today's videos compliments of the house. I'll tell Caroline."

Shelley was walking out of her small office as she spoke. Ned followed so closely she knew all either one of them had to do was trip and they'd land in each other's arms...which didn't seem such a bad idea.

He said gravely, "I wouldn't think of that. Letting you give me the movies, that is."

"Only for a night," Shelley reminded him. "Really, I'd like to."

"No," he repeated. And added, "I'd feel obligated."

He sounded deadly serious. She dared to glance around and found that he was literally at her elbow and he also looked deadly serious.

"Ned," she said, "there's no question of obligation. You did me a big favor last night. So just take a night's free rental as a pre-Christmas gift, okay?"

He didn't answer her. Then, once they were out in the shop again, Caroline called her to help some customers who wanted to buy videos as Christmas gifts.

The tender loving care she'd been giving her customers since the store opened in September was paying off, Shelley discovered, as she became busier and busier. But even at the most hectic moments, she found herself searching for Ned. When finally her eyes caught up with him it was to see he'd gone back to browsing. She watched him pick up a cassette, read the blurb on the box and then replace it.

After a time, she became so busy she lost track of him. And when, in a momentary lull, she went looking for him she quickly discovered that he was nowhere to be seen. Video Vibes wasn't that big. So, there was only one conclusion to be drawn. At some point, when her back was turned, he'd left.

He had every right to walk out of the store and no particular reason to linger, Shelley reminded herself. But she began wishing, fervently, that she'd cast her scruples to the winter winds and peered into his wallet. Any kind of a clue about Ned would be a plus at this point.

During another lull, she approached Caroline to ask, "Did Mr. Alexander take any movies with him when he left?"

Caroline looked puzzled. "Mr. Alexander?"

"Ned," Shelley augmented.

"Ah, Ned." A warm smile broke out on Caroline's face. "Yes." She chuckled. "He picked *Kiss of the Spiderwoman* and *Abbott and Costello Meet Captain Kidd*," she reported. "Then, since it's Saturday, he added *Goldfinger*. I must say the man has the widest range of taste I've ever come up against."

"Mmmm," Shelley observed noncommittally. Then added, "He did tell you the rentals were a perk, didn't he?"

"A perk?"

"Last night he helped me out with the tree," Shelley said. "I told him today's rentals were a way of saying thank you."

"Maybe he forgot," Caroline suggested. "He paid for the movies as usual, Shelley."

"I see," Shelley muttered bitterly, and switched the subject.

There was no opportunity for Shelley to take a lunch break that day, though she insisted that Caroline grab a sandwich and a cup of coffee. Caroline, in turn, visited the small cheese shop-deli in the mall and brought back a succulent calzone for Shelley, but she never found time to eat it.

Business slackened in the late afternoon, though Shelley suspected it might very well pick up again later on. She decided to stay open until at least nine, maybe even later. There were bound to be a lot of people out doing Christmas shopping after dinner now that the streets were cleared of snow and ice.

A few minutes after five, Caroline, who had put in a long day as it was, asked, "Sure you don't want me to hang around? Or come back, after I've had some dinner?"

"No," Shelley said firmly. She pasted on a bright smile and continued, "I don't expect to be that swamped, Caroline."

"Well, why don't I stay while you go get something to eat?" Caroline suggested.

"I still have the calzone you brought me. I'll give it a quick turn in the micro and it'll make a great dinner."

"Humph," Caroline huffed. Then said, "At least drink a glass of milk with it, will you? You could use a few extra pounds."

Shelley was naturally slim. No matter what she ate, she never seemed to gain weight, though, admittedly, she seldom indulged in sweets, drank very little alcohol and simply happened to like things that were both nonfattening and good for her.

Now she merely smiled at Caroline and agreed she'd drink a glass of milk. Caroline had two grown-up children who were married and lived at quite a distance. It was natural that her maternal instinct should resurface occasionally, and Shelley didn't mind being the recipient of it.

It's nice to have someone around who cares, she thought rather bleakly. And had a sudden vision of Ned Question Mark. Were there people around who cared for him? Maybe even more important . . . were there people around he cared for? He came from a good background, that was obvious. There was an innate politeness about him, a certain quality. Everything about him was indicative of someone who'd been taught good manners early in life.

With Caroline's departure, the store suddenly seemed empty and lonely, and Shelley shivered slightly as she thought about the impending Christmas, which she was so determined to enjoy. The people who'd rented her big house had asked her to have Christmas dinner with them. So had some other friends and acquaintances around town. Also, she'd been invited to a number of Christmas parties. And she was still thinking about having the eggnog party herself. But none of those things made up for the fact that basically she was alone.

She'd been alone a long time. Her brother was at the other end of the earth, and there were chasms between them anyway that could never be crossed. They'd never been close to begin with, and his moral sense—or, rather, lack of a moral sense—had only widened the gap.

Her mother had remarried within a year after her father's death. Ironically, she'd married the lawyer who'd been hired to defend Shelley's father but had never had to put in any real work on the case because nature had taken its own toll. Her mother and stepfather lived in Mexico, in Guadalajara, where there was a large American colony and the dollar, reputedly, went a lot farther than it did in the States. From the occasional letter she received from her mother, Shelley gained the impression that they were living quite luxuriously. There was a standing invitation for her to come for a visit, but she felt in her bones it was a token invitation and she'd never felt a real desire to accept it.

The big house here in town had come to her directly from her grandmother, her father's mother, who, in recognizing her only son and only grandson's unfortunate potential had bypassed the men in the family in her will.

Shelley grimaced, thinking about her family and the trauma the actions of parents and siblings and children, as well, could cause other family members. To make matters worse, she'd always had the crazy feeling that her father's actions had stemmed not so much from greed but because of her. She had been the apple of his eye—he had wanted to give her the moon and several stars. And because he was a weak man, he'd evidently seen only a single way of ever approximating that.

If only he had realized that all she ever wanted from him was his love, and his being there. Just being there. So often, business had taken him away from home. Also, too often they had moved from place to place, house to apartment or apartment to house, depending on how the family fortunes were doing. And then everything had crashed down all at once, and she'd been made to realize so fully how fragile the structure of her family life had been. In so many ways, she'd grown up in a make-believe world.

Lost in her thoughts, Shelley heard the store door thud shut. She turned, planning to greet a potential customer with a professional smile and a bright, "Hello," and found herself facing Ned.

The word died on her lips. Instead, she found herself stammering, "I didn't expect to see you. I mean, you were in earlier..."

As she spoke, Shelley noted again that he was hatless. And she would have sworn he'd had a haircut. A very good haircut, so it wasn't obvious. But the smooth, sandy hair was beautifully contoured to a head that was just about perfect in shape.

Also, again, he wasn't wearing the tinted glasses. And the smile he was bestowing upon her extended right to his clear, light blue eyes.

"I wasn't planning to come in again today," he admitted, "but I ran into Caroline at the pharmacy a little while ago..."

"Oh?"

"She said you're here by yourself and she was worried because you haven't eaten anything all day."

"Oh, Caroline," Shelley scoffed. "It's the mother in her, Ned." As she spoke his name, she wondered again if it really was his name. "I'm fine," she finished rather lamely.

Ned Question Mark gestured toward the large brown paper bag he was holding. "I stopped by the supermarket and picked up a couple of things," he volunteered. "I thought I'd fix supper for us. I noticed you've got a stove and a microwave in your kitchenette."

"You don't need to do that," Shelley protested, but Ned was already heading toward the back office.

He said, over his shoulder, "I can play instant chef with the stuff I bought. All strictly gourmet quality, you understand—frozen variety. Nevertheless..."

The end of his sentence was muffled, and Shelley stared after him helplessly.

"What a blabbermouth Caroline is," she muttered to herself. Then her lips curved into a smile and she amended that to, "Bless Caroline!"

Chapter Three

Ned set the bag on the small round table in the kitchenette and expelled an exasperated sigh.

What had come over him, to voluntarily get into such a situation as this?

Curiosity might be part of it, he conceded. Had Shelley looked into his wallet after she found it or hadn't she? Her behavior had given him no clue...which didn't mean anything. Women, most women anyway, were past masters of camouflage. It was congenital with them.

Ned began extracting his purchases from the bag. He'd chosen some fancy puffs to be baked in the oven for hors d'oeuvres. There was a can of consommé which he planned to lace with sherry and garnish with slices of avocado. Then steak-and-mushroom pies, to be accompanied by the finest frozen green asparagus. For dessert, babas au rhum, which he'd discovered in a jar and which he planned to augment with genuine whipped cream straight from a squirt can. He'd thought about having either espresso or cappuccino to finish off the repast, but since Shelley wasn't apt to have equipment in her kitchenette to produce either he'd settled for a tin of Viennese-type instant coffee.

All you need is candles in gleaming brass holders, you idiot, Ned growled at himself. And finally admitted that his interest in Shelley went beyond curiosity as to whether or not she'd snooped in his wallet. It shocked him to think how much she was getting to him without even trying. He was aware she was responsive to him. His senses hadn't become that deadened. But she'd made none of the overtures "interested" women were apt to make. Should she ever do so, Ned thought ruefully, he'd be in serious danger of becoming involved in a love affair that could have only one place to go. Nowhere.

What was there about Shelley that was so enormously appealing? She was beautiful, but he'd encountered any number of beautiful women in his life. Maybe one of the attractions about Shelley was that she seemed so unaware of her beauty. She didn't do much with makeup. She didn't need to—she was lovely enough without embellishment. But he could imagine how she'd look, should some professional in a New York or Beverly Hills or Paris salon take her over and style that mass of almost jet-black hair, then enhance her topaz eyes with makeup that would bring out their glorious, tawny color.

Ned envisioned her draped in expensive couturier clothes which, needless to say, would emphasize her seductive figure in quite a different way than did the rather loose-fitting, practical, relatively colorless workday clothes she customarily wore in the shop. And he realized, to his surprise, that he'd love to encircle her smooth, graceful neck with an expensive necklace—diamond and emeralds maybe—with matching eardrops. Maybe a ring, too, centered with a large emerald, the emerald surrounded with diamonds. Emeralds would suit her....

Fool, Ned branded himself savagely, then grabbed the package of appetizers and read the printed directions, and set the oven to the proper time.

But by the time the hors d'oeuvre were baked—the little puffs nicely browned, and the bottle of chilled Chablis he'd bought chilled even more—Shelley was not ready to come to sample them. In fact, the after-supper business became so brisk that, after a time, Ned shrugged, put the puffs, already beginning to wilt, on top of the stove, and went out to the store to see if he could be of help to Shelley in a more practical way.

He suspected that ordinarily she would have refused his offer. She had made it clear, when she'd wanted to give him the video cassettes free of charge, that she didn't relish owing anyone, which put them in the same corner. But tonight she was so rushed she let him check out the rentals for her while she attended to customers who wanted to buy videos for Christmas-giving, or blank cassettes on which they could record and store their own material. And, after a time, she made no objection when he tried his hand at selling.

It was a quarter past ten when Shelley finally put out the Closed sign, shut the door and locked it. Then she turned to Ned. Her "Thanks" was simple but heartfelt.

"You're more than welcome," Ned returned, resisting the temptation to take his own pulse. His heart, he thought wryly, must be working overtime. Tired though she obviously was, he was sure Shelley had never looked lovelier, nor more desirable. She was literally flushed with victory, and her eyes were sparkling. He sensed that tonight had been a triumph for her, maybe the affirmation she needed that her business was really a success.

He couldn't believe how much he'd enjoyed working with her, even though selling, per se, was totally foreign to him. But he'd found himself promoting some of Shelley's cassettes—easy to do, because a number of them were videos he'd watched only recently, himself. And his promotions had resulted in affirmative nods from the customers.

Now Shelley finished straightening up a few things at the checkout desk then turned to say, almost apologetically, "Ned, I'd just as soon settle up with you right now."

Ned felt as if she'd dashed a cup of ice water in his face. Warily he asked, "What do you mean?," though he was afraid he knew exactly what she meant.

"Well, I do need to pay you for what you've done tonight," she told him.

Ned tried to convince himself he was overreacting. There was no logical reason why Shelley's offer should be such a letdown.

When he didn't answer her, she went on, "You did put in the better part of three hours, you know. Without you, I'd have been in quite a bind. So..."

Ned saw her open the cash drawer as she spoke, and he didn't know whether he wanted to kiss her or to throttle her. Didn't she know he hadn't come to her rescue tonight for money?

"Shelley," he began, but she waved his words away.

"I insist," she said firmly. "Anyway, I have a favor to ask of you and unless you let me pay you when you do things for me I can't ask it."

"What kind of favor?" he queried, an edge of suspicion automatically surfacing.

"Next Saturday morning I'm having a Christmas party for kids. I won't be the first in town, but I want to have it anyway. For years, Nonnie—you know Nonnie's Kitchen...?"

"Yes," Ned conceded cautiously.

"They make the best coffee around," Shelley said rather absently. "Anyway, for years Nonnie has had a Christmas party for kids to meet Santa, one Saturday morning in December. She's set her date for the seventeenth and I didn't want to conflict with her plans, so I set my party for next Saturday from nine to noon. I'm going to serve cookies and fruit punch for the kids, and I've ordered little paperback Christmas stories to be given as presents. But, of course, I need a Santa."

"Mmmm," Ned murmured noncommittally.

"Marty Ferguson was to be my Santa," Shelley went on, "but his wife called earlier today. Marty's a fisherman and would you believe it, he slipped on the deck of his trawler and broke his ankle. So he's not going to feel much like playing Santa in just one more week."

"No, I wouldn't think he would," Ned conceded.

"So..." Shelley drew out the word.

"So?" Ned encouraged.

"Well, I was wondering if you might be able to do it."

"To be Santa Claus?" he asked incredulously.

"Yes. I know you're on the skinny side..."

"Skinny, eh?" he asked, not knowing whether to be amused or insulted.

"Well, for Santa, that is," Shelley temporized, and Ned saw the color in her cheeks. "But we could fill you out with pillows and..."

When he didn't at once answer, Shelley said, "Naturally, I'll pay you."

"Did you plan to pay Marty?" The question shot out.

"Well, no," she admitted. "I planned to get Marty a bottle of bourbon. But..."

"But you think you should pay me?"

"Well," she said, obviously finding this very hard going, "I don't want to be personal, Ned. But... it's not hard to see you could...well, you could maybe use some money."

Ned arched an expressive eyebrow. "Is that so?"

"Please," Shelley pleaded. "Please don't take offense. It's just that... well, you can tell things about people, you know. At least..."

"Yes?"

"Well, all the time you've been coming in the store I thought I could tell things about you."

"That changed?"

"I guess so, in a way," Shelley said, looking so miserable Ned had to fight a brief but intense battle to keep from covering the distance between them, sweeping her in his arms and kissing her the way he wanted to kiss her—even though doing so would be as dangerous as hell...

"I mean," Shelley fumbled on, "that hat you wear, the overcoat..."

"Seedy, eh?"

"I don't mean to insult your clothes, Ned, but... yes, they both look as if they've seen better days. And..."

Ned said, rather stiffly, "I wasn't aware you'd been studying me so intently, Shelley."

"There," Shelley muttered unhappily. "Now I *have* insulted you, and I don't blame you for being annoyed. It's just that I wanted you to know I..."

"Yes?"

"Ned," she said almost desperately, "there's no disgrace in being poor. Or temporarily down on your luck. Or needing money."

"Or a combination of all three?" he suggested.

"Yes."

So she hadn't looked in his wallet after all! Ned suddenly smiled, and it was a smile so dazzling Shelley was blinded by it.

"Thank you," he said unexpectedly.

"Thank me...for what?" she floundered.

"For taking the trouble to consider me as you have," he said. "I mean that, Shelley. But I really don't need money as much as you evidently think I do."

Shelley suddenly remembered the hundred-dollar bill he'd taken out of his wallet. It had been crisp and new, and just one of many bills though of course she had no idea of the denominations of the other ones.

Ned interrupted Shelley's racing train of thought. "I'd like to consider my work for you tonight as Part One of a Christmas present," he said quietly. "And my playing Santa for you as Part Two. All right?"

"Ned, honestly..."

"Look," he said, "let's consider it settled, okay?" He added, with a slight grimace, "Our appetizers are probably beyond repair, but at least we can sip some wine while the rest of the dinner cooks. I'm starved. How about you?"

Shelley didn't need to give the matter much thought to realize that she, too, was starved. Genuinely hungry...something that didn't happen to her too often and automatically evoked memories of her childhood when, according to tales she had been told, she'd grown like a weed, had a hollow leg, and was ravenously hungry all the time.

In the kitchenette, Ned gave the pastry puffs a quick warm-up, then—though they were past their prime—he and Shelley ate them anyway as they sipped the Chablis. Next, Shelley watched him lace the consommé with sherry, and her eyes widened when she saw the brand of sherry he was using. It was widely advertised as a sherry to suit the most discriminating palate and she knew it was expensive.

She was startled when he said suddenly, "I really should have bought some candles, damn it."

Shelley frowned. "Is there a storm forecast?"

"What do you mean?"

"I thought you might have heard we were in for another storm, or that the power might fail again."

Ned laughed. "I wasn't thinking about power failures," he admitted. "Just a more...agreeable ambience. That's a bright ceiling light you've got there."

It was. Shelley tried to blot out the light mentally as she thought about dining by candlelight with Ned, and she suddenly felt as if she'd been cast into some very deep warm water and was tumbling around helplessly, in danger of losing all sense of direction.

Ned had removed their soup dishes, and he had his back to her so she was able to take a couple of deep breaths without his observing her. Also, too, to look at him and think about him without meeting those light blue eyes that were so discerning they made her feel he could see clear to her soul.

She'd never before met anyone like him...and the considerable common sense she'd acquired over the years was warning her that there was danger as well as delight in the pursuit of the unknown. Not that she had any idea of pursuing Ned, in fact she doubted she'd even know where to begin with a man like him, he was that different.

He was so many things. Even though she still knew absolutely nothing *about* him she was beginning to know *him* via the things he said, the things he did. For example, his manners were perfect, without being in the least affected. He was playing host in her kitchenette with an ease that made her suspect it was a role he was thoroughly familiar with, or at least had been at some time in his life. Also, though strong, he was gentle, funny when he wanted to be—he'd had more than one of the customers chuckling tonight—and understanding.

She discovered the understanding part of his nature when, once he was seated at the table again, he brought up some of the small happenings in the shop tonight and she began to recount some of the difficulties she'd come up against in trying to run her own business. Ned, she discovered, was not merely sympathetic and encouraging, he was also thoughtful and astute—this latter quality made evident by suggestions he offered about how things might be done better or more easily.

Caution warned that it would be very easy to lean on such a man as Ned, to draw strength from his strength. And the last thing in the world Shelley wanted to do was lean on anyone. Valiantly she tried to heed the warning and stiffen her backbone. But the fact was that, despite the bright lights in the kitchenette, the wine and food were lulling her to a point where she felt as pliable as clay. Or was clay malleable? she asked herself. Or maybe both?

Whatever clay was, Ned was spellbinding her.

The problem was, she loved being spellbound by Ned.

She chuckled, wondering what he'd say if she told him she loved being spellbound by him. Ned was in the process of savoring the steak-and-mushroom pie, and he looked up quizzically. "Want to share the joke?" he asked her.

"Oh, there isn't any joke," Shelley said a bit fuzzily. She wasn't used to drinking more than one glass of wine at any given time, and so far she'd had two. Or was it three? "I just... well, I guess I'm just not used to being waited on, that's all."

He favored her with one of his dazzling smiles. "My pleasure," he said smoothly and suggested, "Maybe you'd better eat something, Shelley."

"Am I that transparent?" she asked, a bit miffed at the implication she'd had too much to drink. She tried to gather together a few shreds of dignity. "I admit I do feel a little bit woozy..." she began.

"You feel woozy because you haven't eaten anything all day," Ned informed her. "Try the pie. It's good."

It was good, and for a time they ate in silence. Then another surmise about Ned occurred to Shelley and she asked him, "Have you ever been a chef?"

He was genuinely startled. "Me, a chef?" he echoed. "No. Why would you think I might have been?"

"The food, I guess," Shelley murmured.

"Shelley, the food came out of the frozen food cabinet, except for the consommé, and that came out of a can," he reminded her.

"What do you do, Ned?" she asked, the wine giving her a false courage she was sure she'd never have found otherwise. But her curiosity about him had reached the brimming point and was spilling over.

"What do I do?" Ned repeated, and fuzzy though she was Shelley recognized stalling tactics when she heard them.

"Yes," she persisted. "Professionally, that is."

"Well," Ned said, after a long pause, "I guess you might say I'm a wanderer."

Shelley shook her head slightly, touched her ears. "Did I hear you right?" she demanded.

"I think so. I'm a wanderer. Yes, a professional wanderer, actually."

"What do you mean?"

"I wander," Ned said, as if that were the simplest and most logical course of action any human being could possibly take.

"Wander?"

"Yes. In other words, I'm...a human rolling stone. That's to say...I never stay around anywhere long enough to gather any moss, metaphorically speaking."

"You just roam...all over the countryside?"

"All over the country," he corrected. "In fact, all over the world."

"You don't work?"

He shrugged. "Only when I want to. Like helping you out in the store tonight. Or perhaps signing on at a temporary job somewhere for a change of pace."

She stared at him, completely befuddled. And wished she'd stopped after her usual one small glass of wine because she needed to have all her wits about her. She was finding it very difficult to understand what he was saying. To make sense out of what he was saying.

It occurred to her that she would probably find it equally difficult even if she were cold sober.

Ned laughed and said, "Don't look at me like that, Shelley."

"Like what?"

"As if you're doubting yourself." His eyes twinkled. "What's the matter?" he teased. "Haven't you ever met a wanderer before?"

"No," she said, "at least no one who would..."

He finished her thought for her. "No one who would admit he dedicated his life to roaming around as much as possible and doing as little as possible?"

"I can't believe that description fits your life-style," Shelley stated flatly.

"Why not?"

"Because you're making yourself sound like a...a..."

"A bum?" he suggested.

"Well, yes," she admitted, thoroughly flustered. "And you couldn't possibly be a bum."

"Why couldn't I be a bum, Shelley?"

"Because you...you don't look like a bum," she fumbled. "You don't act like a bum. You..." She stared at him helplessly, words deserting her.

"Well," Ned said levelly, "I'm not a bum. At least not according to my own definition of bum or, I imagine, yours. But that's not to say bums can't be fine people...some of them. Life deals out a lot of different hands and people playing the game react differently..."

He broke off suddenly, and frowned. "This is getting a shade too deep for a small supper on a cold winter evening," he decided.

Shelley felt as if he'd closed a door in her face. Desperately, she wanted to open it again. Maybe it was the food she'd eaten, maybe her own agitation, but she felt cold sober as she said, "Ned, I didn't mean to pry. It's just that all of a sudden you appeared from out of nowhere..."

He smiled faintly. "I arrived in the center of town one day in November in an old jalopy which has since died and gone to car heaven, read, the junkyard," he told her.

She stirred impatiently. "What I meant was, you seemed to appear from out of nowhere and I..."

"And you got curious?"

"Yes."

"You're not the first, Shelley," he observed with a wry twist to his lips.

Shelley watched him put down his fork, then lean back to look at her mildly. "If you must know, I'd been in Hawaii," he stated. "There I made the decision to look around New England for a while. I favor places in the off-season. I don't care about being one in a horde of tourists. So I thought Thanksgiving and Christmas would be a good time of year to be on Cape Cod."

"So... you simply packed up and came here."

"Packing's quite easy for me," Ned said, looking slightly, very slightly amused. "Shall we say I travel light? Very light? When I feel the urge to move on, I don't want to be encumbered by possessions. Most of which—" He broke off abruptly.

After a moment Shelley said, "So one day you'll simply feel this 'urge' and you'll move on again?" She discovered she was holding her breath as she waited for his answer.

"Yes," he said, and she couldn't read the expression that crept into his eyes as he looked at her. He shrugged slightly. "Who knows? One of these days I may head somewhere warm. Not every warm place on the globe is necessarily swarming with tourists. Or else I may try the Midwest for a while. Or maybe one of the western Canadian provinces, to experience some real winter. And save the south for summer, when most other people have come north." He shrugged again. "Time enough to think about that later," he said, then stood and cleared off both their plates and put on the kettle to boil water for coffee.

Again his back was turned to Shelley and she surveyed it with mounting frustration. He was wearing a cranberry wool shirt that was a perfect fit. A tan belt, obviously genuine leather, cinched his narrow waist. His jeans contoured his hips, thighs and calves. His physique, she admitted weakly, was terrific. How had he hidden so much under a shabby old, outsized tweed overcoat?

He served their dessert, and her eyes widened again when she saw the babas. She knew they were expensive. He garnished the babas with whipped cream, fixed the coffee, then sat down opposite her again. But he made no move to start to eat the dessert or sip the coffee.

His handsome face was grave as he said, "I don't expect you to understand either me or my way of life, Shelley. That's something I don't ask of anyone. But it's what I want, and you should know that I neither desire to change it, nor have any intention of doing so. The few people who find out anything much about me tend to put labels on me. Loner, eccentric. Whatever. I don't really blame them, but on the other hand what people think doesn't much matter to me. I've found my niche in life, I'm where I want to be."

"Watching two movies a night?" The words exploded before Shelley could hold them back.

Ned's eyelids flickered. "Right now that's . . . an avocation," he admitted. Then added, "Movies, in their way, reflect a lot about life. Last week I watched *It Happened One Night* which goes back, need I say, to before either of us was born . . ."

Shelley couldn't resist the question. "When were you born, Ned?"

"Thirty-nine years ago, come Christmas Day," he said, after only the briefest hesitation.

"Christmas is your birthday?"

"Yeah," he drawled. "And, yes, I felt somewhat shortchanged when I was a kid. Shall we say my birthday tended to be bypassed in the general excitement? However," he continued, before she could comment on that, "to go back to *It Happened One Night . . .*"

Shelley nearly moaned aloud. She didn't want to go back to *It Happened One Night*. She wanted to find out more, a lot more, about Ned Alexander Question Mark.

"The cars in the picture are totally vintage," Ned said. "The clothes, too, so much so they're practically in fashion again. And the vernacular's interesting. Slang, language usage, that's something that does change.

"Then," he continued, "a couple of days later I was watching an old Cary Grant film. Interesting to see Grant looking so young. The same with an early Sean Connery film I rented. It was done before he became famous as James Bond and—"

"Is that why you watch so many movies?" she asked. "To analyze?"

"I do analyze, yes," he admitted, "but it's more than that. It's a way of catching up with a lot of history. Much of it fairly recent history, I admit. Although I take out some period films from time to time, I don't have the greatest faith in their historical accuracy. I may be wrong about that, of course. But I prefer to go right to the source, and the thirties and forties and fifties movies were done then. They accurately reflect those times in so many ways. So, I do go for the details, yes, if you call that analyzing."

"In other words, you're a recent history buff?"

"I haven't thought of myself in that light," Ned said, amused. "But I guess the description fits."

"And a movie buff," Shelley added, stating rather than asking this time. "Have you always been a movie buff, Ned?"

He laughed. "No. Till I spotted your store and decided to give videos a whirl, I couldn't tell you when it was I last saw a movie."

"You rented the VCR, you rent the videos, just so you can . . . catch up?"

He sidestepped the question. "I do enjoy the movies, Shelley," he pointed out, almost reprovingly.

Shelley let that issue go in favor of pursuing another one. Gathering up her courage, she asked, "How long have you been a professional wanderer, Ned?"

He frowned, and at first she thought he wasn't going to answer her. But finally he said slowly, "Since Christmas Day, four years ago." He added, even more slowly, "I gave myself a present for my thirty-fifth birthday. Freedom. I drafted my own Declaration of Independence and from that day on I've been completely my own person. These past four years have been remarkable in more ways than I can tell you. This has been—this is—a mind-boggling experience. I would hate to think I could so easily have missed it if . . ."

Shelley waited for him to continue and when he didn't she prompted, "If?"

"If I hadn't given myself the gift of freedom."

A small silence descended. Shelley couldn't remember when she'd ever felt at such a loss. Where to go from here?

Certainly, she felt totally sober again. So sober, in fact, that she asked rather tentatively, "Do you suppose I could have another glass of wine, Ned?"

"Of course, if you like."

"I'd like. I was giddy a while ago, but that's worn off."

"Okay."

He poured the wine with that natural grace that Shelley had discovered was an essential part of him. She sipped, as if the pale golden liquid might be an elixir that would give her courage. She needed courage, because she had the feeling that at any moment Ned might shut her off. But she had to ask him some more questions.

She took a long breath, then plunged. "Are you saying," she asked him, "that you walked out of your home on Christmas Day, left your family and turned your back on...on everyone and everything? And you've never gone back since? You've just kept on wandering?"

She would have sworn that his eyes literally changed in temperature. Became cool—cold, in fact—and cautious. For a moment she thought she might be turned off even sooner than she'd expected to be. But Ned, his voice edged with steel, asked, "What makes you think I had a home and family, Shelley?"

She stated the obvious. "Don't most people?"

"I suppose so. But not all people."

"Didn't you?"

"I suppose that depends on definitions," he said. "Exactly what constitutes a home? Exactly what constitutes a family?"

"Do you analyze everything, Ned?"

His smile was lopsided. "I suppose it does become a kind of game," he said diffidently.

"I'm not sure it's a game I like," Shelley retorted honestly. "And I'm also not sure, but I'd call it a diversion rather than a game."

"Oh?"

"You sidestep questions with analyses, don't you, Ned?"

Ned reached for the wine bottle and refilled his own glass. He stared rather broodingly at the light gold liquid then, without raising the glass, admitted, "Possibly."

"Then," Shelley dared, "could we go back to my original question? You did have a home and family, didn't you?"

Was it her imagination, or were there really shadows creeping across Ned's face, obscuring his eyes almost as much as the tinted glasses had earlier? "Yes," he said, after a tense moment.

"You decided to become a . . . a wanderer, and so you just severed the connection with everyone and everything close to you?"

"Your incredulity's showing," Ned said briefly. "Also, I can imagine how my answer will make me seem to you. But, yes, I did exactly that."

"As a birthday gift to yourself?"

"Yes."

"And you've never regretted it?"

"Regret? What's regret?" Ned began, and then caught himself short. With a guilty smile, he confessed, "I'm doing it again. I see what you mean."

Shelley stared at him helplessly. She felt at the edge of tears, though she didn't know why she should. Except she was suddenly almost afraid of finding out too much about Ned. Afraid that whatever his past held was so . . . overwhelming it would totally undermine her. Sorrowful, because whatever Ned's past held was certain to be unhappy.

The sorrow and fear churned together inside her, and she shuddered inwardly as she realized how much this man had gotten to her in such a short space of time.

She forced herself to speak levelly. She said as calmly as she could, "I suppose it might be best if you simply told me none of this is any of my business." Even as she spoke she didn't expect him to take her statement seriously.

She was not at all prepared when Ned said—even his gentleness failing to take the sting out of the words—"I agree. It's none of your business, Shelley. Now suppose we make plans for Saturday and your Christmas party, and you can tell me where I'm supposed to get a Santa Claus suit."

Chapter Four

Ned took one look at Shelley's expressive face and could have kicked himself. He wished that he could rephrase what he had just said, but obviously it was too late.

You're right, Shelley. It is none of your business.

The words echoed in his mind, and he couldn't believe he'd spoken them to her. He had hurt her, how the hell could he have expected otherwise? and there was no immediate way to make up for having inflicted that hurt.

Feeling both inept and frustrated, Ned prodded, "About the Christmas party, Shelley..."

"I have it pretty well planned," Shelley said. She added, a shade too abruptly, "Look, Ned, this has been a pretty full day for both of us. I don't know about you, but I'm bushed. I'll see about a Santa suit Monday. The one I was planning to borrow for Marty wouldn't do for you. He's a lot shorter than you are."

It was a rebuff, issued in a tired voice which made it all the harder to take.

Ned began, "Shelley," and then stopped. What could he say after all? Attracted though he was to Shelley, he was not about to bare his heart to her, to share confidences about things he didn't wish or intend to confide to anyone.

Wearily, she asked, "What?"

"If you'd trust me to lock up," Ned improvised quickly, "I'll take care of the few dishes and straighten things and . . ."

"There's no need for that," Shelley said. "You've done enough."

Ned's smile was bitter. He'd done enough, all right. He'd stepped on some very tender feelings, and there was no good excuse for having done so. Naturally she was curious about him; he was curious about her, for that matter. He had even wondered about how to ask some questions of his own without being heavy-handed about it. It wasn't his style to be heavy-handed.

His style? He almost followed the bitter smile with a bitter laugh. Just what the hell was his style? To insult someone who'd come a shade too close to chipping some of his carefully applied veneer?

He watched Shelley pick up some of the dishes on the table, carry them over to the sink, then turn on the hot water and test it with her finger. She was sagging a little, her shoulders drooped slightly. An unexpected feeling of tenderness arose in Ned. He picked up the wineglasses, carried them over and set them at the side of the small sink. Then he reached out and turned off the hot water, firmly placed his hands on Shelley's shoulders and said, "Enough."

He felt her stiffen. Her voice was muffled as she asked, "What do you mean, enough?"

"I mean enough. I'm cleaning up, you go home. You can trust me to make sure everything is secure."

He was staring down at her beautiful jet hair as he spoke. He could smell her soft perfume. She used a slightly Oriental scent that had a nice, mysterious quality about it. It occurred to him suddenly that she was as much a mystery to him as he was to her. They knew very little about each other. But Shelley had shown herself to him as a tender, caring, vulnerable person. As well as being a very desirable woman.

Ned felt an ache that went straight through his groin. Desire twisted. Shelley's proximity, her warm, feminine loveliness, was getting to him, making him realize that a large segment of his life had been a pretty barren desert for longer than he liked to think about.

Involuntarily, he leaned closer to her. Her soft hair brushed his chin. The effect was incredibly provocative. He turned Shelley around. She stumbled slightly as he did so, and he sensed he'd thrown her off balance in more ways than one. She'd also thrown him off balance, damn it. Because he was a wanderer, that was exactly what he was, and he didn't want to be anything else. And being the proverbial rolling stone that gathers no moss meant stepping out of the kind of involvement that lurked beneath his fingertips instead of plunging into it.

Ned tried to resist and couldn't. He looked down into Shelley's topaz eyes and said softly, huskily, "I'm sorry. About saying that what you were asking was none of your business. You didn't deserve that. It's just that I..."

Her look stilled him, was as effective as if she'd clapped a slender hand over his mouth. She said, "You don't have to apologize. I'm the one who was doing the trespassing. It won't happen again, Ned."

Why should that statement incur a feeling of keen disappointment instead of relief? Ned posed the question to himself, but he wasn't in the mood for analysis. He was too conscious of Shelley, her warmth, her nearness.

Suddenly, impulsively, he framed her face with his hands. He kissed her, a kiss that was not meant to be deep and long and lingering but turned out that way. Shelley broke away first. He let her go, watching as she tried to find words, then before she could speak said urgently, "Please, Shelley, don't say anything. Except," he added gently, "perhaps good-night."

As she drove across town after leaving Ned to take care of things in the store, Shelley engaged in a spirited silent dialogue with herself.

Ned's kiss had sent her spiraling into orbit and that, she told herself sternly, was ridiculous. She scarcely knew the man. And though maybe—a few hours ago—she would have said she was getting to know him, that condition had changed abruptly with his telling her gently, politely but firmly, that his life, his past was none of her business.

It was a shock to be told something like that. She'd been nowhere near rallying from the shock when Ned came up behind her and the next thing she knew she was in his arms.

Ned had been attracting her more and more, she didn't deny that. He was an exceptionally attractive man— tweed coat, battered wool hat and all. The added quality of mystery about him had only been all the more enticing. Fuel had been added to the simmering fire when he told her he was a wanderer. Not merely a wanderer, but a professional wanderer...due to a birthday gift he'd given himself nearly four years ago. On Christmas Day, on his thirty-fifth birthday.

He'd had a home, a family, that much he had admitted. He'd walked out on them. Wandered all over the place, ever since, working when he wanted to work, not working when that suited him. Essentially pleasing only himself, being true only to himself. With, evidently, no regrets.

Shelley pulled up to the back door of her cottage, switched off the motor but made no immediate move to get out of the car.

Conjectures about Ned raced through her mind. She tried to sort them out into some kind of manageable order and couldn't. She didn't know enough about Ned to make sense out of what he had done and after that statement of his tonight she doubted she ever would.

Still, she kept on analyzing the little she did know of him. He was reserved most of the time. But not cold. He could be enthusiastic, spontaneous, warm...and God knows he'd put a full quota of passion into that kiss.

He'd shown her that he had a nice sense of humor, he was thoughtful, considerate and, apparently, very wide-ranging in his interests. Yet she was conscious always, except for the duration of that kiss, of a certain distance between the two of them. As if Ned had insulated himself so that no one would ever get too close to him.

Which could mean a lot of things, Shelley concluded rather unhappily. Finally, shivering from the cold that had seeped into the car, Shelley got out, let herself in the kitchen door and was greeted by an irate Puffy. Evidently the cat was getting tired of her mistress coming home on the late side, for she demanded her long-overdue supper with a series of outraged meows.

Puffy became an angry feline princess as she stalked back and forth, her slanted, pale green eyes sending some significant messages Shelley's way. And she was still meowing as Shelley opened a can of cat food and tried to placate her with murmured apologies.

She put the dish full of food in the little niche next to the wood stove that was Puffy's private dining nook. The cat turned her back with the kind of eloquence only cats can manage, and started to eat.

Shelley thought about making herself a cup of coffee, but opted instead for hot milk. She took the milk into her bedroom and sipped it as she undressed. In bed, with the lights out, she gazed at the nearly full moon then watched a cloud drift by to blot out the silvery light.

It was a contrast that made her think, again, of Ned. That same moon was shining on whatever place he'd come from. Shining on whomever he'd left behind. He had walked out on that person—those persons—he had admitted as much. Could it possibly be true that he really had no regrets, felt no remorse?

I feel so differently, Shelley thought, and buried her head in the pillow, trying to blot out the moonlight. *I have no reason to feel remorse, but I think I'll always wish I could have done something to make things turn out differently than they did.*

Did my father really think I was such a spoiled little brat he had to steal from people who trusted him to keep me happy? If my mother and I had been able to communicate better, once the chips were down, could the two of us have helped Daddy and Stan so the tables could have been turned?...people given back their money...the books straightened out...

It was not the first time Shelley had gone through this kind of agonized self-questioning, and she was sure it

wouldn't be the last. Also, her common sense told her
that in actuality there was nothing she could have done
about her father, nor about her brother, for that matter.
Stan was eight years older than she, and his patterns had
been engrained by the father in whose footsteps he followed long before she was old enough to have any idea of
what was going on.

And, she hadn't really had any idea of what was going
on until it was too late. Until her father had been in-
dicted and Stan had fled the country and her whole world
started crumbling.

She had been only sixteen years old. With no voice in
the matter when her parents abruptly bundled her off to
Cape Cod and her grandmother's house. For a time, she
had feared that either her mother or her father was seriously ill and her family was trying to spare her a lot of
trauma. That, as it turned out, had been true enough . . .
though it had been trauma of quite a different kind.

Meantime, she had started her third year of high school
here in Devon, trying to fathom why her mother had become so different, shortly before the decision was made
to send Shelley to her Grandmother Mitchell's. That had
been one of the hardest things to take—the way her
mother had turned, almost overnight, from a charming,
popular, fun-loving person into a bitter, tight-lipped
woman who had been unable to show even an atom of
mercy toward either her husband or her son.

Not that either man had deserved much in the way of
mercy, Shelley admitted. The frauds they had perpetrated had been deliberate, so carefully thought out that
if it had not been for a disgruntled employee who had
tipped off the authorities they might literally have made
crime pay for many more years.

Still, Justin Mitchell had been her father and Stanley Mitchell her brother, and she had fond memories of both men in the earlier years, when life had been very good in the series of houses and apartments they had lived in.

Over the past dozen years, too, Shelley had been able to at least begin to recognize and cope with her knowledge of the weakness that had led both her father and Stan in such wrong directions. No one was perfect, she thought now, sadly. She wasn't excusing either her father's or Stan's imperfections, and what they had done was terribly, terribly wrong. Her father had paid with his life. Stan, which was even more wrong, had gotten away with his actions—ostensibly so, anyway. She wondered how happy he really could be, living incognito in some far-off corner of the world.

As for herself, she had reached the point where she could think back beyond all the misery that had taken place a dozen years ago to the earlier times, the good times. Sometimes, remembering those earlier times, she still suffered tremendous nostalgia bouts. Which was the main reason she had pledged that this coming Christmas season was going to be a holiday time she could enjoy. She'd had enough lonely holiday seasons to last an entire lifetime.

She turned so that she could see the moon again. With no clouds to obscure it at that moment, it reigned supreme in the night sky, a huge and glorious disc, more white than silver.

Was Ned looking at the moon at this moment, by any chance? Didn't Ned ever have to work through nostalgia bouts, as she did? Could it be possible that there wasn't anyone in the entire world he missed?

Shelley got to the store early next Monday morning, and at once started making a list of possible sources for a Santa Claus suit.

She had brought a few pillows from the cottage with her, and she chuckled at the thought of converting slim Ned into a roly-poly Santa.

Ned had been in her mind all day Sunday, then she had awakened a couple of times in the night to the realization that she had been dreaming about him... but she couldn't remember the contents of those dreams. Over breakfast, she had faced up to the issue between Ned and herself and had come to a decision.

They were physically attracted to each other, there was no doubt of that. Some very interesting currents flowed between them, obviously they found each other sensually stimulating and she had the not-so-funny feeling that this tantalizing emotional flow between Ned and herself could become something very special—unless it were checked now. Dammed up.

At 7:45 that cold December morning, Shelley came to the decision that she was going to do a quick engineering job, build a dam and keep the "flow" contained from here on in. She owed that much to herself.

No woman with even a grain of common sense, she reminded herself, would permit herself to become seriously interested in someone like Ned. He'd already admitted that one of these days he'd be moving on again. Evidently, whenever the spirit urged him to do so. At that point, it was unlikely that he would give a damn about her feelings. If, by then, she'd become hopelessly hooked, it would be just too bad from his point of view. He would continue on, playing his rolling stone role, brushing off any shreds of moss that threatened to impede the path of his progress.

When Caroline Marston arrived shortly before nine o'clock, Shelley was on the phone trying to track down a Santa suit that was long enough to fit someone well over six feet tall.

She hung up the phone, momentarily defeated. "Seems like Santas are supposed to be short and fat," she complained.

"Well," Caroline said, "Marty Ferguson is fairly short and fairly fat, if I remember correctly."

"Marty is hobbling around with his ankle in a cast," Shelley reported, "so I've had to find another Santa. I asked Ned Alexander..."

"Hmmm," Caroline observed. "Is he willing?"

"Yes, but I don't know where I'm going to get a suit long enough for him."

Caroline gave this consideration, then brightened. "Wally Burnett plays Santa at the Council on Aging's Christmas party every year," she said, "and I'd say he's as tall as Ned. Since the party isn't till Christmas Eve, Wally might loan his suit to you. Want me to ask him?"

"That would be terrific," Shelley said gratefully.

She was amused at the charm Caroline exuded while making her phone request to Mr. Burnett. And couldn't resist asking, once Caroline had hung up, "What is this Wally Burnett like?"

"He looks like Cary Grant," Caroline confessed.

"Married?"

"A widower."

"Hmmm," Shelley murmured impishly.

"This is strictly a business transaction," Caroline said loftily. But when Wallace Burnett arrived at the store an hour or so later to deliver the Santa suit personally, Caroline was all charm once again and Shelley couldn't blame her. He did look like a rather elderly Cary Grant, and he was a real charmer.

By then, business was becoming brisk and remained so throughout the whole day. But even while she was helping people select videos for Christmas gifts or ringing up sales, Shelley was keeping one eye on the door, waiting for Ned to appear.

The day passed, dusk descended, and there was still no sign of Ned. Benny and Brian arrived to restock shelves and Shelley pressed them into helping with the customers as well. They and Caroline stayed with her till closing time, and she was profoundly grateful to all three of them. As it was, each minute had seemed like an hour and each hour like a day and . . .

Where the hell was Ned?

Tuesday was a repeat of Monday, and by then Shelley couldn't help but be struck by the thought that maybe Ned had decided to move on, after that dialogue Saturday night. She told herself she should have held her tongue. Put the brakes on her curiosity about him. Why had she asked him so damned many questions?

Shelley tossed and turned through that night, and faced the chill gray dawn with a throbbing headache and a sick feeling in the pit of her stomach.

Fortunately, business was brisk again. Dealing with customers was the only thing keeping her going.

During a brief mid-morning lull, though, she couldn't keep herself from approaching Caroline at the checkout desk and asking, "Does Ned Alexander still have any videos checked out?"

Caroline gave her a look that was swift, and much too perceptive, but she didn't say anything. She turned to the computer, programmed Ned's name—or the portion of it the two of them knew about, Shelley thought bitterly—then silently read the information brought up on the screen.

"Well?" Shelley demanded, trying to hold back her impatience.

"Strange, he still has the videos he took out last Saturday," Caroline said. She looked up at Shelley, her pretty blue eyes troubled. "What's the problem?" she asked.

"I wish I knew," Shelley admitted.

"I think it's the first time even a single day has gone by without Ned showing up since he walked in here," Caroline said.

"Yes, I know," Shelley nodded. For a while, as she kept busy, her headache had diminished somewhat. Now it returned full force, and her stomach was churning. Probably a virus, she told herself. *Probably I'm coming down with a virus.* But she knew better.

"The two of you spat about something?" Caroline asked.

"No," Shelley said. And added, wryly, "We're hardly on spatting terms, Caroline."

"I don't know about that," Caroline said. "He's certainly interested in you. I've watched the way he looks at you when you're busy and not noticing him."

"Don't imagine things," Shelley ordered sharply, then relented. "I'm sorry, Caroline," she said wearily. "I didn't mean to snap at you. I'm disappointed, that's all. He promised to be Santa. Now I guess I'd better get busy and find someone else."

"You're giving up on him, Shelley?"

"What else can I do? Chances are he's left town."

Caroline looked shocked. "You can't believe he'd go away without saying goodbye," she protested.

"Can't I? On the contrary, I think that's exactly what Ned would do. Just slip away. It's his style, Caroline, from everything I could find out."

"What have you found out about him, Shelley?" Caroline paused, then said, "If that's an out-of-line question, skip it."

"No, it's not out of line," Shelley said slowly. "But it's a question I can't really answer. That's to say, I've found out very little about him. Only that he wanders."

"What?"

"He's a wanderer," Shelley tried to explain. "A professional wanderer, actually. That's what he does."

"No one just wanders, Shelley."

"Ned does."

"I find that very difficult to believe," Caroline said, after a moment. "Everything about Ned speaks of...well, of background, of breeding. Also, he's well educated. I would peg him as a professional in some field..."

"I just said he's a professional wanderer, Caroline."

"That's ridiculous," Caroline stated. And added, as if she'd been called upon to defend Ned and was going to live up to the calling, "Ned Alexander is a great deal more than a so-called professional wanderer, Shelley. I think—"

Caroline was unable to expound further on what she thought because several customers arrived simultaneously and there were no more empty gaps.

By four o'clock, Shelley felt so miserable she didn't think she could keep going another moment. She touched her hand to her forehead, certain that she must have a fever and was disconcerted to discover that actually her skin was quite cool. Too bad, she thought disconsolately. A raging fever would have given her a valid excuse to close up the store and go home.

As it was, at five o'clock she faced Caroline and Benny and Brian and said thickly, "I think we'll close."

Three incredulous "What?s" were fired at her simultaneously.

"I feel rotten," Shelley confessed. "Probably one of those twenty-four-hour viruses. I've been hanging in all day but frankly, people, I've had enough. I want to go home and crawl into bed and blot out for a while."

"Why didn't you say something sooner?" Caroline admonished. "I thought you looked peaked, but I assumed it was because you've been working so hard. Shelley, for heaven's sake go home. The boys and I can handle things here and close up later."

"No," Shelley protested. "No, that would be an imposition. Look, let's just put out the Closed sign, okay? The world won't come to an end if people can't get their videos till tomorrow."

"Well," Caroline said, "maybe it's my inborn sense of Yankee thrift but I don't agree with that at all. It just doesn't make sense to lose holiday business, Shelley, when you have the boys and me on board here. Unless, that is," Caroline added rather stiffly, "you don't think we can manage on our own."

"Of course you can manage on your own, Caroline," Shelley said quickly. "It's just that—"

She broke off, because Ned was walking through the door.

Shelley had never in her life been so glad to see anyone, yet her heart sank as she looked at him. He was wearing the oversized coat, and the battered hat was placed firmly on his head. He looked as if he could use a shave, he was stony-faced as he confronted her, and he was wearing the camouflaging tinted glasses.

She imagined she could feel a thick wall of insulation between them and suspected that over these past three days Ned had rewrapped himself in whatever it was he used to keep the world at bay. She couldn't imagine the two of them ever again sharing the intimate kind of supper they'd shared in her shop kitchenette.

He was remote, this man facing her, more remote than he'd ever been, suddenly a complete stranger to her.

There were other people coming into the shop, too. As if on cue, Caroline literally nudged Shelley's elbow and said, "Will you help that lady over there, the one with the red coat, Shelley? She was in yesterday trying to make up her mind about some videos, and I think she needs guidance."

Shelley quickly muttered, "Excuse me," to Ned and sought out the woman in the red coat. A lot of people needed help, she was thinking rather incoherently. Herself among them.

It was a relief, though, to plunge into work for a few minutes, to help the red-coated woman choose a selection of videos for Christmas-giving, and to know that she now had yet another satisfied customer.

She turned away from wishing this new customer a merry Christmas to find Ned at her elbow.

His face was still impassive, she couldn't read his eyes and she wished he'd dispense with the damned tinted glasses for once and for all.

"I brought back some tapes," he said, as if he needed an excuse to come into the shop. "But, while I was here I thought I'd better speak to you about the Santa Claus suit. Maybe if you haven't found one yet I can try to. It suddenly occurred to me your party's not that far off."

Shelley's head was throbbing, her stomach was burning and she felt sick and miserable. Resentment toward the cause of all her misery suddenly surged. "That's right," she said, the resentment lacing each word. "But I'd suggest, Ned, that you just forget about playing Santa Claus." She finished, scathingly, "I don't think it's a role you were ever cut out for, anyway."

Chapter Five

Shelley turned her back on Ned and approached a man and his wife who were studying a rack of videos for sale. Ned heard her ask, "May I help you?"

He watched her reach down and select a cassette, knew she must be discussing its merits with the couple, but couldn't quite hear what she was saying. Not that it mattered. Shelley, though perhaps not quite as thoroughly as he had, had learned the art of camouflage and he was sure that right now she was being an alert, interested salesperson and would probably wind up having these people choose more than one video as a gift.

Ned was accustomed to making diagnoses—in fact he'd once had a reputation as an excellent diagnostician and was called in for frequent consultation for that purpose by his peers. Now, watching the way Shelley was standing, the tautness about her, he verified a diagnosis already made. Shelley was unhappy, on edge, and although he didn't want to attribute an importance to himself that wasn't valid he was sure he was the cause of her present misery.

He looked up to find Caroline Marston's eyes fixed firmly upon him. Caroline was at the cash register, and Ned strolled over to her. She, too, was busy, but when she had a free moment he said, "Tell me something, will you, Caroline? Has Shelley already gotten another Santa Claus for Saturday?"

Caroline frowned at him, and it didn't take diagnostic skill to realize he wasn't very high on her preferred list at the moment. She said shortly, "No, she hasn't."

"Did she find a costume, do you know?"

"Yes, she found a costume."

"Caroline, look, it's not my intention to let her down." Ned stopped short, aware that he actually was pleading for understanding from this woman, something he couldn't remember having done with anyone, ever before.

"How could you expect her to know that?" Caroline demanded bluntly.

"I couldn't, I suppose," Ned admitted. And, the fact was, he'd come pretty close to letting Shelley down. He'd come very close, a few hours ago, to taking a walk out of town.

He mumbled, "I'll go look over some videos, and wait till Shelley's free."

Caroline said grimly, "You may have quite a wait."

Was that to imply Caroline knew Shelley didn't want to talk to him? Equally grim, Ned said, "I have all day. All night, if necessary."

He *thought* he detected a faint smile in Caroline's blue eyes. But her face remained impassive and all she said was, "That's up to you."

It was a while—quite a long while—before there was a lull, and at that point Shelley immediately began restocking some of the shelves herself.

For over an hour, Ned had been watching her deliberately keeping herself as busy as possible. Almost pouncing on customers as they came into the store, offering her services. Again, it didn't take an expert to know that she was bent on avoiding him.

When she started stocking shelves, though, he moved in. There was an unconscious note of authority in his voice as he said, "Shelley, I need to talk to you."

She looked up, not quite meeting his eyes. "I really need to get these cassettes back on the shelves," she said.

"Let the twins do it," Ned suggested. "Brian was just wandering around with his hands in his pockets, whistling."

"The twins are staying overtime as it is," Shelley snapped defensively. "I was about to tell them to go home."

"Would you prefer that I leave, too?"

Ned's tone was like a dash of ice water. Shelley put the stack of videos she was holding down on the nearest empty space, and hoped she didn't look as helpless as she felt. Just being with Ned undermined her. She had been determined to tell him again to forget about playing Santa Claus for her. She didn't want any favors from him.

"Can't you answer my question?" Ned demanded, and the edge of anger to his voice startled her. It was an emotion she'd not seen him display before.

She said hesitantly, "I want you to do what you want to do."

"What kind of an answer is that?"

Unconsciously, Shelley put a hand to her aching temple. "You should do what you want to do," she said.

"I usually do," Ned said, but there was a flatness to the way he said it and his tone was mirthless.

Shelley became aware that he was scrutinizing her closely, behind those tinted glasses. He said suddenly, sharply, "You don't feel well, do you?"

"I'm okay," she managed, both startled and surprised. "I have a headache, that's all."

She felt long, slender fingers touching her forehead. She had the crazy feeling that in another minute Ned was going to grab her wrist and take her pulse. He said, "It's a shade more than that, I'd say. Frankly, you look like hell..."

"Thanks a lot," Shelley managed.

"What I'm saying is, you look exhausted. Wrung out. You've been working too hard," Ned decided. "Go home. I'll help Caroline and the twins close up."

Shelley was exasperated as she faced him. Did he think he could come into her life one minute and then go out of it the next? Then slide back in again? If that was his style, it wasn't hers.

She said stiffly, "Thanks, but I'm perfectly all right. Also, I don't intend to close the store for another two and a half hours. It's the twins who are doing overtime, not me. Nor Caroline, for that matter. Caroline has volunteered to work nights until Christmas, in addition to her daytime stint."

Ned didn't answer that. His gaze was still centered directly on Shelley's face, nor did it swerve as he said, "I understand you got the Santa Claus suit."

"Yes," she said, too tired to argue about it. "I got the Santa Claus suit."

"Where is it?"

"In the office, in a white cardboard box."

"Don't you think I'd better try it on? If it's not long enough, there's not much time to rustle up a duplicate."

"Try it on if you like," Shelley said, feigning an indifference she could only hope would come across to him.

He gave her a long, level, unreadable look, turned on his heel and stalked to her office. She finished restacking the shelves, saw that Caroline and the twins had all the customers well in hand, and was sorely tempted to go back to the office herself and get a couple more aspirin. But she was not about to walk in on Ned.

It was another ten minutes or so before he came walking across the store toward her. She saw that he had removed both the hat and the tinted glasses, though he still wore his oversized coat. There was a hint of both mischief and humor in his arresting, light blue eyes and a trace of laughter in his voice as he said, "It's long enough. But, you were right. I'm going to need some stuffing."

"I brought some pillows," she said.

"You should have told me," he chided. "But then, I guess that part can wait till Saturday. I'll be here early on Saturday, incidentally, in plenty of time to help you get ready before I change into costume."

Shelley nodded, at a temporary loss for words. She was seeing concern on Ned's face she hadn't expected to see there, and his voice was surprisingly gentle as he said, "Get out of here, Shelley, and go home and get some rest, will you? Make yourself some hot milk and take a couple of aspirin, and try to relax, okay?"

She found herself nodding like an obedient child. "Okay," she said.

"See you Saturday, bright and early." As Shelley watched, Ned gave Caroline and the twins a farewell wave then turned and walked out of the shop.

* * *

For half an hour after he left Shelley's store, Ned literally did wander, up and down the streets in the vicinity of the small shopping mall. Then he came to a junction and struck out on a road that led across the town to a wide strand of beach that bordered Cape Cod Bay.

He'd been told that the Cape was one of the few areas along the North Atlantic coast where the salt water literally froze during the winter months, creating a vast expanse of ice floes that looked like pictures of either the Arctic or Antarctica. Today, the image was a valid one. Standing at the water's edge, Ned looked out upon a frozen wasteland that stretched clear to the horizon.

He let his eyes and his mind fill up with the white emptiness. He tried to keep things that way, but other visions kept intruding, and finally he turned and stalked along the water's edge, the frozen sand crunching beneath his feet.

The visions had started coming back to him Saturday night, after he'd finished cleaning up the supper things in Shelley's kitchenette.

On his way to the small studio apartment he'd rented over a garage, in a house a quarter mile or so from the mall, he'd passed through a residential section of lovely homes and they, like the mall itself and the streets and everything everywhere, were decorated for Christmas. He'd seen the lighted Christmas trees twinkling in living-room windows, and a terrible feeling of desolation had swept over him. He knew he wouldn't go back even if he could go back. But sometimes the memory of all he'd lost swept over him and became near-catastrophic. A memory centered primarily on Lucy, who had had coppery red hair and topaz eyes very much like Shelley's eyes, and who would have been eight years old this past October, had she lived...

Ned's eyes had blurred with tears as he struck off down the side lane that led to the house where he was staying. The couple who owned the house both worked, and they hadn't gotten around to putting up Christmas decorations as yet, for which he was thankful.

Alone in his studio apartment he'd poured himself a hefty measure of Scotch then had sat down with a book he was reading and tried to concentrate on the printed page as he sipped the Scotch. It was a futile effort, though. He fingered the cassettes he'd rented from the store, but knew he didn't have the patience to watch them, either. The movies usually provided distraction and served a second purpose, as well. They made him feel as if he was catching up on life. For a lot of years he'd been too busy for much in the way of diversion, like movies or plays or sports or concerts. He'd lost a certain kind of pulse beat, or so it seemed to him, and the movies were helping him get it back again.

Ned gave up after a time and went to bed, but sleep was a stranger that night. It was nearly dawn when, finally, he dozed and he awakened feeling groggy and out of sorts.

He told himself, irritably, that he had been a fool to come to New England at this time of the year. He should have gone somewhere in the tropics where there was no snow, no carols echoing in the crisp cold air, nothing to make him remember...

His mood was heavy all that day and the next and the next. So much so that he didn't want to inflict himself on Shelley or anyone else. He had learned that when he got into those deep, dark moods he was his own best companion. He walked the Cape Cod beaches, drank more coffee than he should have and subsisted on canned soups for his lunches and suppers.

He knew Shelley must be expecting him to come in about the Santa Claus suit. And he went to bed Tuesday night promising himself that he'd head for Video Vibes first thing in the morning. But again he had a terrible, nightmare-plagued night, and by morning decided that there was only one thing to do and that was to start roaming again. To wander to another place in another climate.

He nearly succumbed to the urge, was on the verge of packing up and catching the bus for New York, via Hyannis, that stopped in front of the movie theater up on Main Street. But then he thought about Shelley, and her Christmas party, and remembered he'd actually promised her he'd be Santa Claus.

He, of all people, playing Santa Claus...

He'd started out for Video Vibes shortly before noon. And he was passing the toy store at the edge of the mall when he saw the little girl. She was climbing out of a station wagon, and a woman, evidently her mother, was holding the door open for her. She was wearing a bright blue coat whose hood framed her face, but he still saw the copper-colored curls and his heart constricted. She had chubby little legs and a cherubic little face and—yes, oh God—topaz eyes, Ned saw, as he came closer to her.

He met those eyes and when she smiled at him, a sweet, childish smile, the wrench of pain that jolted through him nearly took his breath away.

She was just about three, he estimated. The same age Lucy had been when she'd run out into the street in front of his home in Scarsdale....

Ned had veered away from the mall, walked to the movie theater, waited for the New York bus and climbed aboard it. But he got off in Hyannis and went into a cinema and, in the darkness, tried to lose himself for a while and then to regroup.

Most of the time he had much better control of himself. But Christmas, he acknowledged, and Shelley were getting an upper hand.

It would be very easy to love someone like Shelley and, he reminded himself, love was the one thing he couldn't afford. So he would be Shelley's Santa Claus, as he had promised. But, right after Saturday, he'd move on.

On that note, Ned started back to Devon and his rendezvous at Video Vibes.

Shelley had yet another headache when she woke up Saturday morning. It was a bright, sunny day, perfect for her Christmas party, but she couldn't bring herself to rejoice in it.

Wednesday night, after Ned had left, she had sensed that Caroline was holding back all sorts of unspoken questions. Even the twins had looked curious. It had been a relief to shoo them all out of the store a few minutes before nine, then to lock up and go home herself.

In the night, Puffy had come in and curled up on the foot of her bed. Impulsively, she had reached down and tugged the cat toward her until Puff was resting in the crook of her arm, purring contentedly. She had dropped off to sleep, thankful for that warm, furry presence. She had been feeling singularly alone.

Now, as she put on a bright, Christmas-green dress, paid special attention to her makeup and, as a final touch, tucked a fake white poinsettia into her dark hair, she wondered if Ned was going to show up for the party. She felt she'd talked him into playing Santa Claus, very possibly against his will. And, subsequently, he'd simply been too polite to come out and tell her he didn't want to get dressed up in a bright red suit and heave out a lot of ho-ho-hos.

On the other hand, Ned had looked terrible Wednesday night. As if he'd been through some kind of private hell. And she was a little bit ashamed because she'd been thinking so much about herself, the aching head, the upset tummy that had lingered all week, that she now felt she'd shortchanged him.

On the other hand, what could she have done? She didn't know Ned very well, but she knew him well enough to have already learned that he disliked personal questions, didn't want to talk about himself and probably would detest having a solicitous fuss made over him.

He, on the other hand, had been solicitous of her. She remembered very well that touch of his finger on her forehead, the way he'd admonished her to close up the shop and go home. She'd had the funny feeling that Ned was used to looking out for people, which didn't make sense. Certainly the one thing that could be said about anyone who was a wanderer was that he must also be a loner.

But then, Ned hadn't always been a wanderer.

As she left her house, Shelley remembered the song about the little boy who only wanted his two front teeth for Christmas. She was thinking that if she were given the choice of a single Christmas gift she would ask for a crystal ball, but a very special kind of crystal ball. Instead of possessing the power to look into the future, her crystal ball would come with the capability of reversing directions, and peering into Ned's past.

Shelley stopped at the small coffee shop in the corner of the mall and bought a container of coffee and a big bran-and-raisin muffin. Then she parked in her usual place and made her way to Video Vibes.

She hadn't been in the store five minutes when the door opened and Ned walked in.

The bag with the coffee and muffin in it was still standing on the checkout counter. Ned looked at it and grinned, and held up a similar bag. "Case of great minds running around in the same direction," he proclaimed, as he drew forth two muffins and two cartons of coffee.

"Mmmm," Shelley said, slightly shamefaced, "I'm afraid I wasn't as considerate as you were."

"Bought sustenance for yourself alone, is that it?" he teased.

"Yes, I'm afraid so. I..." She let the sentence trail off. She didn't want to tell him she hadn't expected him to show up.

Apparently he got the unspoken message for his face darkened briefly. But then he said, "Okay, so we'll share equally. A cup and a half and a muffin and a half apiece. In the kitchenette, maybe? It might be an idea to nuke the coffee for a few seconds. It's probably getting on the cool side."

Ned picked up both paper bags as he spoke, and headed toward the back of the store. Shelley watched him, and experienced a mix of emotions. This man made her churn, because he frustrated her, intrigued her, attracted her, and dismayed her all at once. And, as well, because something deep inside her cried out with a need to get to know him better. She'd never before known anyone even remotely like him ... and she doubted very much she ever would again.

And the problem is, she admitted to herself honestly, I don't want to let him go...

After a moment, she followed him. Ned had the coffee containers in the microwave and he'd gotten out two plates and put an exact muffin and a half on each of them.

With an extravagant, courtly gesture he pulled out a chair for Shelley. She was happy to sit down. Being around Ned when he acted like this made her knees start to tremble.

He sat down opposite her and started buttering a muffin. Shelley watched his hands at work, and wondered how much you could really tell about a person by his hands. A lot, she thought, if you were observant enough. Ned, for instance, might have worked at a lot of odd jobs in the course of his wanderings, but basically she was sure he'd never done anything like manual labor. There was a very special kind of dexterity to his fingers.

The question popped out. "Where were you this time last year, Ned?"

"In Aruba," he said.

"Aruba?"

"Yes. It's a Caribbean island, down near the coast of Venezuela...."

"I know where Aruba is. But what were you doing there?"

"It was just a way station," Ned said. "I stayed there for a couple of weeks around Christmas and New Year's and did a little casino gambling."

"You?" She hadn't meant to sound quite so incredulous.

"I wield a wicked slot-machine handle," Ned said urbanely.

"I thought you said you worked everywhere you went."

"No," he corrected. "Not everywhere. Just when I want to work, and I had been working. I had been in St. Thomas for a couple of months, where I bartended in a little place down near the docks where the cruise ships come in. I might say that I learned to make what is un-doubtedly the world's best piña colada. As I may prove to you, one day when the weather is warmer."

One day when the weather is warmer. Ned got a funny look once he'd said that and Shelley didn't need anyone to spell out the look's meaning for her. They both knew he wasn't going to still be around Cape Cod by the time the weather got warmer.

She said, "Well." Then repeated herself and said, "Well," again. "I guess I'd better start getting ready for the party," she told him.

"Shouldn't that be 'we'?" Ned asked her.

"I beg your pardon?"

"I somehow thought today's party was going to be a joint effort. I'm not mistaken about that, am I, Shelley? I admit, the other night I got the impression you weren't all that eager to have me saddle up my reindeer. By any chance, have you gotten someone else to play Santa?"

"No," Shelley said. And added frankly, "Matter of fact, I was going to be Santa Claus myself if you didn't come in time."

To her surprise, Ned grinned. "Don't you think you would have tripped over those pant legs?" he queried. Then he grew sober, and said, "Look, I know I've been rather conspicuously absent the past few days. I don't blame you for thinking I wasn't going to show up at all for the party. Something came up I just can't go into with you, Shelley. But there is one thing I want you to know."

Ned paused. "I'm going to ask you to accept what I'm about to say," he told Shelley then. "Please just accept it, will you? Right now it's all I can tell you, but it's the truth. I discovered I couldn't let you down."

Ned spoke with an intensity that couldn't fail to register. Shelley suddenly felt tuned in to him in a new and different way. Ned certainly hadn't offered her anything in the way of an explanation for his actions. Yet she knew that what he just had told her was significant, very significant.

She said shakily, "Thank you," not sure exactly what she was thanking him for. Except she had the strong feeling that what Ned had just told her had been a revelation to him ... and, somehow, marked a kind of turning point.

She realized her confusion must be showing on her face when Ned slanted a long, light blue gaze at her and said, "Don't try to figure out too much, Shelley. I've found it's better to just let things happen. At least, sometimes not to try to dissect too much."

Shelley couldn't think of a right answer to that. Ned stepped into the gap and asked, "Through with your coffee?"

"Yes." She nodded.

He stood, picked up her paper carton and his and the plate that had held the muffins. "We'd better get a move on and start putting our act together," he said. "Otherwise, the kids will be beating on the door and we won't be ready for them."

Chapter Six

Shelley glanced at the clock as Ned spoke. He was right. It was eight o'clock, so they had exactly an hour to get ready for what she hoped would be a horde of children.

She thought about that and had a moment of apprehension. "Suppose no one shows up," she worried, her voice not much more than a whisper.

Ned chuckled. "You're borrowing trouble," he advised her, "and that's a waste of anyone's time. I've seen posters all over the mall advertising your party, plus that ad you put in the weekly newspaper. What do you bet we run out of cookies and punch in half an hour?"

"I hope you're right," Shelley said, her apprehension still showing.

Ned laughed, bridged the distance between them and to her astonishment gave her a hug which could have been called brotherly, except that it set off a series of small electrical charges up and down her spine. "Look," he advised, "think positive, will you? This is going to be the first of a long series of annual Christmas parties for kids, and it's going to be an absolute smash. Believe me."

He gave her another hug for emphasis, and the little imaginary electrical charges overloaded. Shelley said weakly, "We'd better get you into that Santa suit."

"Shouldn't we set up your refreshment table first?" Ned suggested. "And what about balloons? You do have balloons, don't you?"

"Yes," Shelley said.

"Shouldn't I start blowing them up?"

She shook her head. "No. I ordered balloons from the balloon lady, you know, she has a shop at the other end of the mall. She promised to bring them by herself around eight-thirty."

"Do you have the little paperback storybooks you were planning to give out?"

His memory surprised her. "Yes," she said. "In cartons, behind the checkout counter."

"Where is the table you're going to use for refreshments, Shelley?"

"It's a fold-up job, it's in a long carton back of the boxes of paperbacks."

"And you do have some sort of tablecloth and napkins?" Ned prodded.

"Yes."

"Shelley..."

His tone was patient, indulgent, and the expression in his eyes made her melt all the more. He was looking at her with a tenderness that was very disconcerting. It took an effort to pull herself together, precede him into the store and, as he'd put it, to start getting the act together.

She still wasn't in full gear, and though she tried to prod herself Shelley was only too aware she was lagging.

Ned, in contrast, was a model of efficiency. He set up the table with a minimum of effort and Shelley breathed a sigh of relief over that. She'd read the instructions on the carton and had been contemplating a long, arduous struggle with the various parts. She'd intended, in fact, to ask the twins to come over and help, but then the twins had mentioned that they both had an early basketball practice scheduled but should be able to be at the shop by ten, at the latest.

Now, following along in Ned's footsteps, Shelley spread out the bright holiday tablecloth and stacked up napkins. She put out paper cups for the fruit punch she was going to serve, then suddenly remembered she had a big basket in her car, decorated with red and green ribbons, which she'd brought along as a container for the books.

At that point, Ned said, "I'd better get the Santa suit on, don't you think? I'll need your help when it comes to adding the stuffing."

Shelley nodded, and said, "I think I'll go ahead and fill the bowl with the first batch of punch. Kids won't care if it isn't icy cold."

Ned nodded agreement, and disappeared in the direction of the office. Shelley followed, bent on getting the punch out of the refrigerator. But Ned waylaid her to ask, "Where did you put the Santa suit, Shelley?"

"I hung it on the back of the bathroom door," she said, and busied herself with the punch.

She'd filled the bowl and was returning the empty gallon jugs when she almost bumped into Ned on the threshold. She took one look at him, and couldn't repress a giggle. He was the most streamlined Santa she'd ever seen.

"Okay," he said with mock severity, "go ahead and tell me I'm too skinny for the job."

Shelley stared at him and felt her throat closing up on her. Even in a baggy Santa suit, Ned was anything but skinny.

"How about helping with the pillows?" Ned suggested.

Shelley swallowed. Stuffing Ned's trousers with pillows meant a kind of proximity she wasn't ready for. She'd stashed the pillows to one side of her desk. Now she retrieved the first of them and blindly held it out to Ned.

Ned grunted, stuffed, then said, "It'll take more than that. A couple more front ones, anyhow. To say nothing of some backside ones. Why don't you take care of the backside first, Shelley?"

There was no escape route. Shelley nodded, and approached him with a pillow tucked under either arm. She tried to apply herself to the job at hand without becoming personal about it, but the effort was useless. She had to get close to Ned, very close, to accomplish what needed to be accomplished. With fumbling fingers, she pulled out the elasticized band of his Santa pants with one hand and started stuffing the resulting space with a pillow with the other hand. In the process, her fingers brushed his smooth, cool skin and Ned yelped.

"Hey," he protested, "you're tickling me."

"Sorry," Shelley said briefly, and started in with the other pillow. Ned wriggled this time when she touched his skin, which did nothing to help her. The pillow was only partway in, her fingers fumbled, everything went lopsided and the pillow slid to the floor.

"Damn," Shelley mumbled.

"Having trouble?" Ned asked calmly.

"Yes. The casing's slippery." She tried again, and this time he helped her by holding out the elastic band himself. But this assistance on his part only revealed the snug-fitting dark blue jockey shorts he was wearing.

Shelley was reprieved by the peal of the doorbell. "Must be the balloon lady," she said hastily, and took off toward the front of the store.

It was the balloon lady, and the next ten minutes were spent positioning bunches of red, green and white balloons around the store.

As the balloon lady left, Shelley spied several children heading toward the store, most of them young enough to be clasping the hand of an adult.

She sped back to the office. Ned had already completed the pillow stuffing, had fastened on a luxurious white beard, mustache and eyebrows, and was putting into place the white-trimmed Santa cap, which came complete with a white wig lining so there would be no chance of his true hair color peeping through.

The transformation was terrific. She watched Ned redden his cheeks with a little blush she'd set out for him, then he threw his shoulders back, let out a resounding "Ho ho ho," and his fake tummy quivered like the proverbial bowl of jelly.

"Will I do?" he asked then.

"I think you were made to play Santa Claus," Shelley assured him a little breathlessly.

"I think you were made to play the part of a beautiful princess," Ned told her softly. "You look like the spirit of Christmas, Shelley, in that dress, with that flower tucked in your hair."

The store bell tinkled, announcing someone's entrance, and Shelley seized the opportunity. She said hastily, "That must be Caroline," and peeked through the curtains. "It is Caroline, and there are kids lining up," she reported. "Oh, Ned, Ned, I think you're right. I think, just maybe, we're going to be a big hit."

Ned watched Shelley go out into the store, pulling the door that closed off the office behind her. They had decided that he would wait until there were a lot of kids in the store and then make his grand entrance. Shelley was to cue him when the time came by knocking on the door.

Meantime, she had put on a Christmas record and he heard the strains of "Jingle Bells." He stiffened. Lucy, at age three, had already learned to lisp the first words of "Jingle Bells."

He thought about Shelley saying he'd been born to play Santa Claus. She couldn't be more wrong. He shouldn't be here, Ned told himself, suddenly miserable, actually a lot more than miserable as he became afraid that he wasn't going to be able to get through today. He might have to walk out on Shelley's party to save his own sanity....

The minutes inched by. Ned knew that Shelley had some bourbon around, they'd shared a drink the night he helped her trim the Christmas tree. He thought about finding it—there weren't that many places to look in, in this small space—and taking a couple of slugs for courage. But he knew, from experience, that drinking wouldn't help. A long time ago he'd learned that, for him at least, all a bout of drinking produced was a monster hangover. But no respite. The memories, the problems were still there, always still there, when you woke up.

Ned willed himself not to think about anything at all for a few minutes...one of the many tricks he'd learned in the course of his wanderings. He went into a kind of mental limbo, but when the knock came he still was not ready.

He fought back the impulse to run wherever he could run, to climb out the bathroom window, if necessary, and then race through the mall to wherever he could get ... someplace as far away as possible from the scene of Shelley's Christmas party for kids.

But then something seemed to snap. Maybe because he saw the expression on Shelley's face, as she peeked in, change from smile to worry; heard her soft, questioning, "Ned?"

Ned walked by her and out into the shop, booming, "Ho ho ho, merry Christmas," and he tried to put all the considerable discipline he possessed into making himself believe that, for this small segment of time, he really was Santa Claus.

The punch and the cookies were in danger of running out within less than an hour after Shelley opened her shop doors to the children. Caroline was dispatched to get new supplies of both. An hour or so later, the twins were sent forth on the same errand again.

By noon, Shelley decided that just about every child in Devon must have stopped by Video Vibes. An urgent plea was conveyed by Brian to the balloon lady. Fortunately, the balloon lady had stocked a good supply of holiday colors and Brian came back carrying such a huge bunch of balloons in each hand, Shelley marveled they hadn't caused him to become airborne.

Ned, on the spur of the moment, elicited a little help from Caroline and the twins while he continued roaming among the kids, and the next thing Shelley knew a makeshift throne had been erected and Ned was sitting on it, holding audiences with the kids one by one.

Why hadn't she thought of that? Shelley asked herself.

The twins appeared with a camera that made instant prints. Caroline lugged the basket of paperbacks across the store, and set it on the floor on Santa's left side. As each child descended from the throne, one of the twins took a picture and the other twin offered a paperback Christmas story.

Shelley had planned her party to last from nine to eleven. But the kids kept coming, some of the older ones on their own, as the morning progressed, and she didn't have the heart to turn any of them away.

Around noon, things began to abate. Ned climbed down from his throne, stretched, and said with a laugh, "I was beginning to feel muscle-bound. Shelley, I have an idea."

There was genuine enthusiasm in his voice, and she looked at him curiously. There had been a bad moment, when she had opened the door to see Ned slumped at the table in an attitude of terrible defeat. She had been afraid he was suddenly going to walk out on her after all. He'd glanced up, and she'd felt herself immersed in an aura of profound sadness. When he had looked at her, she had flinched from the pain in his eyes.

Now, those eyes were sparkling and so was Ned.

She asked, her voice a shade huskier than usual, "What's your idea?"

"Well, why don't we keep this party going a while? In fact, why don't we expand it to include grown-ups?"

She stared at him. "What in the world are you suggesting?"

"Just that." He turned to Caroline. "Could you or the twins print up a sign saying, 'Closed till four, when, by popular demand, we will continue our Christmas party

for both children and adults, until our nine o'clock closing time'?''

Caroline was already saying she could work up such a
sign in no time flat, using some cardboard and green and
red markers. But Shelley raised a detaining hand. "Wait
a minute, wait a minute," she said. "We're not prepared
to offer refreshments for the adults. And we've already
gone through so many gallons of punch I've lost
count...."

"No problem," Ned said quickly. "We'll give the
grown-ups cookies and eggnog. We can have both 'with'
and 'without' eggnog...that's what you were planning
anyway, wasn't it?''

"Yes, but just for a few evenings before Christmas,"
Shelley said.

"Well, you can do it then," Ned said. "Seriously,
Shelley, I think this would be a good investment. People
won't forget you; you'll attract a whole load of new customers." He paused. "Look, Caroline and the twins and
I can work out the details," he said, "while you see if you
can find some sandwich makings in the fridge. I'm cav-
ing in from hunger and I'd better eat in a hurry if I'm to
climb back on that throne. I don't think we should close
up until Caroline has the sign ready to tack to the door."

Shelley glanced at him suspiciously. She had the feeling that, in a nice way, he was telling her to get lost. Still,
she didn't doubt that Ned must be hungry. Hours had
passed since he'd consumed a muffin and a half and a
cup and a half of coffee.

She sighed, went out to the deli and then ferreted some
ham and Swiss cheese out of the fridge. She also found a
jar of pickles and some rye bread and built a very large,
very thick sandwich for Ned.

She had just finished putting her creation on a plate, cutting it in two and adding a couple of pickles when Ned stepped in.

"We'd better close the door," he advised. "There's no way I could eat with this beard on without totally messing it up."

He was stripping off the beard as he spoke and doffing the Santa cap with the built-in wig. The result made him look ludicrous, for he still had bushy white eyebrows that were at total variance with the rest of his face, as well as with his smooth, sandy hair. Shelley smiled inadvertently.

"Funny, eh?" Ned challenged, as he sat down at the table and started wolfing the sandwich. He chewed vigorously, then paused, to ask tentatively, "Shelley?"

"Yes?"

"Look, I didn't intend to take over a few minutes ago. It just seemed like such a golden opportunity. Continuing the party, I mean."

"It seems to me maybe you've just worked yourself up into a party mood, Ned," Shelley said quietly.

Ned stopped eating, and looked at her. "Maybe I have done that," he admitted, and could not have sounded more surprised. "And . . . I guess I was out of line. It is your store, after all."

Shelley noted that the light had gone out of his eyes, and although she could see no real reason why she should feel ashamed she felt ashamed, anyway. He'd been thinking of her, her business, after all. And she'd been so totally unresponsive.

She said carefully, "Continuing the party's a good idea. I just wasn't ready for it, that's all. Maybe I should learn to get in gear faster, I don't know. This was an experiment for me, and I guess I didn't go too far in my thinking about it.''

"I wouldn't say that," Ned protested. Gently, he asked, "Is this your first business venture, Shelley?"

"What do you mean?"

"Well, have you ever had your own business before?" She shook her head. "No."

"I guess this isn't the best time to ask, but what made you start Video Vibes?"

"Well, when I decided to stay here I knew I'd need to do something," Shelley confided, the words coming slowly. "I've had a variety of jobs over the years in selling, also in advertising. But this time I didn't want to work for someone else, I wanted my own business. It occurred to me that while you could rent videos in the supermarket, there was no separate store for videos in town. I found out a lot of people went over to Orleans to get their videos, so it seemed to me there'd be quite a market for a local enterprise. . . .''

"And you were right, of course."

"It looks that way, yes."

"Are you maybe a little bit afraid of success, Shelley?"

"I've never thought I was," Shelley said honestly.

"A lot of us don't think we are, or think about it at all, until the moment comes," Ned said. "Then, well, I guess then maybe it's more than some people can handle.

"Look," he added hastily, before she could reply to this, "I didn't mean to get in so deep. I need to put my beard back on and return to the throne. If, that is, I have a public awaiting me.''

Shelley opened the door a crack. "You have a public awaiting you," she assured him.

"Okay, then. Suppose we keep going until two. Then we'll put out Caroline's sign and call a halt for a couple of hours. That will give us time to get the eggnog together, maybe send the twins out for some more Christmas napkins and such, if you're running out..."

Again, there was curiosity in Shelley's glance as she surveyed him. "You've thought of everything, haven't you," she said.

"I doubt that," Ned replied, with a rather cryptic smile. And busied himself with getting his beard on straight.

It was well after nine o'clock before Caroline was able to shoo the last customer-reveler out the door and put out the Closed sign.

She turned and surveyed Shelley, Ned and the twins, her face wreathed in a wide smile. "Well," she exclaimed, "what a day!"

The twins turned to Shelley. "Now how about our having some of that 'with' eggnog?" they asked in unison.

"No way," Shelley said firmly. "As it is, I think you've consumed at least a quart each of 'without.' How about you, though, Caroline? I'd say you're due a hefty jolt of 'with.'"

"Not tonight, thanks," Caroline said. She was already shrugging into her heavy, fur-collared coat, then sat down to pull her boots on. "I sampled a couple of cups of the plain stuff myself when Wally Burnett stopped by, and a little eggnog goes a long way with me."

The twins and Caroline left. Shelley switched off the shop lights. Only the Christmas tree lights still glowed.

Behind her, Ned asked, "Well, how about us?"

She turned. "What about us?"

"Don't you think we both deserve a hefty jolt of 'with'?"

She laughed. "Yes, I'd certainly say so."

"How about adjourning to your private sanctum?" Ned asked her.

Was he suggesting they do their eggnog-drinking at her place? Before she could come to a conclusion about that Ned said, with a toss of the head toward the door at the rear of the shop, "Back at our favorite table."

Shelley didn't know whether to be relieved or disappointed. She started toward the back of the store, en route glancing at the refreshment table. "A mess," she pronounced.

Ned followed her gaze. "It's almost all paper stuff," he reminded her. "I'll just roll it up in a big ball and we can consign same to the trash."

Shelley was pulling the door open. Over her shoulder, she said, "You make everything sound so simple."

"Well," Ned told her, "sometimes things are. It's we, ourselves, who complicate matters."

To her surprise, he reached in the fridge and withdrew a capped plastic container of eggnog. "Some of the good stuff," he said. "I managed to snitch it from a batch Caroline made a while back. I might add that I sampled it, and the lady knows her proportions."

Ned was pouring the eggnog into two coffee mugs as he spoke. He glanced around, found some nutmeg and said, "You like this, don't you?"

"Yes," she said, sitting down at the kitchen table and watching him, unable to take her eyes away from his hands. She loved the way he used them, even when doing the simplest task.

"Would you happen to have anything in the way of a snack that might go with this?" Ned asked her. "And I don't mean cookies. I munched my share of cookies."

Shelley stood up, intending to check her cupboard for some crackers and the refrigerator for some cheese. She got the crackers down without difficulty, but as she approached the refrigerator she had to pass Ned, busy sprinkling nutmeg on the eggnog. He was still wearing the plumped-out Santa suit, and they bumped. Ned reached out his arms to steady her. She could feel his pillows rolling against her, and she burst out laughing.

"What's so funny?" Ned demanded, still holding her arms.

"You," she gasped.

"Elaborate, lady," he ordered.

"You feel like I'd think a very, very fat lady in a circus might feel. All soft and sort of plushy."

Ned raised an eyebrow. "Do I, indeed?" he countered.

In the next instant, he tugged her toward him and Shelley felt as if she'd fallen into a feather bed. But there was nothing soft about his kiss when his lips descended to claim her mouth. It was initially a hard and demanding kiss, but then suddenly the mood changed. Ned combined tenderness and passion so exquisitely that Shelley, yielding to him, felt an unbelievably wonderful wave of ecstasy engulf her.

Ned's hands moved from her shoulders to the nape of her neck. She felt his fingers lacing through her hair, then they slid to her temples, lingering on her throbbing pulse, and his touch washed her with a pure delight that was like distilled moonlight. She rocked against the pillows, knowing dimly that she was in danger of drifting away on an exploratory voyage that could have only one ending.

But, regardless of consequences, in no way did she want to head back to shore again.

It was a shock to hear Ned laugh. "This'll teach me never to get fat," he joked as he released her and moved back.

Shelley, her emotions still supercharged, saw that his eyes looked darker, his mouth suddenly was taut, and there was a fine sheen of sweat on his forehead. That, of course, could be because of the Santa suit. It was warm in the kitchenette and the Santa suit was made from heavy cloth.

Shelley's own laugh was silent, and also mirthless. She wasn't wearing a Santa suit . . . but she felt as if she were on fire.

Ned put the mugs full of eggnog in the refrigerator and said, "Excuse me a minute, will you, and let me get this crazy costume off?"

He disappeared into the bathroom and for a long moment he stood with his back pressed against the door, breathing heavily.

What the hell had he been thinking of?

He posed the question to himself angrily, and followed it with a platitude.

Did he have to prove that fools really did rush in where angels fear to tread? Did he need to make that much of a fool of himself?

He drew a long breath, trying to regain at least a vestige of self-control. Then he took off the Santa suit and put his own clothes back on again. All the time warning himself that he was playing with fire, dynamite, whatever the hell you wanted to call it, where Shelley was concerned. Which wasn't fair, either to her or to himself.

Since he had started wandering, Ned had made it a habit to start each New Year in a new location. He might only stay in the new location a few days, a few weeks, maybe for a couple of months before the urge to move on came over him again. But it was a new-year, new-leaf kind of concept with him.

Now he reminded himself that the New Year wasn't all that far away. Three weeks, actually. But he didn't think he could wait that long to pull up stakes. It would be better for both Shelley and himself if he got the hell out of Devon as soon as possible.

On the other hand, he didn't want to hurt her, and he knew it would be far too easy to do exactly that. No, this time he couldn't simply take off, leave town, as he always had before. He was going to need a rationale of some kind, an excuse that would make sense to Shelley.

As he splashed some water on his face, then ran a comb through his hair, Ned warned himself he had some heavy thinking to do.

Chapter Seven

Shelley was still sitting at the table when Ned walked back into the kitchenette. Her hands were folded and she was staring down at them.

He took the eggnog out and slid her mug across to her. "May you have a very merry Christmas," he toasted softly.

He looked up, saw the surprise in her eyes and wondered what it indicated. Had she assumed he wouldn't be staying around for Christmas? Did it really matter to her what he did or didn't do?

Could be, he warned himself, that you're presuming too much.

He sat down opposite her, and tried not to think about the sensations just being near her aroused in him. The truth was, no matter how she felt about his being in or out of her life, he was becoming increasingly aware of the perilous fact that it was going to be hard as hell to leave her.

Over the past four years he'd made a lot of acquaintances in the course of his travels. He had a notebook full of names and addresses and phone numbers. He didn't send Christmas cards, but now and then he thought of someone he'd met and sent them a postcard from wherever he happened to be at the time. He never could give a valid return address because he never knew how long he was going to be anywhere. Which was the way he wanted it. He welcomed companionship as long as it didn't turn into friendship and, thus, threaten to probe beneath the surface. What he didn't want was involvement.

He'd been a lot of places, worked at a variety of odd jobs just for the experience such jobs would give him. But it had never, until now, been difficult for him to leave anyone or any place.

With Shelley, that wasn't going to hold. Without even trying, she had gotten a grip on him. There was something good and honest and beautiful and caring about her that reached out to him and touched him profoundly. He knew almost nothing about her, yet deep down inside he felt he knew all he really needed to know... at least to be sure of the kind of person she was. That wasn't something he'd ever been able to say about anyone else.

How could he possibly put her out of his life? Ned posed the question to himself, already knowing the answer.

He had to.

He grimaced, and Shelley saw the grimace. "What's wrong?" she asked quickly.

Ned shook his head by way of answer, and took a long draught of the eggnog. Watching that small bit of action Shelley suddenly felt sick at heart. He was shutting her off again. She tried to tell herself she was overreacting. It didn't work. Ned had a tendency, too often, to go in and out like this with her. One moment she felt she was at least beginning to get to know him. The next he was a stranger again.

Despite herself, tears stung her eyes. She was tired, the party had been a strain—she hadn't shared Ned's conviction about its being bound to be a success—and between all of that and Ned's abrupt change of attitude her nerves were fraying. To her dismay, the tears spilled over. She grabbed for one of the holiday-decorated paper napkins and wiped hastily, hoping he wouldn't notice.

He noticed. He noticed and suddenly stood, came around the table and drew Shelley to her feet. Shelley's pride surfaced and she pushed him away, turning blindly toward the shop, thinking only of escape.

She got as far as the Christmas tree. There Ned caught up with her. "Shelley," he said, his voice deep and husky.

Shelley stood still, the tears gaining in force and streaming down her face. A lot had been pent up and now nature was forcing its release. But she felt trapped. At the moment, she was a captive in her own store. The only place she had to go was out, and how could she rush into the snowy night, crying her eyes out? With her luck, she thought bitterly, she'd probably immediately bump into the biggest gossip in town, as well as a lot of *other* people she'd as soon not see right now. For, though the stores were mostly closed in the mall, the pharmacy and the two restaurants in the complex were still open, and there would be late Christmas shoppers still milling around.

She felt Ned's hands on her shoulders, and the breath went out of her. He urged gently, "Shelley," and she gave a long, shuddering sigh. His voice alone played arpeggios on her emotions. There was a quality to his voice, something special and different about it. It was a voice she'd recognize if she didn't hear him speak again for ten years.

He said again, "Shelley." Then, in a tone wrought with contrition, "God, I never intended to do anything like this to you. I want to make you happy, not miserable, can you understand that?" His laugh was short, bitter. "I'm not doing very well, am I?" he queried rhetorically. "Oh God, Shelley, please, darling, stop crying."

Please, darling. It was such a slender straw, but Shelley grasped at it. She turned very slowly and faced Ned. The lights from the Christmas tree softened his features and she was seeing him through the blur of her own tears, anyway. But everything about him was so incredibly beloved.

Ned smoothed back her hair and kissed her eyelids. His lips trailed over her damp cheeks, then came to settle on her mouth. His tongue probed her closed lips, urging them to part. Shelley, without even being aware of her body, pressed against Ned. Felt him, and knew his wanting was as great as hers. For she wanted him, oh God, yes, she wanted him. Desire streaked, flamed, wrapped her in a blanket of fire.

Ned's hands moved, circling her waist, curving under her loose-fitting sweater. She felt his heat against her skin, and as his palms covered her breasts she moaned softly, wanting more and still more.

Then Ned broke off, suddenly, so suddenly that only his grip around her waist kept Shelley from tumbling to the floor. Still clasping her with one arm, he managed to put a distance between them. A small, but very definitive distance.

She looked up into his eyes, startled and bewildered and hurt. She saw a smouldering passion that didn't make sense, in view of his actions. Then his mouth curved in a crooked smile and he said, "We can't, very well. Not here." He added, gently, "There's no place."

He was right, of course. There was no place, unless they both were willing to settle for a very hard floor. As it was, they'd put on quite a performance, and Shelley wondered if anyone, passing by, might have been able to see them through the decorated store window.

Ned said suddenly, "I don't know what to say to you."

Shelley clutched at normalcy. "There really isn't anything to say, Ned. We both got carried away for a moment, that's all." Her words sounded trite and unconvincing to her.

Ned said, "Oh yes, we got carried away. But I'd say it was a lot more than that for both of us, Shelley. This has been brewing for days and days. You know it. I know it. The question is," he went on, his voice so low she had to strain to hear it, "what are we going to do about it?"

There was an agony to the next phrase when it came; Shelley felt the words were being wrenched out of him. "I'm no good for you, Shelley," Ned said. "No good for you at all. I'm a person without a future, because I don't want a future. Which means that I have nothing to offer you. Absolutely nothing. I'd never forgive myself if I didn't make that clear to you. Because, regardless, I want you so damn much that every atom in me is aching from the wanting. And believe me, I'm not being quixotic when I say I have no right to even contemplate making love to you. Yet...I have the strong feeling you want me the same way. In which case I can only say we're both adults. We should know what we're doing. I would just have to be very sure there was no doubt you know what *you're* doing..."

Shelley walked across her shop to the big front window and looked out into the mall. It was a crystal night. The streetlights and the stars alike sparkled like faceted diamonds. Snowbanks edged the parking lot, heaped up mini-glaciers. There were only a few cars still around. The quiet was heavy in her ears. She imagined she could hear the sound of her own breathing, and that was heavy, too.

Ned had just asked nothing of her, yet at the same time he had asked everything of her. In a strange and oblique way he had put his cards on the table and was leaving the next move to her.

She had the strong conviction that whatever small part of the future they might be able to share lay squarely within her hands.

Whatever small part of the future? Shelley's imagination went into overdrive and she suddenly was sure she'd discovered what Ned's problem was, and it was a shocking, overwhelming discovery. He was suffering from some terrible terminal disease, he had only a very limited time left to live. That's why he felt he must wander, the proverbial rolling stone that does not permit itself to gather moss. That's why he was saying that he had no future, and could offer her nothing. He *literally* had no future, Shelley thought, and with that thought her hands went cold and her pulse began to throb and she shuddered as she met fear and horror head-on.

Fright surged and thoughts raced, her mind twirled like a mental kaleidoscope from which a single pattern emerged. Then she shook herself. How could she assume something like that? What if she took what he said merely at face value? Then what? In a split second she decided. If she and Ned were to be together for only one single night in her life, it would be better—infinitely better—than never being together at all.

She turned to him. He was a dozen or more feet away from her, standing in silhouette. She could see only his outline, and for a moment he seemed to her more ghost than man and she had to forcibly repress a choking sob.

Still on the edge of a sob, her voice was unsteady as she said, "Please . . . come home with me tonight."

Ned had not expected the invitation. He had been staring across the store at Shelley's back, and knew by her taut stance that her nerves were stretched to the breaking point, for which he certainly couldn't blame her. He saw her convulsive shudder, even from this distance, and fought the impulse to go to her. He had flung down his gauntlet. It was up to her to either sidestep it or pick it up.

Evidently she had elected to pick up the gauntlet. Why did that surprise him so? He knew they shared the same desire. He tried to tell himself that it was an easily identifiable flow, a natural, primitive, age-old element that surfaced between a man and a woman when they were attracted to each other. Why not accept that? Why not let it go at that? Ned wished he could, knew he couldn't. What he was feeling for Shelley went a step beyond the obvious, and that was what frightened him. He couldn't palm it off so easily.

He'd had a few contacts with women over these past four years that couldn't rightfully be called either affairs or relationships. They had, rather, been brief encounters, motivated by the same kind of a wanting that was motivating Shelley and himself. But there the similarity ended. He'd always been careful to limit himself to women he was sure he wasn't going to hurt. Women who wanted exactly what he wanted. Momentary gratification and escape. No regrets the next day. No difficult goodbyes.

It could never be that way with Shelley.

She was waiting for his answer to her invitation. He stared at her through the semidarkness, not knowing what to say. If he vetoed the suggestion, the veto was going to be a tremendous blow to Shelley's pride. If he went home with her, he was in danger of edging toward a commitment he couldn't make.

Shelley said, "I turned the heat down a long time ago. It's getting awfully cold in here. Also it's late, I'm tired. I think maybe I'd better just ... get going."

She was trying to let him off the hook, bless her. Ned recognized true, pure generosity and at that moment he knew he was dangerously close to falling in love with her.

She brushed by him, went back to the kitchenette and returned almost immediately, buttoning up her short coat as she moved toward the door. "Thanks again, Ned," she said, then waited for him to leave so she could lock up.

Ned retrieved his own coat. He paused by the tree. "Want me to switch the lights off?" he asked her.

"Yes, please," she said.

Ned stepped through the doorway and watched as Shelley became very busy turning the key in the lock. As if it had been preordained, he fell into step beside her. He felt her stiffen, saw her thrust her chin up in a determined way that was, in itself, a giveaway. A person shouldn't have to try so hard to be resolute.

They reached her car. Ned held the door for her then walked around and got into the front seat next to her. He saw her hand tremble as she fitted the key into the ignition switch, but she didn't let her emotions affect her driving. There were still icy patches on the roads. She handled them with the skill that comes from having done a lot of winter driving. Then she turned down a dirt lane and they bumped over frozen ruts toward a huge house, touched by moonlight.

Her house? Ned wondered. But Shelley drove past it, pulling up outside the door of a fairly small cottage.

"This is where I live," she said simply, as she got out of the car.

He followed her up a few steps to a back porch. As she opened the door, she said, "I should have left the back light on." She pushed a switch, and light flooded a small kitchen, decorated in blue and white with touches of yellow. Ned felt something rub against his leg and looked down to see a huge gray cat welcoming him.

"Hmm," Shelley said, "I guess Puffy likes you. She usually doesn't take to strangers so quickly."

Ned reached down and picked up the cat, and heard instant, ecstatic purrs. "I like cats," he murmured, and an involuntary picture of the little black kitten he'd given Lucy for her third birthday came to mind.

Shelley filled a kettle with water and she put it on the stove. "Take off your coat," she invited. "I'll make some coffee. It's a wonder Puffy isn't meowing her head off. It's past her dinnertime, and she has an enormous appetite. You must have hypnotized her." The words were spilling out of Shelley; Ned recognized them as a product of tension.

"I imagine you must be hungry," she went on. "I probably have some sandwich makings around, or I could fix some scrambled eggs...."

"Relax, Shelley," Ned said softly, an unconscious note of command creeping into his tone.

Shelley was opening a can of cat food. The cat wriggled and Ned put her down. Shelley, her voice so choked up she sounded hoarse, said, "I don't seem to be able to relax."

Ned crossed the room to her, took the dish of cat food out of her hands and set it down on the floor for Puffy. "Look," he said gently, "nothing's ever going to happen between us that you don't want to happen, Shelley."

"It isn't that . . ." she began.

"Then what is it?"

"I don't know," she said. Ned saw her frown. "I don't know," she repeated. She gestured toward the doorway at the end of the kitchen. "There's wood laid in the living-room fireplace," she said. "Would you go touch a match to the kindling? It's kind of cold in here, too."

Shelley's living room was a mixture of the old and the new. Ned recognized a couple of excellent antiques. There was no particular color scheme but there were splashes of vivid hues and bigger areas of muted tones, lots of books, lots of pictures on the wall, a kind of pleasant confusion. Shelley wasn't messy. On the other hand, she also wasn't neat.

He got the fire going, then sat back on his heels and watched the flames licking the chimney bricks. He was discovering that there was something very personal about this room, yet because Shelley's decor was so unorthodox, her taste so eclectic, it was hard to pinpoint any absolutes about her and Ned was also discovering he wanted a few absolutes.

He tried to recall everything she'd ever said to him about herself. Not much, he conceded. He didn't know much more about her than she knew about him. And it was funny, but when the shoe was on the other foot it didn't fit so well.

Part of his problem, he conceded, was that he was used to getting a lot of answers while at the same time being questioned very little. It was a condition, he supposed, that might be considered a perk of his profession. Doctors, traditionally, did most if not all of the questioning.

Doctors. Ned stood, and strolled restlessly over to the windows at the back of Shelley's living room. They looked out on a snow-covered field, sprinkled tonight with silvery moon motes. He knew he was almost deliberately churning himself up, and he couldn't tolerate too much of that kind of churning. His profession, he reminded himself, was something else he'd put behind him. Medicine had no place in the kind of life he was leading now, and intended to keep on leading.

It was a hell of a lot easier to drift through the months and the years with no ties, no restrictions, no obligations. Especially when one no longer had anything, anyone, to go back to.

Shelley came into the room. He heard her footsteps, soft upon the wide-boarded pine floor, and swung around. She'd slipped off her shoes and was walking barefoot. Her green holiday dress emphasized her figure and dramatized her vivid coloring. The white flower tucked into her hair brought out that dark glossiness.

She was carrying a tray with a silver coffeepot on it, cream and sugar, cups and saucers. Ned watched her set the tray down on the coffee table in front of the fireplace and in a sudden, intense moment he wished he could have Shelley painted just as she was now, dressed in holiday colors and looking so unutterably beautiful it hurt to look at her.

She poured his coffee, added the cream and sugar she knew he took without asking him about it. Ned accepted the cup from her, noting it was fine English bone china, a family heirloom, he suspected. Shelley sat down on the couch; after a moment Ned sat down next to her. He set his cup and saucer on the low, round table, reached across and took Shelley's cup and saucer from her and placed them on the table, too. Then he drew her into his arms and did what he had been aching to do. He kissed her gently, eloquently, caring and concern and passion merging so that the kiss went beyond being a kiss and became a bond between them, all the stronger because it was invisible.

Shelley melted into Ned's embrace and stopped asking herself a lot of questions she couldn't answer. She'd already told herself that if she could be with Ned only for tonight it was far better than never being with him at all.

Finally their lips parted and Ned leaned back, drawing her with him. Close to him, with his arm around her, Shelley experienced an unexpected feeling of peace.

For a long time they were silent, Ned making no move to touch her again. And gradually the tension ebbed out of Shelley.

Only then did Ned ask, "How long have you lived here, Shelley?"

"The better part of two years."

"But you didn't open your shop until last fall, did you? I seem to remember Caroline telling me that."

"That's right," she said, surprised that he had talked about her with Caroline and wondering what else Caroline might have said about her. Had rumors, gossip, traveled to the point where they might have reached Caroline? She hoped not.

Here on the Cape, the old-timers still thought of her late grandmother as a Nickerson, not a Mitchell. Agatha Nickerson, who had come from an old Cape family and just happened to marry a man from Maine who had traveled to the Cape to teach school in Devon. Because of her grandmother's status in this town, much that would not otherwise have been squelched had been squelched. There were few people still around who would remember or care about Justin Mitchell's dereliction. Justin was not a product of Devon. His father had died when he was very young. Agatha, for reasons never fully explained, at least to Shelley, had sent him back to Maine, where his paternal grandmother had reared him. Just as he, later, had sent his daughter back to his mother, at a time of crisis in his life.

There had been mention that, at the earlier time, Agatha had been suffering from a severe illness from which she wasn't expected to recover. She had, of course, recovered and lived on to an old age, lived ten years longer than her only son. Maybe the illness story had been invented to cover up something else. Maybe Agatha had been so grief-stricken by her husband's death, at a relatively young age, that she hadn't been able to cope with bringing up a child, especially a boy child.

Shelley brushed away conjecture, because the answers to such family questions had been lost in the mazes of time and, she'd come to believe, should stay lost.

She addressed herself to Ned's question about her store. "That's right," she said. "I opened Video Vibes last fall."

"You said you wanted your own business, once you decided to settle here in Devon."

"Yes. Years ago, I went to business college," she confessed. "In Boston. After graduation, I went to work for an advertising agency. My field was the statistical end of the operation. After holding a few other jobs, I found I liked selling, and for a while worked for a rather famous shop in Copley Place. Then, a couple of years ago, my grandmother became quite ill and so I transferred jobs and went to work for a small computer sales company in Hyannis. That way I could be closer to her, visit her a lot more often. I'd expected, in fact, that I'd be taking care of her, living with her, anyway. But as it happened she went from the hospital directly into a nursing home, because she needed a lot of specialized care, and she died in the nursing home."

"She lived in this cottage?" Ned asked.

"Oh, no," Shelley said quickly. "In the big house. We passed it on the way in, remember?"

"Your family homestead, Shelley?"

"Yes. My grandmother's family, that is. The house was in her branch of the Nickerson family for a long time."

"You sold it?"

"No, I still own it," Shelley said. "It's rented year-round to Regina and Dale Clark. Dale owns that big hardware store up on Main Street. As it happened, not long after my grandmother died the Clarks had a fire in their house. It was so badly destroyed it had to be razed. It was a terrible experience for them. Regina hadn't been too well at the time, and she just wasn't up to rebuilding. I wanted to rent the house, and that proved to be the perfect solution all the way around. The Clarks still have no particular desire to rebuild—there are just the two of them, and they're in their late-fifties. I'm sure one of these days the spirit will move them and they'll start looking at house plans. But for the moment we're all happy with our arrangement."

"If they do decide to build, will you move back into the big house yourself, Shelley?" Ned asked her.

"I don't know," she said. "I doubt it. On the other hand, I wouldn't want to rent to anyone I didn't know very well. Still, I'd hate to ever sell the house."

"A matter of roots?" Ned asked quizzically.

"Yes, I suppose you could say that."

"I take it you were the sole person to inherit the house."

"Yes."

"Don't you have any family, Shelley?"

Shelley hesitated. It occurred to her that Ned was asking her an awful lot of questions, but he was doing it so smoothly she hadn't been conscious she was being interrogated. Suddenly on the alert, wondering if maybe Caroline *did* know about her father and had passed the knowledge on to Ned, she said, "My mother lives in Mexico with her second husband. My father died a long time ago. I have a brother, but, well, we drifted apart a long time ago. We don't communicate."

"That's too bad," Ned said.

Shelley darted a suspicious glance at him. "Did Caroline tell you about my family, Ned?"

She was sure his surprise was genuine as he said, "Why, no. Is there something to tell?"

Shelley sat up straight, and reached for her coffee cup. The coffee was lukewarm, but she started sipping it anyway. If she was ever to get to know Ned, really get to know him, and if she was ever going to permit him to really get to know her, she was going to have to tell him about her father. She knew that, though she hated the knowledge.

She began very carefully. "There's quite a bit to tell, actually. Though it can be said quickly. My brother was—is—a thief, Ned. That's why I want no contact with him. My father was also a thief, a fraud. That's to say, he perpetrated frauds. He was in the insurance business. My brother went into business with him, right after college. They ripped off people who were not only clients but friends, as well. They were clever, very clever. But finally it caught up with them. My brother managed to skip out of the country, taking a good chunk of money and he's stayed away ever since. The last I heard he was living on some island in the Orient. I have absolutely no idea what he does today for a living. Maybe he's gone legit—isn't that what they call it? I don't know, and I don't care to know. We are much, much better off, both of us, out of each other's lives and at this date we would have absolutely nothing in common.

"My father would have stood trial, but almost on the eve of the trial date he died of a heart attack. Later, my mother married the man who had served as my father's attorney. I'm sure he's a good person—but there, again, we have nothing in common. He's retired now. He and my mother have made their lives in Mexico. I have no desire to visit them, though I've been asked. It's a long time since my mother and I have been close. My parents, you see, sent me here, to my grandmother's, for my last two years of high school . . .

"I didn't think people in Devon had ever heard about my father," Shelley admitted unhappily. "I thought my grandmother, who was a very strong and wonderful woman, was not someone about whom people voiced scandal, and as far as I know this was a family skeleton she managed to bury completely. Now I guess I was naive to assume that. If Caroline knows . . ."

"What makes you think Caroline knows?" Ned asked.

"She told you, didn't she? That's why you started asking me about my family, isn't it?"

"Dear God, no," Ned protested. "I asked you about yourself, about your family, because I want to know about you, Shelley. It was no more than that. Caroline's never gossiped about you, if that's what you're implying. I think she has the very highest regard for you and admires you tremendously for starting your own business and making a go of it. As do I," he finished quietly.

Shelley looked at him, weariness and vulnerability etched on her lovely face. Ned discovered he wanted to comfort her, console her, take care of her...and to make love to her. Shaken by the force of that wanting, he said aloud something that sprang, suddenly, from his subconscious.

"Trust me, will you?" he asked Shelley.

Shelley met his eyes, and she didn't have to be told that there was a lot to that simple question, a very great deal. In effect Ned was telling her that he couldn't return her confidences, couldn't tell her about himself. Not yet. But, this time around, he was not closing the door on her.

Impulsively, she reached her hand out and touched his cheek. Ned jumped as if she'd scorched him. But then he took her hand and held it against his face, and his eyes became full of messages, a whole chain of unspoken communications that somehow spoke volumes to Shelley.

Finally he said simply, "I want you. Oh God, Shelley, I want you so much." His voice was hoarse, ragged with pent-up emotion. And Shelley felt herself come alive, every vein in her body pulsing in response to him.

This time, when he drew her into his arms, it was a beginning with only one possible ending. Ned kissed Shelley and caressed her, molded her flesh with his palms, cupped her breasts in his hands then tantalized her nipples with his warm, soft mouth while those hands roamed lower and lower, to center finally, with exquisite finesse, upon the throbbing core of her whole being.

Ned gave to Shelley, first. He let her soar into her own realm. But then gradually she drifted back to earth and she began to return his gift, shyly, at first, giving in her own way but with such caring and such sharing that Ned was deeply moved even as the passion he'd been keeping under such strict control began to escape its bounds. This time he joined Shelley in a culmination that stretched toward the edges of infinity.

Chapter Eight

Ned woke up to find lemon-bright December sunshine filtering through the filmy white curtains at Shelley's bedroom window. He closed his eyes tightly and held his breath, afraid to move, equally afraid to open his eyes again and really look. Then he felt her stir at his side.

She was there. This wasn't an illusion. He wasn't hallucinating. Shelley was there, at his side, beautiful and warm and extremely alive.

He turned and discovered that her topaz eyes were wide open, surveying him as if she had been equally disbelieving. A surge of something he didn't want to put a name to—because it felt too much like love—infiltrated Ned, burrowing deep. He reached out his arms to Shelley and she came into them as if she belonged there. He nuzzled the soft hollow under her ear, tasted the sweetness of her skin. Ached with the sudden resurgence of his need for her. And knew she wanted to satisfy that need as much as he did, because she was sharing it as she'd shared so much with him since last night, every step of the way.

They made love without the initial urgency that had possessed both of them last night. Lazy lovemaking, each giving more than taking, so that the result was even better, even more wonderful, even more sublime, Ned thought a trifle incoherently when—a while later—Shelley was again within the circle of his arms. But this time they were both quiet, unmoving, wanting only the warm knowledge of each other's presence.

After a time they got up and fixed some breakfast, then sat at the maple table in Shelley's kitchen looking at each other as if each had discovered a new continent holding more marvels than could be either enumerated or envisioned.

Then Ned became possessed of the need to move, just to move, just to let his muscles and his joints—and himself—ambulate with a new kind of unrestrained feeling. When he communicated this to Shelley she laughed and said, "Me, too," and they dressed quickly, bundling up with some extra wool scarfs Shelley unearthed from a shelf in her closet. They drove all the way out to Provincetown, at the tip of Cape Cod, where they climbed down long wooden steps to a sandy stretch they could almost claim as their own that December morning. There were hardy souls out exploring the winter beach but not that many.

They walked close to the tide line, the sand crunching under their feet. Ned stopped and picked up a handful of pebbles and scanned them. Watching him, Shelley said, "You're holding glacial rubble. The glaciers passed this way and actually molded the Cape millions of years ago."

"I know," Ned said, to her surprise, because this was something most casual visitors to Cape Cod didn't know.

He explained, "I was reading a book on Cape Cod geology a few days ago. Got it at the library. It was fascinating."

"What other sorts of things do you like to read?" Shelley asked, wondering if his taste in literature was as varied as his taste in movies.

He smiled. "Biographies, mostly biographies of contemporary people, mysteries, best-sellers, horror, now and then. I'm not too much for science fiction, though I dabble in it occasionally. I suppose you might say that primarily, except for absolutely pure escape, I like to delve into people and events over the past fifteen or twenty years. What about you?"

The return question came quickly. Shelley said, rather absently, "Oh, I like a variety of subjects, too, in my reading." She knew the answer was vague, but it was the best she could do because she was thinking about him. When she analyzed the matter, it came across that his concentration in films was primarily centered on the past fifteen or twenty years, too. It was almost as if that had been a time gap in his life, and he was trying to fill it up again.

Where had Ned been, these past couple of decades? she wondered. And what had he been doing to take and keep him so out of the mainstream?

He was still holding the handful of pebbles. Now he tossed them back down on the damp sand. "Sometimes there are semiprecious stones mixed in with the rubble," he informed her. "But there weren't any in that lot. Shelley..."

She was still thinking about him, wondering about him, a situation which seemed to have become one of her principal avocations. "Yes?" she asked.

"Don't," Ned said.

That injunction brought her to. "Don't what?" she asked, with a frown.

He smiled faintly. "Don't get to thinking too much," he advised. "There are times for it, but this isn't one of them. At least, that's how I feel about it. It's so beautiful out here. I want to share the moment and the beauty with you...no past, no future, just the here and now. For just a little while. Okay?"

He was too perceptive, Shelley thought. Much too perceptive. But he also was right. They owed each other this little space of time to be together. So that, for a little while longer, they could keep together the magic fabric that had been woven between them last night.

An hour later, having walked and explored a long length of the beach, they retraced their steps to Shelley's car. Then, chilled through, but exhilarated, they drove into the center of town and found a restaurant that served Portuguese kale soup. They feasted on the soup and crusty bread and red wine, and then they strolled along Provincetown's narrow Commercial Street, arm in arm.

There were quite a few stores open, ready to lure Christmas shoppers. Ned and Shelley window-shopped, but when she saw a pin she liked, silver filigree set with purple wampum—that part of the quahog clamshell the Indians once used for trading money—Ned insisted they go inside and take a look at it. He further insisted on buying it for her, and Shelley was at once conscience-stricken. It was a lovely but relatively costly piece of jewelry, and she was sure he couldn't afford it. But then he brought forth that expensive leather wallet and she saw again that it was bulging with bills. Ned extracted a couple of the bills, the transaction was accomplished and he insisted on pinning the pin to the white sweater she was wearing, then and there.

"To good luck, forever and ever," he murmured, as he fastened the clasp.

Shelley could only say, "Ned, you shouldn't have." And despite her pleasure in his gift, a small cloud had intruded into the clear day. The wallet, the abundance of money, had made her remember something she had been forgetting. Ned, when all was said and done, was as much of a mystery to her as ever. Except in a personal sense, a highly personal sense. There, they were kindred spirits, so totally in tune it was a miracle.

No matter what happens, that's the part I must remember, Shelley told herself as they left the little shop and emerged into the sunlight of Commercial Street.

The afternoon was waning as they started back to Devon. Ned was driving—Shelley had asked him to—and suddenly he deviated from the main highway, striking along a side road toward Cape Cod Bay.

The road ended at a beach, high on a bluff. Ned, bringing the car to a stop as close to the edge of the bluff as possible, said, "I hope you don't mind. But I thought we should see the sunset...."

They clambered down the bluff and huddled together in a little hollow in the sand where they were out of the wind and protected from the cold, as well. The sun was performing magnificently on the western stage, still emperor of the heavens as it slowly descended toward its rendezvous with night. Ribbons of gold spiraled across the water, Shelley saw Ned's face bronzed by them and she felt a love for him so intense she was momentarily consumed by it.

She was frightened by the depth of her own emotion. Frightened and also saddened because, for all she knew, this might be the only time they'd have together. She searched his face, and saw that he was watching the sunset's afterglow fill the sky with glorious colors.

A few minutes later, Ned's hand upon her elbow was strong and firm as he helped her climb back up the bluff. But the sand shifted, she slipped back now and then and each time realized she was depending on his strength.

Once they reached the top, she told herself that she was going to have to start standing on her own feet again, here and now.

Ned had never promised her that theirs would be a forever time.

Shelley had just arrived at the shop Thursday morning when Caroline called. But Shelley didn't recognize her voice because Caroline was so hoarse she could scarcely speak.

"Flu, I think," Caroline croaked. "Some damn bug, anyway. I should be fine by this afternoon."

"Don't be ridiculous," Shelley snapped, then mellowed her tone. "Sorry, Caroline," she amended, "but *don't* be ridiculous. I hope you're tucked into bed and have taken some aspirin and have plenty of fruit juice to drink. Soon as I can, I'll sneak away from here and make sure of that."

"Don't *you* be ridiculous," Caroline rasped. "There's no way you're going to be able to leave that store today without losing a lot of business. You tend shop, do you hear, and don't worry about me. I'll be fine. What concerns me is that I'm letting you down."

Caroline barely made it through that speech before her voice gave out entirely. Shelley hung up the phone and knew that business or no business she was going to have to sneak out and look in on Caroline a couple of times during the day, taking along a supply of fruit juice and bouillon with her. What had started out as a casual business relationship had merged into a real friendship between her and Caroline.

The first customers were on hand by the time the store opened, and subsequently the morning began to take on a nightmare quality. It was impossible to handle everyone and everything and still give the kind of service she wanted to give, Shelley soon realized. She settled for doing the best she could do, but wasn't happy about it.

Unfortunately, she'd given the twins the day off. So, she thought resignedly, as she rushed from cash register to checkout counter to VCR displays and video shelves, there was nothing for it except to do the best she could do.

Then Ned walked in.

Since Sunday, he'd reverted to his old customer status. He'd appeared each day to bring back some videos and take out some new ones. Since the store had been consistently crowded and busy, there had been no chance for any real conversation with him. Nor, Shelley thought somewhat resentfully, had he exactly gone out of his way to create any opportunities for close encounters. He had been pleasant, charming, actually had spent more time chatting with Caroline than he had with her.

Now, he was hatless, and instead of the oversized tweed coat he was wearing a heavy, dark green hooded jacket that looked warm, new, expensive, and fit the way clothes were supposed to fit.

Shelley saw him glance around, and was sure he had assessed the situation even before he approached her to ask, "Where's Caroline?"

Shelley had just rung up a sale and was in the process of gift wrapping a cassette for a customer. She explained, "Caroline has the flu or something. Anyway, she's sick and I'm worried about her and—oh, damn it."

A sharp edge of the gift-wrap paper had nicked the side of her finger, and a small red line appeared.

Ned said, "Here, let me. You go take care of another customer." With that, he stepped behind the counter, deftly handling the gift paper, scissors, cassette and tape, with an efficiency that made Shelley groan.

Two young housewives who watched movies together while their respective youngsters were in kindergarten were waiting to return several cassettes and simultaneously check out some new ones. Shelley started to say something to Ned then yielded and went to help out her customers. When she'd finished with the housewives, an elderly man who came in regularly and loved to have her assist him in his rental choices claimed her attention. After that, she dealt with a few customers who wanted to buy videos for Christmas gifts.

The morning sped by, and Shelley was grateful to have Ned substituting for Caroline, though that was the last thing in the world she would ever have intended to have happen.

She glanced at Ned as frequently as she could. Again, he was surprising her. He was dealing with customers, handling transactions, as expertly as if he'd been in retail sales all his life.

Had he?

That was one question Shelley was sure she had the right answer to. No, Ned had not been a shopkeeper or a salesman, she was certain of that. Nor a banker nor a stockbroker nor a bus driver nor a restaurateur nor a pharmacist nor, she thought, a lawyer. None of those occupations "fit" him.

She still felt that whatever he'd done had something to do with those marvelous hands of his. Though maybe not as directly as she imagined. It occurred to her that he could have been a writer. Have been? He could *be* a writer. This wandering ploy could be the cover for gathering material for a book about becoming a wanderer late in the twentieth century when people, allegedly, were far too programmed to give themselves free rein to do anything like that.

Were that the case, she, Caroline, the twins, everyone else Ned met and would meet until he got all the material he wanted for his book, would be grist for his mill.

Shelley's imagination was going at full speed, and the resentment that brimmed at the thought of Ned using her in such a manner was genuine. At that moment, he happened to glance her way to find her looking at him with such ferocity that his eyebrows rose interrogatively and then he frowned.

As soon as he could, he crossed to her side. Shelley had just handed a customer her change and for the moment was free. Ned, she saw, was again frowning as he looked down at her. "May I ask just what that was all about?" he demanded.

Shelley tried to look innocent as she asked, "What?" and knew she was failing.

"Shelley, you're just no good at dissembling," Ned informed her. "A couple of minutes ago you looked at me as if you'd like to run a knife through my heart. What did I do?"

"Nothing," Shelley said.

"Come on," Ned protested, the frown developing into a scowl.

"It's true, Ned," Shelley insisted. "You didn't do anything. I was thinking, that's all."

"I hope you won't feel I'm leaping to conclusions if I suspect those thoughts included me," Ned said, his light eyes suddenly touched with frost.

"All right, they included you, I was just thinking about you, wondering a few things..."

"I don't think I'm exactly flattering myself, either, when I say I suspect you do a fair bit of wondering about me," Ned announced.

"Well," Shelley challenged, "if our positions were reversed, wouldn't you be doing the same thing?"

Ned gave her a long, level look. The irritation faded from his face. Watching him, Shelley had the funny feeling she was seeing his mental gears shift, and she wondered just what that might imply. She saw Ned take a deep breath, then expel it fast. "Yes, if our positions were reversed I'd wonder about you, Shelley. I *have* wondered about you. I still do. Even though," he added with a slight smile, "I know more about you now than I did. Whereas the shoe is not on the other foot, is it? I realize that. I'll have to think about it. That's all I can say. I'll have to think about it."

With that, Ned turned on his heel and sought out a customer he might be able to help.

At noon, Ned insisted that Shelley go back in the kitchenette and fix herself a sandwich which, he instructed, she was then to sit down and eat slowly. "I want you to take a half-hour break," he said. "I'll handle the store."

It wasn't the first time she had gotten the impression that Ned was used to giving orders and having them obeyed without question. She looked at him curiously, and was glad that he wasn't looking at her at that moment. Her telltale face had already given enough away for one day.

She trotted back to the kitchenette like an obedient child, opened a can of tuna fish and concocted a quick tuna salad, and then used about a third of the mixture to make a sandwich. She had to smile at herself as she did so. Without even thinking about it she had left enough tuna salad so there would be plenty for Ned to share.

Shelley sat down at the little round table, munched her sandwich and drank a glass of milk, and was slightly surprised when she felt a flow of new energy taking over.

She stretched out her legs and willed herself to relax. Limp shoulder muscles, limp arms, limp hips, limp legs, limp feet. She deliberately slackened her body, then took a couple of deep breaths, in and out, and stretched. By the time she finished this small routine she could understand why cats like Puffy seemed so blissful after doing a series of stretches. She actually felt like purring.

She was smiling when she went back into the shop. Ned caught the smile, and at the first opportunity came over to ask, "What happened? You look as if you just won the lottery."

"I relaxed," Shelley told him.

"Ha," he said with a knowing grin. "Something you don't normally do too much of, right?"

"I guess that's right," she admitted, then turned the tables. "I left the makings for a couple of sandwiches for you," she told him. "Now it's your turn to go on back there and let the troubles of the world slip off your shoulders."

Ned gave her a knowing look. "Why do you think I wander?" he asked her. And with that headed back to the kitchenette.

Shelley thought about that remark during the afternoon, when she had the chance to think of anything at all. Had Ned really managed to divest himself of the world's troubles—or, more specifically, his own troubles—by turning his back on home and family and setting forth to become a professional wanderer?

She doubted it. There were moments when Ned looked incredibly weary, sad; when she felt that he was being haunted by memories he couldn't escape.

Late in the afternoon, Shelley approached him to say, "I think I'll close at six today."

"Why?" Ned asked promptly.

"The twins couldn't come in today—they had to do something for their parents. Or didn't you notice they weren't on board?"

"I guess I've been too busy to notice much of anything," Ned admitted.

"Well, without the twins and without Caroline it seems wise to close up early."

Ned looked at her skeptically. "Am I to take that personally?" he asked. "In other words, am I being fired even before I've formally been hired, boss lady?"

"Neither," Shelley said. "Ned, look, I really appreciate what you've done today but I can't let you keep on doing it."

"You do need help, don't you, Shelley?"

"Yes, I need help," she admitted wearily. "A lot of people are probably eating early suppers about now so they can get out and do some Christmas shopping. That's why I think it would be wise to close before we get an influx."

"You don't think the two of us could handle an influx? We've been pretty busy today and I thought we were doing reasonably well."

"Ned," Shelley said desperately, "there's just no way I'm going to let you stay here and work. Unless," she added flatly, "you'll let me pay you for it." She stole a glance at Ned as she said this, and she didn't like either the look in his eyes or the set of his mouth.

He was a shade too calm as he asked, "Do you measure everything in dollars and cents, Shelley?"

"Of course I don't measure everything in dollars and cents," she snapped. The nice, relaxed feeling that had lasted since lunch began to dissipate fast.

"Then," Ned said, "why can't you accept help when you need it and it is offered to you? Or is it just me you can't bring yourself to accept help from?"

"I don't want your help," Shelley sputtered. And wished she could bite back the words. She hadn't meant to put it that way at all.

"I see," Ned said coldly.

"But you don't see," she protested. "Look, Ned, you could get all kinds of temporary holiday jobs around the mall and make some money. So why should you spend your time working free for me? It isn't that I don't appreciate it—it's just not right, that's all."

"Again, do you think only in terms of money, Shelley?" Ned's voice was icy.

"Of course I don't think only in terms of money," she said, as heated as he was cold. "But most people do have to think of money, Ned. Am I to assume that you don't?"

"That's right," he said. "I don't."

That remark, spoken with absolutely no intonation, stopped Shelley. She stared up at him, not knowing what to say. There had been moments when she'd thought she was at least beginning to understand Ned. But now any vestige of understanding had been hopelessly obliterated because she simply couldn't comprehend what he was saying.

He sighed. His mouth twisted in a wry smile. He said, "Do you know, we just had our first quarrel?"

"What?" Shelley asked, her mind going around and around in little circles.

"We just had our first quarrel," Ned said. "And over money, at that. Sounds almost conventional, doesn't it?"

Shelley came to. "We did not have a quarrel over money," she sparked. "If you want to call it a quarrel, what we were quarreling about was your... your attitude about life."

"My attitude about life?" Shelley saw Ned's amusement and gritted her teeth. "Shelley, love, that's an awfully big order," he observed.

"It certainly is," she agreed tightly. "Because your attitude is... absolutely insane."

To add to her fury and chagrin, Ned laughed. "Are you saying I'm absolutely insane?" he queried lightly.

"No. Yes. Maybe. How the hell would I know?" Shelley demanded. "Every time I think I know anything about you or what makes you tick you shoot it down. And how can I make sense out of anything that involves you anyway when I don't know where you came from or why you're here or where you're going—"

Shelley broke off. "Excuse me," she said. "A customer just came in."

"Damn the customer," Ned suggested softly. "We need to talk."

"We can't talk now," Shelley gritted out. "This is a business I'm running, remember? Maybe money's nothing in your life, but I have rent to pay and gas for my car..."

"And food for your cat?" Ned put in, teasing.

Shelley didn't accept the teasing. She glared at him. Then, without a word, she walked over to the door and hung out the Closed sign. With that, she headed for the person she'd designated to become the last customer of the day.

On her way, she called sweetly to Ned, "You might as well leave now. I'll be closing up as soon as I finish with this lady."

She didn't look at Ned as she spoke. She focused all her attention upon her customer, a worthwhile action, as it turned out, since the lady in question wanted to buy a VCR for her husband for Christmas and also to make a selection of movie cassettes to go along with it.

As Shelley discussed the merits of the different VCR models she heard the shop door close. She glanced up in time to see Ned's retreating back through the glass panel, and she cursed the mixture of pride and temper that had made her act as she had.

He was right. She had been swamped in the store today, so much so that there hadn't been a single minute when she could have escaped to check on Caroline. And that had been with Ned's help. He had offered his help to her, certainly she had needed it, in fact she had taken it and if she'd had any sense at all would have been both gracious and thankful to him. Also, if money wasn't important to Ned, who was she to question his attitude? He lived alone, probably very simply; perhaps it didn't take much money to keep him going. Maybe when Ned did work he made enough money to carry him through other times. He'd mentioned going to Aruba and gambling. Maybe he had won enough cash at the Aruba casino to keep him solvent for quite a spell.

Shelley's imagination went into high gear and she envisioned Ned at roulette tables, crap tables, twirling slot-machine handles, placing bets at racetrack windows or maybe in a jai alai fronton.

Was that what he did? Was Ned a professional gambler? Maybe a card shark? Those long, supple fingers could do a great job maneuvering a pack of cards.

But then Shelley thought about Ned, himself. The way he carried himself, with that definite assurance, almost an air of command. The way he looked great, somehow, even in shabby old clothes. The character stamped on his face. The clarity of his light blue eyes.

The gambling image didn't fit. Nothing fit. That was the problem. And as Shelley locked up her store she faced an even greater problem.

Had her dismissal of Ned tonight been all he needed to walk out of her life? Would he come back again?

She went to bed that night praying that Ned would come back again.

Chapter Nine

Shelley was restocking the display case that held gift cassettes shortly after eight o'clock the next morning when she heard a rap at the window. She turned to see Ned signaling toward the door, which was locked and still displayed the Closed sign.

She was sure that her heart leaped into her mouth, and it still felt very peculiar as it sank back into its usual position. Her pulse was doing overtime.

She let Ned in. He was carrying a white paper bag—evidently he'd brought coffee again—and he smiled at her as cheerfully as if nothing had ever happened. Bewildered, Shelley followed him back to the kitchenette and watched him take two cartons of coffee and two huge, thickly iced French crullers out of the bag.

"Sugar energy," he grinned, motioning toward the crullers.

Just looking at him turned Shelley's knees to rubber. She had been so afraid she would never see him again. She sat down with a sudden thump and propped her elbows up on the table. Her arms felt weak, her chin felt weak, her head felt weak.

Ned seemed to be blissfully unaware of her condition. He put a cruller on a paper napkin and passed it across to her with a carton of the coffee. He took a bite of his doughnut then paused to say, "Got these right here in the bakery in the mall. They're good."

Shelley could only nod in return. She had temporarily lost her voice. Also her power to swallow and chew. She stared at the coffee, at the cruller, and made no move toward either of them.

Ned sounded worried as he asked, "Is something the matter, Shelley? You're not coming down with Caroline's bug, are you?"

"No," she managed faintly. "At least, I don't think so."

"Did you eat a big breakfast or something?"

"No." The fact was she hadn't bothered with any breakfast.

Ned put down his coffee carton. "What is it?" he asked her directly.

Shelley pushed back threatening tears. Tears, in her opinion, denoted weakness, and she'd already shed a few too many in front of Ned. On the other hand, she had to say what she had to say because she was brimming over with it.

"I didn't think I'd see you again," she told him.

He reeled back, shocked. "Why in God's name would you think that?" he demanded.

"Last night," Shelley said. "The things we said to each other. The way I...well, the way I practically kicked you out of here."

"Shelley, my God, do you think I'm that thin-skinned?" Ned asked her. "You and I bickered, for a while there we didn't see eye to eye. Remember, I told you we'd had our first quarrel? That sort of amused me." He considered what he had said. "Amused isn't quite the right word," he admitted. "I suppose what I was feeling was that a first quarrel between two people is a kind of milestone. But regardless of that..."

"Yes?"

"I'll admit I was pretty angry when I left here," Ned said. "Principally because I thought you were being ridiculously stubborn. I wanted to help you out because you needed help and because...I like being around you. I like the feeling of working with you."

Shelley lost her voice.

"You, on the other hand, kept insisting that I should find a paying job somewhere in the mall since I wouldn't accept pay from you," Ned continued. "I tried to tell you I wasn't interested in making money and I couldn't seem to get that across to you."

He shrugged. "Oh, hell," he said, "that's all behind us. What's important is that you know I will never leave here without saying goodbye to you, Shelley. We've come to mean too much to each other for me to walk out on you without a word. It's not just what went between us the other night...though I admit that was pretty powerful chemistry. I think we've touched each other deeply on a number of levels..."

Ned broke off, looking more than slightly distracted, and Shelley discovered she was holding her breath. She wanted to say the right thing to him. She suspected he had said more than he'd intended to say, and maybe was trying to think of a way to retract a little of it. She saw him close his eyes tightly, sensed he was wrestling with himself in a way she didn't understand. But then, there was so much she didn't understand about Ned.

He opened his eyes and looked at her directly. No attempt to evade, she found herself thinking. He's leveling.

"Okay," he said, "I've come to care about you, Shelley, and I think you've also come to care about me. Let's just accept that, all right? You know my life-style. I think you can easily understand that I don't let myself get to the point of caring very often. But you," he added, with a smile that melted her, "seem to have slipped into my life. I'm not apt to ever forget you. I don't want to ever forget you. I hope you feel, or will feel, the same way about me."

Ned held out a long, slender hand. "Friends, eh?" he suggested.

Shelley accepted his hand, felt the warmth of his clasp, but at the same time a small cloud settled on top of her head. *Friends.* Oh, she was more than willing to be Ned's friend. She wanted to be his friend. Friendship was great. But they'd already gone a long, long way beyond friendship. Was Ned so blind he didn't know that? Or, rather, was it just that he didn't want to see it?

Ned went back to his coffee and cruller. Shelley couldn't eat, but she did drink some of the coffee. After a moment, Ned asked, "Heard from Caroline?"

"No. I thought I'd call her later."

"If she's been having a routine, short-term virus she should be starting to feel better," he said. "Look . . ."

"Yes?"

"Well, I don't want to push my way into your business, but I'm here today to help, if you'll accept that help."

Shelley wasn't about to make the same mistake twice. "I'll accept it," she told him.

Shelley and Ned put in another busy day at Video Vibes. The twins arrived early in the afternoon to help out, and the steady stream of customers kept all of them going till the nine o'clock closing time.

It was only when she was locking up that Shelley said, guiltily, "Once again, I never did get around to calling Caroline." She glanced at her watch. "It's rather late now," she said. "That's to say, I would imagine she's probably sleeping."

"Chances are she'll be back tomorrow," Ned assured her.

But Caroline wasn't back the next morning, and when Shelley called her around noon it was to discover that Caroline sounded very fuzzy.

Ned accepted this report with a minimum amount of comment, but his professionalism was surfacing, despite himself. By late afternoon, even though he knew he might be letting himself in for something, he made a decision.

The twins were on hand, and with the dinner hour nearing there was probably going to be a lull in the volume of business anyway. Ned approached Shelley and said diffidently, "Look, I'm going to have to cut out for a while. Just for an hour or so."

"All right," she said, but she was puzzled and afraid she was showing it. It occurred to her that most people would say where they were going, under similar circumstances. Ned, on the other hand, was being his usual, mysterious self.

"Would you like to use my car?" she offered, not so much because she was trying to pin him down as because she wondered if he might need transportation.

"Thanks, no, I can walk," he said, and Shelley fought back irritation.

She watched him leave the store. He was wearing the heavy green parka, he was bareheaded, and he looked terrific. Desire twisted, to be almost pushed away by something else. Love. Genuine love.

Oh, damn it, Shelley thought helplessly, I love him so much.

An instant later she was berating herself. How could she have *done* this? How could she have permitted herself to fall so hopelessly in love with a man who had made it very clear from the start that he had no intention of ever putting roots down anywhere?

She wanted roots. She wanted a home, a husband, a family, stability. She wanted all of those things perhaps even more than most people did, she conceded, because once she'd thought she had them all and then they had been ripped away from her.

When her parents had sent her to stay with her grandmother she had been forced to leave so much behind. School friends. Her school itself, where she was on the honor roll. Possessions she cherished, since she couldn't take everything with her to Devon.

At the time, her father had said it would be for just a little while, till things got settled. She hadn't known what "things" meant, she had assumed he was going through some financial problems and felt the need to cut back. Later, of course, she had learned the whole bitter truth.

Grammy had been wonderful, bless her. From the beginning, Grammy had tried to make her feel like the big old Mitchell homestead was *her* house. But Grammy had also been frugal, strict, anyway, about the spending of money. Later, Shelley had discovered that her grandmother had lived on not much more than half of her income, conservatively investing the rest. That, of course, had provided the inheritance that had enabled her to keep the house and cottage and to finance the Video Vibes venture. But when Shelley was in her teens, Grammy's frugality had also kept her from having a lot of the things the other kids in her class took for granted. Not that it had really made that much difference. She had done well in her new school, made a number of good friends, but living with Grammy still had seemed a temporary situation and it was a long time before she could accept the fact that her father was dead and would never be coming to take her home with him.

Ned had made the sudden decision that someone should look in on Caroline and that he was the logical choice.

He quickly covered the relatively short distance to Caroline's apartment, the address of which he had looked up on the computer when Shelley had been involved with a customer. The sky was gray today, there were clouds in the distance and an icy nip to the air. He suspected it might begin to snow again before morning.

Caroline's apartment was on the second floor of a condominium complex only a couple of blocks from the shopping mall. To date it was the only condominium complex in Devon and from what Ned had heard it had been built over considerable protest from many of the townspeople.

He couldn't blame the protesters, in a way. The condominiums were nicely designed and attractive, and a lot of people needed space like this to live in. But the complaint on the part of the locals was that the Cape was turning into a series of suburbs, and Ned had to admit he would hate to see that happen, himself. In his short time here, he had been captivated by the charm of the Cape, though, again according to the locals, it was a lot harder to find than it had been even a few years ago.

Ned climbed the stairs and rang Caroline's bell. He waited for quite an interval, then rang again, beginning to feel alarmed about her. He knew that if she were well she'd be back working at Video Vibes right now. Could she have taken a turn for the worse and maybe called an ambulance to transport her to the hospital in Hyannis?

Ned was about to decide that was probably exactly what had happened when he heard the door chain jangle, and Caroline slowly opened the door.

She looked terrible. Ned didn't like the putty color of her skin, her lips were parched and there was an unfocused glaze to her blue eyes.

"Ned," she exclaimed, her voice both weak and hoarse. "Whatever are you doing here? I thought it must be Wally."

"I'm going to get you back into bed to begin with," Ned said, and reached down and scooped her up into his arms because she looked so wobbly he was afraid she was about to fall flat on her face.

He felt the heat of her body, and didn't have to take her temperature to know she was running a fever. Muttering to himself that he should have thought about looking in on her sooner, he carried her through her living room into a small adjoining bedroom and plumped her down on the rumpled sheets and blankets.

"Well," Caroline said, managing a giddy little laugh, "that was quite an experience. I don't think I've been carried by anyone since my husband carried me over the threshold on our wedding night."

Ned plumped up the pillows under her head, smoothed the sheets slightly before drawing them, then pulled the blankets over her, all the while thinking grimly that doctors simply were not very good nurses. He needed a lady in white to go into efficient action here—then imagined what Caroline would say if he were to make such a suggestion. He suspected that Caroline was every bit as spunky and independent as Shelley.

Shelley. Ned smiled a bittersweet smile. How the hell had he ever let himself fall in love with her?

He glanced at Caroline and saw that she had closed her eyes. He reached for her hand, put an experienced finger on her wrist and clocked her pulse.

Caroline's eyes fluttered open. Ned saw her surprise and knew that some questions were certain to follow.

"You give me the impression you've done this before," she commented.

Ned nodded. "I've done it before," he acknowledged grimly.

"In what capacity, may I ask?"

His eyes met hers, held them briefly. "I'm a doctor," he said. "A surgeon, actually. But right now I think I'll try out a little family practice. Have you seen anyone, Caroline?"

"You mean a doctor?"

"Yes."

"No," she said. "No, I haven't seen a doctor, that is."

"What have you been taking?"

"Oh, some aspirin, fruit juice and such. Wally has been a dear. He's been getting soup from one of the local restaurants and bringing it to me each evening for my supper."

"That's good enough as far as it goes," Ned said. "But obviously it isn't going far enough. Are you allergic to anything?"

She shook her head. "Nothing I know of."

"Okay, I'm going to fill a prescription for you. I'll cut over to the pharmacy and get the medication and bring it back as quickly as possible. But first, do you have a flashlight?"

"In the top desk drawer in the living room," Caroline said hoarsely.

A minute later Ned was sitting on the side of the bed again, requesting politely, "Will you open your mouth, please? Wider, Caroline, you can do better than that. Umm," he said then. "Okay, now you can close."

"What did the 'umm' mean?" Caroline croaked.

"The umm means that I'm pretty sure I've verified my diagnosis," Ned said. "It would take a throat culture to be absolutely sure, but the point is I'm pretty certain your problem is bacterial rather than viral. That's to say, something an antibiotic can work with, or rather against."

He stood, and flashed her a smile. "Be back directly," he promised.

Outdoors, it seemed even colder and darker. Ned walked rapidly to the pharmacy, consulted with the pharmacist on duty, and wrote out a prescription. His medical license, fortunately, was recognized in Massachusetts. His license was one of the very few things he'd retained and kept updated.

Was that a sign that subconsciously, right from the beginning, he'd known one day he would go back to his profession? Not for the first time Ned thought about that, and came to the same conclusion he always came to. If there was anything he missed from his former life, it was surely the practice of his profession. But that didn't mean he wanted to go back and pick up his career, even were he able to do so. And he wasn't sure whether or not he would be able to do so. It was something he had never investigated.

Ned headed back to Caroline's condo, on the way pausing to pick up some sherbet. With a sore throat, the cold sherbet would go down well.

He left Caroline half an hour later, having started her on antibiotics and firmly cautioning her to keep taking the medicine at six-hour intervals, setting her alarm clock, so she'd be sure to do so, if necessary.

"And don't stop taking it until the bottle's empty," he admonished. "Even if by then you feel strong enough to run the Boston Marathon."

Caroline chuckled. "That'll be the day," she rasped. But then she reached out and grasped Ned's hand, twining her fingers through his. "What you've just done for me was pretty wonderful," she said.

There was a sadness to Ned's smile. "Just a case of the old fire horse hearing the whistle and having to gallop forth to the blaze," he said.

"Nonsense. I'm not going to go into it, Ned. I haven't enough voice, for one thing. I know you must also have reasons for whatever you're doing. But I imagine you must be every bit as fine a doctor as you are a man."

Caroline added, a mischievous twinkle in her eyes, "If I were Shelley's age, I'm afraid I'd fall head over heels in love with you."

Startled, it took Ned a minute to rally. Then he said, "Caroline, incidentally... about Shelley. Don't tell her about this, all right? Let's keep my playing doctor strictly between the two of us.''

Shelley was on the telephone when Ned returned to Video Vibes. She saw him look around for her, and then he smiled and Shelley nearly dropped the phone receiver. It was ridiculous, the effect this man had on her, she chided herself. With considerable effort she forced herself back onto the subject of VCRs and was sufficiently explicit so the man at the other end of the line said he'd be over, probably to make a purchase, sometime the next morning.

By then, Ned was standing at the counter. "Didn't mean to take so long," he said.

"That's all right," Shelley said, then added, "For heaven's sake, Ned, you don't need to clock-watch. It's enough that you're doing what you're doing at all."

She knew she sounded irritable, or irritated, or both. Her curiosity was overwhelming, and it wasn't eased as Ned blithely went back to work again without offering any information as to what had caused him to stay away from the store for the better part of two hours.

Before very long, the clock hands were pointing to nine and Shelley put out the Closed sign. The last customers in the store drifted off and, with them, the twins. Shelley straightened a few papers, put a few cassettes back into their proper places, then tore the page off the wall calendar as she always did.

"Rushing things?" Ned asked pleasantly, watching her.

"Oh, you mean the calendar? I always tear the page off before I leave so the date will be right when I open up," she said.

"Only a week from tomorrow to Christmas," Ned observed, then added in a low tone as if speaking to himself, "time really is rushing by."

Shelley looked at him sharply and wished she could read his mind. Then she told herself she shouldn't forever be assuming he was thinking about leaving, wandering again. But it was hard not to.

Christmas. Suddenly the dual significance of that date hit her. Christmas was also Ned's birthday. As she remembered that, Shelley suddenly knew that somehow, some way, she was going to have to make this Christmas memorable to him. She was going to have to do something very special for him, get him a gift he'd really like . . . and want to take with him wherever he went.

Thoughts and ideas raced through her mind as she watched Ned switch off the tree lights and together they left the shop.

He didn't seem to care much about clothes. And, evidently when he wanted something he did buy it. Witness the parka, which was new. Also, he was wearing a cranberry-colored wool shirt today that she was sure was new, too.

He liked books, she'd discovered that much about him. Maybe a book about the Cape's history? Books, though, could be difficult to carry with you when you were traveling light and she was sure that Ned must travel very light.

She could pick out a really special movie and give him the video cassette. But he'd watched so many movies of late.

Something personal. Yes, definitely, she wanted to get him something personal. Something he'd keep forever that would remind him of her every time he looked at it. Which was asking quite a lot of one gift. Yet . . . there had to be a gift that would do exactly that. The problem was finding it between now and Christmas. Her personal shopping time at the moment was close to zilch.

Momentarily lost in her thoughts, Shelley suddenly realized Ned had said something to her. She turned to find him so close she nearly bumped into him.

He smiled and asked, "Are you with me?"

"Yes, of course."

"I wondered," he admitted. "I could almost hear the wheels turning and you seemed off somewhere."

"I was thinking about something," Shelley confessed.

"It must have been something pretty important, the way you were concentrating."

"In a way, yes. What was it you asked me before, Ned?"

"I didn't ask you anything," he said. "I said good night, that's all."

"Good night?" she echoed.

"Yes. It's that time, isn't it?"

The question sprang out before she could give it any thought. "Have you had dinner?"

"I thought I'd stop for a pizza over at Casa Italia on the way home," he said. He hesitated, then asked, "Would you care to join me?"

Maybe she was unduly sensitive where Ned was concerned, Shelley conceded, but she felt she'd more or less edged him into issuing that invitation and it was an invitation he hadn't really wanted to issue at all.

"Thank you," she said rather stiffly, "but I have some chowder at home."

Ned looked at her, and she saw sudden laughter in his eyes. "Enough for two?" he asked her.

Shelley was taken aback. It was the last suggestion she had expected to hear from him at that particular moment. The last thing he had said to her, of what could be considered an intimate nature, had been the expressed hope that they would always be friends.

He said gently, "Hey, don't look like that. I didn't intend to throw you a curve."

"You didn't throw me a curve."

"No?"

"I . . . well, all right, you did throw me a curve." Shelley looked at him, and decided that she was going to let the matter of their perpetual friendship become his problem, not hers. Right now, she wasn't feeling very "friendly" toward him at all. Rather, it was all she could do not to throw her arms around him here in the middle of the mall, press her lips to his, cling to him, show him how much she wanted him, needed him . . .

"Yes," she said, "I have enough chowder for two."

Chapter Ten

Did you think I didn't want to be with you?" Ned asked softly.

They were lying side by side in Shelley's bed. Outside the wind moaned, splashing soft snow against the window. Hearing the wind, seeing the snow, made Shelley feel especially warm and snug cuddled with Ned under an heirloom patchwork quilt that had belonged to her grandmother.

"At times you are such a goose," Ned chided her. "Don't you see...it's an awkward position I'm in. I don't have a place where I can invite you. So I guess I feel I have to wait for you to suggest..."

"I never know," Shelley said.

"You never know what?"

"I'm never sure," she amended. "I'm never sure about you, about what you want."

"Then shall I show you how much I want you?" Ned suggested.

He reached for her, took her into his arms. He was an experienced lover, she already knew that. He touched secret places; arousing her, then evoking pure delight. He was tender at first, and then increasingly ardent until they were both caught up in passion and for a while, in the snow-spattered world, they became lost in each other.

They subsided, still entwined. Shelley, her head on his shoulder, laughed softly.

"Share," Ned said.

"All right," she conceded. "I was thinking that even when you make love you have such very good manners."

He raised himself on one elbow and peered down at her. "Just what is that supposed to mean?"

"What I said. You do have very good manners, you know. You must have been tremendously well brought up."

It was just a statement. For once, she wasn't fishing but merely stating a fact.

Ned scowled, pretended anger. "Making fun of me, are you, you little witch?" he taunted.

"No," she said.

The quilt was up to her chin and her nearly jet hair spread over the white pillow. Her eyes were glowing, trusting. For an instant, they reminded him of Lucy's eyes. He had the sudden, crazy wish that Shelley had been Lucy's mother. Then, maybe, Lucy would be alive today, and the three of them would live happily ever after in a beautiful big house in Scarsdale....

The mock anger faded from his face. He was wondering how old Shelley would have been when Lucy was born. It occurred to him he didn't even know how old she was now. He asked her.

She stared up at him, surprised. "Twenty-eight," she said. "I'll be twenty-nine next July."

She would have been twenty when Lucy was born. Clare had been twenty-six. Twenty-six and blond and, admittedly, as beautiful in her way as was Shelley.

He wrested himself away from memories he didn't want to remember and concentrated on the question of their ages. He was ten and a half years older than she was. Chronologically. A thousand years older, in other ways. He looked down at her, looked at her loveliness, and felt older than anyone else, older than time.

His face, his eyes, graphically expressed the suffocating bleakness he felt. Shelley saw the bleakness and, as a result, felt inadequate. She knew they'd shared the same ecstasy, just moments before. Now Ned was locked in his own private world again.

Damn it, she had to find a key to that world!

She stirred. Ned, catching the movement, quickly said, "Not cold, are you?"

"Wrapped up in this quilt? How could I be?"

"Thought maybe when I propped myself up I let some cold air under the covers."

"Is it that cold in the house? Maybe I'd better turn up the thermostat."

Drivel, drivel, we're just tossing a lot of drivel back and forth to keep from talking about real things, she thought impatiently. She became newly aware of all she didn't know about Ned. Good God, she didn't even know if he was married.

That particular lack of knowledge became overwhelmingly important. She blurted out the question, "Ned, are you married?"

Shelley saw a strange play of emotions across his face. She yearned desperately to be able to read them, to understand their significance. But then he said, quietly, "No, I'm not married."

There was something about the way he said it. "But you've been married?" Her voice sounded a pitch higher than usual.

"Yes," he said. "Yes, I have been married."

He didn't wait for her to pose a third question. He said flatly, "My wife is dead."

Defeat thudded inside Shelley, dark and hollow. Conclusions tumbled. She had no idea, of course, how long ago his wife had died, but she would have been willing to guarantee it was four years ago. At which point, Ned had started to wander.

Shelley pictured the intensity of his grief, and wanted to weep for him. She had experienced the effect of Ned's passion; she could imagine, only too clearly, what it would be like to be loved by him. Ned would love with a consuming intensity, the woman he loved would be supremely important to him. He would never get over her loss. He would never love again. Ever.

Shelley suddenly felt sick all over.

Then she felt Ned's hand on her shoulder and became aware that she had shut her eyes tightly and that there were tears oozing behind her eyelids.

"Look at me," Ned urged.

Shelley looked at him, seeing him through a watery blur.

"I'm afraid you are taking this entirely the wrong way," Ned said. "You are so terribly transparent it scares me, Shelley. Someone could hurt the hell out of you . . ."

He withdrew his hand, sat up, reached over and turned the switch on the dimmed bedside lamp so the bulb glowed brighter. "Shelley," he said, "for the record, let's get one thing straight. I didn't love my wife. I hated her."

With that, he swung out of bed. Through a new haze, this one of shock, Shelley saw him pick up his clothes and head for the bathroom. Moments later she heard the front door thud shut and knew he'd gone.

Shelley didn't sleep at all the rest of that night. It was almost daylight when she finally dozed off and so she overslept. The clock hands were pointing to eight-thirty when she woke up. She felt a momentary sense of panic, because there was no way she could get to the store in time to open up at nine.

This was the first time she'd ever contemplated opening up on a Sunday. Most of the other stores in the mall had opted to open on this Sunday before Christmas, so she had decided to join the crowd, especially when the twins had expressed their willingness to work.

Now she sank back again the pillows and fought the tightness in her chest, made herself relax. Whether she opened the store at nine or nine-thirty wasn't all that world-shaking. In fact, she was almost at the point where she really didn't give a damn if she opened the store at all.

She brewed a cup of strong tea and drank it while she showered and dressed. She looked like hell, she decided, surveying her face in the mirror. Sort of a preview of the way she would probably look when she was forty, or sixty, or maybe eighty. She put on a bit more makeup than usual, hoping the added touch of blush would detract from the shadows under her eyes.

It was a mess outside. Snow everywhere, and it was a heavy, wet snow that bent down tree boughs. It was a marvel they hadn't had another power outage. Shelley struggled out to her car and then faced the task of getting the accumulation off the windshield and windows.

She brushed and scraped and wished she had accepted her tenants' offer to use half of the garage. Her own garage, after all. The problem was that the garage was a lot closer to the big house than it was to the cottage, so usually it was more convenient to simply park at the back of the cottage, outside the kitchen door. And she hadn't been thinking about snow, anyway, when she and Ned drove home last night. She hadn't been thinking about anything, anyone, except Ned.

When, finally, the windows and windshield were clear enough to give her good visibility, Shelley discovered that the car didn't want to start. Hoping her battery hadn't run down, she coaxed and coaxed and finally got the engine started, but then she had to allow plenty of warm-up time before she dared risk driving. There was no saying whether the roads leading uptown would be cleared yet or not.

Some of the roads were, some of them weren't. It took her full attention and skillful, careful driving to negotiate the couple of miles between the cottage and the mall successfully. As she parked, Shelley glanced at her watch and was dismayed to find it was ten o'clock. Regardless of her earlier indifference, she had what she supposed might be considered an overly strong sense of obligation toward her customers.

It was still nasty out. Cold, with a strong wind. She hugged the side of the mall as she headed toward Video Vibes, thankful for the shelter of the roof overhangs. She rounded the corner, reached the entrance to her store, then stopped short. Inside, business was going on as usual.

Ned was presiding behind the checkout desk and handling the cash register. The twins were helping customers. Shelley pushed the door open, feeling as if she'd been caught midway in a dream.

Ned handed a woman her change, put the two videos she was taking out in a plastic bag, then looked up and saw Shelley. She was surprised at the look of relief on his face, and his voice was almost a shade too casual as he said, "Well, there you are."

"Yes, and here you are," she answered. She knew she should be grateful to him. So why, she asked herself, was she feeling annoyed with him instead? "How did you get in?" she snapped.

"Through the door, naturally," Ned said calmly.

"Where did you get a key? Or did you break the lock?"

"I stopped by to see how Caroline was doing and she gave me the key," he said. Then added infuriatingly, "Shelley, if you don't mind, I told this gentleman I'd help him locate the second cassette on *The Sound of Music.* It seems to have been misplaced."

She had to let him get away from her for the moment. She'd based her business on the precept that the customer always came first. So she gritted her teeth and watched Ned find the second cassette in question, and yet another satisfied customer departed Video Vibes.

During the noon hour, though, when there was a lull, Shelley spotted Ned heading for the office and she followed him. He was pouring coffee and milk into a mug, and as she watched he put the mug into the microwave and pushed the On button. Only then did he turn, see her, and invite, "Why don't you get rid of whatever's on your mind?"

"It's not that simple," Shelley said. "For a starter, I'd like to know how you happened to go see Caroline and also how you were able to persuade her to give you the shop key. I trusted her with that key, damn it."

All traces of expression faded from Ned's face. He was stony as he faced her, and his voice was hard, as well. "Are you saying you don't think she should have given me the key?" he asked.

"Exactly," Shelley said. She was fuming inwardly, and she couldn't analyze why, which made matters all the worse. Logic told her that Ned had been doing her a favor, opening up the shop for her so she wouldn't lose business. Why didn't she appreciate the favor?

Maybe because Ned's action seemed high-handed to her, and even though his motivation might have been good what he'd done was presumptuous? No, it wasn't that. Shelley faced the truth, which was that she was still upset, very upset, over the revelation about Ned's wife. She was dead, and Ned had said he hadn't loved her but had hated her.

Shelley shuddered at the memory of his words, and the coldness in his eyes and rigid set of his face as he'd spoken them.

Now he looked as rigid as he had at that terrible moment. And he said, his voice icy, "I'm sorry you feel that way. I knew you'd advertised this Sunday opening, and that you'd need help. So when I came over this morning and you weren't here I was afraid maybe you'd come down with the same kind of throat infection Caroline has, which can be rather nasty. In other words, that you'd caught it from her."

She stared at him. "I thought Caroline had the flu," she said.

Ned shook his head. "No," he said, "her problem is bacterial, not viral. Anyway..."

Shelley frowned. "How would you know that?" She answered her own question. "From Caroline herself, I would presume. But how did you happen to go to her place?"

"I was concerned about her," Ned said simply. "If she had come down with a twenty-four-hour bug, she would have been getting better instead of worse. So I decided to stop by and see her yesterday..."

"Yesterday?"

"Yes." Ned paused. "Look," he said, "it doesn't really matter. I had intended to break away at some point today to check on Caroline. When you weren't here at the store and when you didn't answer my phone..."

"When did you call?"

"Around eight-thirty, I guess, the first time," Ned said.

That, Shelley knew, must have been at just about the time she had staggered into the shower.

"I went back over to Caroline's and asked if I could borrow her key," he went on. "Then I opened the shop, and every now and then I tried to reach you. Then the twins called to find out when you wanted them in, so I asked them if they could come in early. I was about to borrow their car and head out to your place when you walked in. I was afraid you might really be sick."

"You did think of everything, didn't you," Shelley observed nastily, and immediately detested the sound of her own voice.

"I wasn't trying to butt in, if that's what you're inferring, nor to usurp anyone's authority. Your authority, to be more specific," Ned said. He turned and took his coffee mug out of the microwave, tested the coffee and muttered, "Ouch! The damned stuff's scalding."

Shelley watched him, and knew he was rattled. It was the first time since she'd known him that he'd fixed coffee or anything else for himself without asking her if she didn't want some of whatever it was. Those good manners she had commented on were such a basic part of him that it was natural for him to be a shade more polite and considerate than most of the people she knew.

She was beginning to see that he was also more knowledgeable in some areas than most of the people she knew. She asked suddenly, "How did you happen to know that Caroline's problem was viral rather than bacterial, Ned?"

"I looked at her throat," he said. "It was fairly evident that—" He broke off and grimaced. "Okay," he said wearily, "I'll spare you asking the next question. I'm a doctor. That's to say, I was a doctor. So when I looked down Caroline's throat, yes, I knew what I was seeing. Call it an educated guess, but I was so certain of the diagnosis I prescribed an antibiotic for her and I'm happy to say it seems to be doing the job."

Ned took the mug over to the sink and poured its contents down the drain. "Too bitter," he said. "Now, if you don't mind, I think I'll get back to work."

"I do mind," Shelley said. Once again, her head was whirling. Ned, a doctor.

He was standing by the door that led out into the shop. "Why do you mind my being here?" he asked. "All of a sudden, you don't want me around—is that it?"

"I think you must have better things to do than working for nothing in a video store," Shelley said.

Ned's laugh was harsh. "Do you, now?" he challenged. "Suppose you spell them out for me, whatever they are. No, on second thought, please don't spell them out. I'm sure I wouldn't agree with you and though I'm equally sure there are probably a lot of things you'd like to discuss I don't want to discuss them. Now or any time," he said and added, "I've already said a hell of a lot more to you than I ever intended to say."

Shelley didn't answer him. She couldn't. Of course there were a lot of things she wanted to discuss with him. A thousand things. But Ned, she saw, was not about to vouchsafe any more information about himself. Not now, anyway. Maybe never. Which meant, certainly, that the two of them couldn't go much farther together. There was no way, to think of one example, that she could let him make love to her again until she knew a great deal more about his marriage. Maybe to his way of thinking that part of his past didn't have anything to do with the relationship the two of them had forged. But from her point of view, a terrible kind of ghost had been wedged between them. A dead woman whom Ned had hated, not loved . . .

"There is no point, Shelley, in your looking at me like that," Ned said, speaking into a brittle silence. "No point at all. What I'd like, if that matters to you, is to go back in the store and get busy again . . ."

"So you won't have time to think?" Again the question sprang forth from her before she had time to measure her words.

"Yes," he said, after another brittle silence. "Exactly. So I won't have time to think."

It began to snow again in the late afternoon. The snow put a damper on business. A few shoppers already browsing round the mall straggled in, mostly to rent cassettes. And that was it.

Around five-thirty, Ned announced, "I think I'll take off."

It was one of the twins this time, who asked, "How about a ride? Our jalopy's got snow tires."

"Thanks, no," Ned answered promptly. "I don't have that far to go, and I rather like walking in the snow."

He took off, again wearing the oversized tweed coat and the crumpled Irish wool hat, and some huge black, rubbery overshoes Shelley couldn't remember having seen before.

With the door closed behind Ned, Brian said reflectively, "He's a strange one."

Benny was restocking the shelves with rental cassettes that had been returned during the day. "Whaddya mean?" he asked his brother.

"Oh, he's a cool guy," Brian said. "But it's kind of hard figuring someone who'd want to walk through all that slop outside when he has the chance to hitch a ride."

"So," Benny said with a shrug, "he's a nature freak."

"Maybe," Brian conceded.

"I like him," Benny announced unexpectedly.

"I didn't say I didn't like him," Brian put in quickly. "I just can't figure him, that's all. Where does he live, Shelley?"

Shelley felt foolish to have to admit, "I don't know."

"You don't know?" both twins echoed.

"He's never said, I've never asked," Shelley reported, and salved her conscience with the realization that essentially that was true. She never had come out and asked Ned directly where he lived. Rather, she had given him every possible opportunity to tell her.

"How come he started working here?" Benny asked.

"It just...happened," Shelley confessed. "I mean, he's been a customer for quite a while..."

"I know," Brian put in wisely. "I've checked out cassettes for him and he picks the weirdest stuff."

"You can say that again," Benny concurred. "Once I sort of asked him about it, about the kind of stuff he likes, that is."

"What did he say?" Shelley asked.

"He said he was trying to make up for something."

"Make up for something?"

"Lost time, I think he said," Benny told her, and disappeared toward the back of the store carrying a towering stack of videos.

With his brother temporarily out of earshot, Brian said calmly, "He has a thing going for you."

Shelley felt her cheeks flame. "Are you speaking about Ned?" she asked.

Brian grinned. "Well, I'd say maybe Benny has a thing going for you, too, but yeah, I was talking about Ned," he said.

"Brian, you are absolutely impossible," Shelley protested.

"That's what my mother tells me."

"And incorrigible."

"That's what my mother tells me, too," Brian responded with a grin. "I do think the guy's got it going for you, though, Shelley. When you're not watching, his eyes follow you all around the store. Ask me, I'd say that's why he hangs around."

"Don't be ridiculous," Shelley sputtered, and quickly made her way over to the checkout counter and started going through a heap of papers that actually already had been straightened out.

Brian got out the small carpet sweeper and started using it, all the time whistling, *Near You*. Shelley wanted to throttle him. The twins were terrible teases, but she was also a little disconcerted to think that they'd noticed something between Ned and herself.

When Brian had finished his carpet sweeping and Benny had replaced the last of the rental cassettes, she said, "You two should really take off. It looks to me like the snow's coming down heavier. And it is Sunday, after all."

"How about you?" Brian asked. "Want us to follow you home in case you get in any kind of trouble?"

"What kind of trouble could I get in?" Shelley asked him.

"You could skid. Go off the road," Brian suggested.

"Thanks a lot," she retorted.

Fifteen minutes later, though, she thought that it would have been rather nice to have the twins following her in their beaten up but mechanically sound old jalopy. The roads were treacherous, she did go into a couple of minor skids, and by the time she got inside the cottage her nerves were jangling.

She built a fire in the fireplace, poured herself a glass of sherry, then sat down in front of the blaze and tried both to get warm and to relax.

She still was not being very successful at either when the telephone rang.

At the other end of the line, Ned said, "I just wanted to be sure you got home safely. It really is rotten out. Driving must be pretty bad."

"It is," Shelley admitted.

"You made it all right, though?"

"Yes."

"Did I interrupt something?"

"What might you have interrupted, Ned?"

"I don't know," he said. "What were you doing when the phone rang?"

"Sitting in front of the fire with a glass of sherry trying to get warm," she told him.

"Your power's okay, isn't it? I mean, your furnace isn't about to go out on you?"

"I doubt it. Of course you can always get a power outage if the snow weighs the lines down too heavily. But..."

"I hope that won't happen."

"I hope so, too." As she spoke, something dawned on Shelley and she had to pose another of her unfortunate questions.

"I thought you didn't have a phone," she reminded him.

"I don't," he said. "I stopped in at the Port and Starboard before leaving that mall and that's where I am, still. Loitering over some bourbon."

Shelley sensed his hesitation, then heard him say under his breath, "Oh, hell!" Then, "Shelley, I couldn't leave it the way it was when I left tonight. You looked as unhappy as I felt. I walked around in the snow until my coat was wet through and I felt like I was a candidate for frostbite, then I came in here.

"I keep thinking of the things we've been saying to each other," he went on. "What I've been saying to you, principally. I can understand how you must find it— me—pretty difficult to deal with. I'm sorry about that. Genuinely sorry. Believe me, I care far too much about you to relish making you miserable."

"You don't make me miserable, Ned," Shelley said, which wasn't entirely the truth because there were moments when he made her extremely miserable. "You do put me...at such a loss," she admitted. "I don't know how to deal with you, or what you're telling me. Whatever you have told me, for that matter, I've felt I had to force out of you, and then you were sorry you said it at all. I don't want it to be like that. I don't want to pry. I . . . I want to know you, that's all."

"Oh my God, darling," Ned said, his voice ragged. Then Shelley could visualize him squaring his shoulders, could imagine that she was seeing the faint smile that probably was playing around his lips. "Whatever else," Ned told her, "you do know me, Shelley. Oh, yes, very definitely, you know me."

Chapter Eleven

There was no point in rushing to get to Video Vibes the next morning. A glance out her window at the snow-covered winter world convinced Shelley that, even though Christmas was almost here, shoppers wouldn't be in any great hurry to get out.

Regardless of the road conditions, though, she soon discovered that she was too restless to stay in the house. Once again, she scooped snow off her car windows and windshield, got the engine going and pretty much kept the snowplows company on her way uptown.

Then as she approached the mall entrance, she made a sudden decision and kept on down the road. A moment later she was sliding into a parking space outside Caroline Marston's condo.

Caroline opened her door, looking pretty and comfortable in a soft blue quilted robe. Though pale, she also looked well rested, Shelley observed. She, on the other hand, knew that she'd seldom looked worse. Her face showed the results of sleepless nights and emotional tension.

"Well, come in," Caroline exclaimed. "What an absolutely delightful surprise! Is someone else minding the store?"

"No," Shelley said. Then wondered if that were true. Would Ned have taken it upon himself to struggle uptown on foot and open up the store for her?

Somehow she doubted he'd be doing that again. Not after the way she'd reacted the last time.

Caroline gave her a curious glance. "I just brewed a pot of coffee. You will have a cup, won't you?"

"Thanks, no," Shelley said. "I had two cups before I left home and that's all the caffeine I need at the moment."

She followed Caroline into the living room and sank down in an armchair. Caroline, looking rather worried, asked, "Is something wrong, Shelley? If you'll forgive my saying so, you seem nervous. Oh, I am *so* sorry I've let you down as I have. Getting sick, at the busiest time of the year."

"You haven't let me down, Caroline," Shelley said quickly. "The twins have put in a lot of extra time...and so has Ned."

His name drifted between them. Shelley waited for Caroline to say something, then realized that was exactly what Caroline was waiting for *her* to do.

She said heavily, "I know he's a doctor, Caroline."

"Whew," Caroline said, making no secret of her relief. "I didn't want to tell tales out of school, Shelley."

"No," Shelley said rather morosely. "I was sure you wouldn't do that. I do understand, though, that Ned's been taking care of you."

"Yes," Caroline said, and smiled. "He's been absolutely wonderful, though now he's chiding me about getting busy with finding a family physician for myself. He says I'm healthy, but he also thinks I've been awfully lucky never having felt sick enough for a long, long time to feel the need to consult a doctor. This time, he says, fighting the bug I've had on my own would really have run me down.

"As it is," Caroline went on, "I feel ninety percent better than I did a couple of days ago. If I had my way, I'd be heading for Video Vibes right about now."

"Don't be ridiculous," Shelley protested sharply. "In this weather? You'd almost certainly come down with pneumonia."

"Well, if I were to go to the store before Ned gives me the okay I must say it would be hard to face him," Caroline admitted. "Ned can be quite stern."

"I can imagine," Shelley murmured.

"And he's right, of course. I do plan to get a doctor and to have a complete physical, as Ned suggested. He was right when he said it was just lucky he was here and decided he'd better see if I needed help. He won't always be around..."

Caroline's last words might as well have been bullets. They struck straight at Shelley's heart, and they hurt.

"Has Ned said when he's leaving?" she asked, trying to make the question sound casual. But her voice choked slightly over the word "leaving."

"Not precisely," Caroline said. "He did say that he makes it a habit to start a new year in a new place, though."

"Oh," Shelley said.

"Shelley, please," Caroline said. "Don't look so stricken. You make me feel I shouldn't have told you that. But I thought..."

"Yes?"

"I thought you should have some warning, Shelley. Not, I'm sure, that Ned would ever go off without telling you he was going..."

Ned had as much as promised he wouldn't do that to her, Shelley remembered. Which didn't mean that when the time came he wouldn't leave with very short notice. The parting wasn't going to be easy for him either, it suddenly occurred to her. So chances were high that he would feel "the quicker the better." He wasn't going to give her brooding time, she'd be ready to swear to that. Nor was he going to give her time to implore him to stay...if, that is, he had an idea that she might implore him to stay.

Would she? Could she? Shelley couldn't readily answer either question. Pride didn't seem nearly as important as...her love for Ned. A love that, right now, was coming close to overwhelming her. But a love her common sense told her, which was absolutely hopeless.

She had no idea why Ned had given up medicine, turned his back on home and family, and simply started off on his own to wander wherever the spirit of the moment led him. She had indulged in flights of fancy but there was no way of knowing, either, if there were any grains of truth sifting through the products of her imagination.

What she did know was that Ned had made a life that seemed to satisfy him. And that he didn't want commitment.

No moss. A smooth rolling stone, who could tumble through the rest of his life without encumbrance.

Caroline said suddenly, "Oh, Shelley, my dear, my dear."

Shelley looked up to see Caroline gazing at her unhappily. She saw conflicting emotions pass over Caroline's face, culminating in determination.

"I'm going to rush in," Caroline announced. "Whether that makes me a fool or not, I'm still going to rush in. I've grown too fond of you, Shelley, to simply sit by and watch you becoming more and more unhappy. You've fallen in love with him, haven't you?"

It was more statement than question.

Shelley's answering smile was slight and sad. "Does it show that much?" she queried.

"No. You're like Ned in that respect. You carry off things very well, camouflage your feelings so that someone needs to know you quite well to see what's beneath the surface. And though I haven't known Ned very long he's—well, I'd say he's somewhat let down his guard when he's been here looking after me. He speaks about you, and I see the look on his face, in his eyes, when he's not trying to put up a facade.

"It is really ridiculous, you know," Caroline decided out loud, "that he should even think of leaving here, feeling as he does about you. From the little he says, I have the idea he has developed a sort of compulsion about packing up and going on to somewhere else. It's as if he's programmed himself to follow that course of action."

Shelley said slowly, heavily, "He must have a reason, Caroline. Ned's a highly intelligent man. He has to have a reason for what he does."

"True," Caroline agreed. "But sometimes we can talk ourselves into believing we have to do what we've set out to do when that's anything but true. Or maybe it was true but isn't any longer. Things do change, Shelley. Times change. But we can become habit-bound and go right on in the same rut. Ned's is a different kind of rut, I don't deny that. He must have had a tremendously strong motivation to start out doing what he does."

"He has been a wanderer for four years," Shelley pointed out. "He had a home, a family. And also, obviously, a profession. He walked away from all of that."

"But you have no idea why?"

"No. And I don't think he's about to tell me. He's an intensely private person; telling would mean losing some of that privacy." Shelley paused. "I had hoped," she admitted, "that maybe he'd told you. I wouldn't have asked you to break a promise and tell me. It just would have helped to know that he had told you. To know that you, at least, know about him."

"I don't," Caroline said. "We've almost always spoken about general subjects. But...he's managed to draw me out about myself. I've found myself talking about my husband and our life together. Things I haven't mentioned much since Dan died. I guess I've been keeping a lot in... when it's really better to let it out. Ned is quite an expert at drawing people out about themselves."

"Yes, isn't he?" Shelley agreed wryly. She got to her feet. "I do need to get to the store," she said.

"I wish I were going with you," Caroline murmured.

"No chance," Shelley informed her briskly. "You just keep on doing what you're doing, and in a few more days you'll be better than new. You look terrific."

Caroline did look terrific. And it was true, in a few more days she probably would be better than new. *But I can't say the same about myself,* Shelley thought bitterly as she drove her car out of the condominium parking lot.

The snowplows had done a good job on the road leading toward the mall. But the skies were still dark, it looked as if it might start snowing again any minute, and suddenly Shelley yearned for the sun. For bright sun and palm trees, hot, golden sand and warm turquoise water. A tropical paradise, where she could become a total sybarite. Sleep late, play late, plunge into a fun-filled existence with no worries, no responsibilities and no breaking heart.

Maybe Ned didn't have such a bad idea!

When things get tense or too demanding, he just moves on, Shelley told herself. And then suddenly her senses went on alert because she saw a familiar figure wearing a dark green parka, trudging along the roadside, the hood pulled up over his head.

She slid smoothly to a stop. Ned looked up. She waited for his smile. It didn't come. But after a moment of hesitation he opened the car door.

"Can I give you a lift somewhere?" Shelley asked him sweetly.

"My plan was to cut over to Nonnie's for some breakfast, then head for the mall," Ned said.

"Would you care to buy me some breakfast? I haven't had any."

It was a suggestion he could hardly refuse without being rude. Shelley knew that as she posed it, and was surprised at herself. Where had her pride gone?

"Sure," Ned said easily, and slid in beside her.

Shelley stole a glance at him, and noted that he looked as tired as she felt. Was he having trouble sleeping, too?

As if she'd asked the question aloud, he said, "I had a real bout of insomnia in the middle of the night. I read for a couple of hours before I could get back to sleep again. Then, I overslept."

He rubbed a hand over his chin. Shelley saw that he could do with a shave. He said, somewhat grumpily, "That kind of sleep makes you feel rotten."

"Yes," she said. "I know."

She was aware that Ned had slanted a glance in her direction, could feel his eyes lingering on her face. "You're working too hard," he diagnosed. "It's showing, Shelley."

She wanted to tell him that it wasn't hard work that was making her look the way she looked. He should know that, damn it, she thought irritably. She was tempted to say, "Go look in the mirror, and you'll see what my problem is." But she bit back the words, subsided into silence.

Nonnie's was packed with people, some just now having their breakfasts, other taking mid-morning coffee breaks. Shelley was surprised at the number of people who greeted Ned by name as the two of them headed to a corner table. He seemed to know more of the men and women than she did.

She ordered toast and tea, Ned ordered pancakes topped with strawberries and whipped cream. His night of poor sleep certainly hadn't interfered with his appetite, Shelley noted. He put away what she considered an enormous amount of food with relish, and asked for a second cup of coffee.

Their conversation during all of this time, though, was minimal. Nonnie's restaurant was fully decorated for Christmas, and they both admired two big and beautifully dressed, movable angel dolls and a matching Mr. and Mrs. Santa Claus.

There were red and white poinsettia plants everywhere in the little restaurant, and a tree decorated with ornaments collected by Nonnie and her family over a period of many years. The atmosphere was highly conducive to engendering Christmas spirit, but Shelley felt as bleak when she left as she had when she'd arrived.

There were just not going to be any bells jingling for her this Christmas, she thought somewhat resentfully, despite all her good intentions to make this holiday season an especially happy one.

Once in the car, when she asked Ned where she could drop him off, he looked at her as if she'd suddenly lost her mind and said coolly, "I assumed we were both going to Video Vibes."

Shelley had already said often enough that there was no need for him to work as he'd been working at the store. She was tempted to say the same thing all over again, but decided not to repeat herself.

The twins had left a note tucked in the door announcing that they'd come by, ready to work, but would go on and do a little Christmas shopping and check back in an hour or so to see if she'd opened by then.

It was cold, gray and cheerless inside the store. Shelley pushed up the thermostat and was about to turn on the tree lights when she saw that Ned was already taking care of that small chore.

"Looks like more snow," Ned observed, as he went around switching on a few other lights.

"I hope not," Shelley muttered. "I've had enough of winter."

He chuckled. "Winter's only starting," he reminded her.

"I've still had enough of it," she said. "Anyway, all this snow in December is unusual for the Cape. We usually get snow much later on..."

She shivered. "I wish it was June," she said. "The spring's long and damp and miserable, for the most part. But by June everything's out and beautiful."

"Sounds like you need a change of scene," Ned observed. He was busy rearranging the display case that held the for-sale videos and wasn't looking at her.

"I was dreaming, just a while ago, about taking off for a tropical paradise," Shelley admitted.

He turned and faced her. "Well, why don't you?" he asked.

"I have a business to run, Ned," she reminded him. "Responsibilities. Obligations."

"It's not good when your business owns you, Shelley," Ned said seriously. "It should be the other way around. You can't let your obligations overwhelm you to the point of taking total control of your life. I know sometimes that can't be avoided. In your case, though, it certainly can. You have only yourself to think of."

Why should that simple comment—simple, true comment, Shelley amended—sting? But it did.

She said stiffly, "It's important to me to make a success of this business, Ned."

"I'm sure it is," he agreed. "I'd say you already have, for that matter. You've built up a good clientele already."

"Which is all the more reason why I can't let my customers down," Shelley said.

"Nonsense. Do you seriously think you'd be letting your customers down if you closed for a month or so during the doldrum time?"

"That's exactly when they may want to rent videos more than ever," Shelley pointed out. "So they can get through the doldrum time."

"They'd survive without your being here," Ned said bluntly. "And, I'm sure, would be so happy to see you back they'd appreciate you more than ever."

Ned paused, then asked quietly, "When I leave, why don't you come with me, Shelley? We'll go somewhere south where it's warm and beautiful and simply enjoy it for a while."

The suggestion totally rocked Shelley. It had never occurred to her that Ned might issue such an invitation. If she had thought about it, she would have said it was the last thing that ever could possibly happen. Ned, when he left, would want to go his way alone. She would have sworn to that.

She saw he was watching her intently. After a moment, when she didn't answer him—she couldn't answer him—he said softly, "You seem so shocked."

"Well, I am shocked," she stated.

"Shelley, do you doubt that we'd have a wonderful month together?"

"No," she said, speaking with difficulty because her mouth felt absolutely dry. "No, I don't doubt that."

"Then think about it," he urged. "Think about it and—"

The bell over the door jangled. The twins burst in, clutching brightly wrapped Christmas packages. Whatever Ned was about to say faded into oblivion.

Shelley was in a trance the rest of the day. Customers began to brave the weather and come in, business became relatively brisk. But she found it almost impossible to concentrate and was thankful to have Ned and the twins on hand to help with people.

Also, maybe it was the sight of the brightly wrapped packages the twins were carrying, but she remembered, anew, that Christmas Day was Ned's birthday. And more and more she wanted to make it a birthday he'd never forget.

She'd been somewhat blocking that whole subject, principally because Ned seemed so unpredictable to her. There was no way of being sure that he'd welcome a birthday celebration. But by late afternoon Shelley was deciding that this was becoming a "nothing ventured nothing gained" situation. And she had very little time left to make any preparations.

For all she knew, she realized, Ned might have made other plans for Christmas. It was the one day of the year when nostalgia was apt to take over, and sometimes chasms were bridged and misunderstandings healed. For all she knew, Ned might be thinking about going home for Christmas. Back to his own home. The place, wherever it was, that he had left four years ago.

The only way to find out was to ask. Maybe to issue an invitation to Christmas dinner at her place. Then, if he had something else to do, he'd have to tell her so.

But time passed, and although there were moments when she could have issued an invitation, she didn't do so. Maybe, she conceded ruefully, because she was afraid he might turn her down. Or that she might find out he did have something to do. Really was going home.

Snow was still threatening again, and the weather report wasn't good. Toward eight o'clock, with no customers in the store, Ned announced he thought he'd take off.

The twins promptly offered to run him home in their car. Ned sidestepped the offer by saying he wanted to stop by and see how Caroline was doing, and that it wasn't that long a walk over to her place.

The twins lingered. A few last-minute customers came in. Then Benny announced that he planned to catch the nine-thirty movie with a girl who worked as a checker in the supermarket, and he departed. Shelley was left alone with Brian.

Ned had teased her a couple of times that he thought Brian had a crush on her. She had found this amusing, considering the fact that though she actually wasn't old enough to be Brian's mother—there was only an eight-year discrepancy in their ages—she usually felt like she was. There was a wide gap between being in college at age twenty, full of zest and enthusiasm for what lay ahead, and being twenty-eight, with a fair bit of living and disillusionment behind you.

It was true, though, that Brian seemed in no hurry to leave. He got out the carpet sweeper and attended to the rug. Straightened a few things that didn't need to be straightened. Indulged in some conversation about the chances of the Celtics to win the NBA championship this year, or of the Bruins to win the Stanley Cup—neither subjects in which Shelley had much expertise.

He talked about a few of the newer videos he'd tried out on his VCR, and recommended a couple of them to Shelley. And, at that point, Shelley said, "I think it's time we both call it a day, Brian. Is Benny going to be using your car? Do you need a ride home?"

"I'd appreciate that," Brian said. "Yeah, Benny wanted the wheels tonight. I was going to thumb."

"Well, I'll drive you," Shelley said. "It's too cold out for hitchhiking."

Brian settled down in the car beside her and automatically switched on the radio. Music blared, and with a glance at Shelley he turned the volume down. Then he plunged into a discussion about heavy metal rock, hard rock, oldies rock, and Shelley, figuring these were things she should know about if she was going to be as contemporary as she probably should be, half listened to him. But she couldn't push Ned all the way out of her mind.

She was startled when Brian said suddenly, "You know, Shelley, neither Benny nor I can figure Ned out."

"What do you mean?" she asked.

"Well, like we said way back, it seems kind of weird for a guy to keep refusing rides in this kind of weather. I'm into running, you know that..."

Shelley hadn't known that Brian was into running, but she merely nodded.

"It's one thing when you're into running," Brian said. "But lately it's been so lousy out there was no way I could get any running in. Just too much snow and ice, you know what I mean? Even people who have to walk their dogs do it as quick as they can and get it over with," Brian stated solemnly.

Shelley repressed a chuckle and said, "I see what you mean."

"Okay, so then we have Ned. I like the guy, I think he's really cool, Benny feels the same way. It would be easy to say he's just plain spaced out, but he doesn't come on like a space shot. So you wonder..."

"True," Shelley agreed, and thought few things Brian could ever say would be any truer.

"Like tonight," Brian persisted. "You know? It's cold out, miserable, all day it's looked like it's going to start pouring down snow again. Benny asks this guy can he run him home when he leaves the store, and he turns him down and says he's going to stop at Caroline's first, anyway."

"Well, I think that was true enough," Shelley said. "Ned's been concerned about Caroline because she's been quite sick." She hesitated, thought about telling Brian that Ned was a doctor, then decided against it. "He wanted to help her, that's all."

"Yeah," Brian said, "but you'd still think . . . I mean, have you noticed? He's never said anything about himself at all. He just appears from the blue, walks away into the blue. It's like he came from nowhere."

"Outer space?" Shelley suggested.

"Hey, look, if you have any faith in UFOs and aliens it's not that far out of sight."

"I'd have to see a UFO and an alien to believe in either," Shelley told him. "Thus far, it hasn't happened."

"Shock you if old Ned turned out to be from another planet, wouldn't it?" Brian teased.

"You might say so."

Brian leaned back, stretched out his long legs. "Seriously," he said, "I wish I could figure him out."

"So do I," Shelley admitted, and hoped she wasn't letting on just how much she wished she could figure Ned out.

"You still don't know where he lives?"

"No. But . . ." An idea suddenly hit Shelley, and she paused.

"Brian . . ." she began then.

"Yeah?"

"Christmas Day is Ned's birthday," she said. "I don't know what Ned's plans are for Christmas Day itself, but I've been thinking . . . maybe you and Benny and Caroline, if she's feeling well enough to go out, could stage a little surprise party for him Saturday night. Christmas Eve."

Brian thought that over, and said, "Sounds pretty neat."

"I could make a cake," Shelley said, "and maybe get a bottle of champagne. We could each buy a couple of small things and wrap them up. And then maybe, once we were sure Ned was home, all burst into his place yelling happy birthday."

"Sounds cool," Brian pronounced, after brief reflection. "But . . ."

"Yes?"

"How are we going to burst into Ned's place when none of us knows where he lives?"

"Well that," Shelley said, her mind clicking into overtime, "is something I think maybe you can find out."

Chapter Twelve

The phone rang as Shelley was getting ready for bed. Although there was no reason to assume it was Ned calling, she couldn't help but hope she'd be hearing his voice, as she picked up the receiver. Brian's youthful tone was a letdown.

"What is it, Brian?" she asked rather dourly, after he'd identified himself.

"It's about our little caper," Brian declared mysteriously.

Shelley kicked herself mentally. She'd been an idiot to get Brian involved in tracing down Ned's place of residence, she told herself irritably. From the moment she'd enlisted his help, Brian's enthusiasm had been boundless. Now he evidently was plunging into a mixed game of cops and robbers, spies and sleuths, good guys and bad guys, all tossed together on one playing board.

"Brian," Shelley said carefully, "I've been thinking."

"So have I," Brian assured her quickly.

"No, no," she said, "not plotting further, just thinking. If Ned wants his privacy, he's entitled to it. That's to say, I think we'd better bag the surprise party. At least, staging it at his place."

"You've got to be kidding," Brian said.

"I'm not kidding."

"Shelley, I'm psyched for this," he told her.

"Then get yourself unpsyched, Brian," she instructed.

"What made you change your mind?" he countered. "You're not afraid of the guy, are you?"

Shelley didn't need to waste thought on that. "Of course not," she snapped.

"Then why—"

"Brian," she interrupted, "haven't you ever thought about something you intended to do and then decided it might be better not to do it?"

"I don't know," Brian said gruffly.

"Well, think," she urged. "If Ned wants his privacy that's his right, wouldn't you say? If it were you . . ."

"It wouldn't be me," Brian informed her. "If it was freezing cold out and about to snow and there was a gale wind blowing, I wouldn't refuse a ride home if someone offered it to me. And that's not the only thing, Shelley."

"What else?" she asked wearily.

"He's flaked out over you and he won't even tell you where he lives," Brian announced.

"What?"

"Hey look, both Benny and I have eyes in our head and we've compared notes," Brian advised her. "Like I already told you, you should see the look on Ned's face when he looks at you and you're not looking at him. Like a kid staring in a candy-store window at stuff he can't have.''

"Brian!" she interjected sharply.

"Shelley, come on," Brian urged. "Look, I don't blame him. You're a lot older than I am, but even so..."

"Brian!" This time there was authority mixed with just a slight edge of panic in Shelley's voice.

"Okay," Brian said. "But I still don't understand why you two don't get together. That's to say—"

"I know what that's to say," Shelley informed Brian. "What I'm saying still stands. When it comes to following Ned, bug off."

"Mmmm," Brian said. Which was neither yes nor no but, for the moment, would have to do.

Shelley hung up before she realized she'd not heard what Brian initially had intended to say about what he referred to as "their little caper."

Well, she reasoned, as she trotted off to bed, whatever it was didn't really matter now. She was glad he'd called. She had intended to take him aside the minute he walked into the shop tomorrow, and to tell him the scheme was off.

They had not planned to implement "the scheme" until that night. Brian, agreeing with Shelley that too many cooks might spoil the broth, even if one of the cooks who would have been involved was his twin brother, had agreed to make a logical excuse to Benny so Benny would leave fairly early and head home. Or, Brian had said, maybe he'd be the one to cut out early and then he'd come back. Not to the shop, directly. He would lurk in another store whose window offered a clear view of Video Vibes. Or maybe in some outside corner, if it wasn't too cold.

Whatever the primary logistics, the plan had been that Brian would let Ned leave, give him a little room, and then follow him.

Brian had assured Shelley that following Ned would present no problem. He confided that in earlier years, "when I was younger," he said, he had gotten a Boy Scout merit badge in Indian lore—and Indian lore had involved "scouting" which, in that instance, had meant trailing someone.

"Like through a woods, without snapping any tree branches or making any other sounds that would give you away," Brian had explained.

Tracking through summer woods and along an icy winter street offered two different kinds of challenges, Shelley had pointed out. Brian rather loftily had insisted that the latter would pose no problem. And, since she'd enlisted Brian's help in the first place and he was offering to do exactly what she wanted him to do, Shelley had gone along with that.

Only to repent, not very much later.

The snow that had seemed so imminent didn't materialize after all, taking that capricious license afforded the elements when it comes to staging winter weather. Shelley opened up Video Vibes on time, customers began to arrive, but then, though busy, she began to clock-watch.

Ten o'clock came, and there was no sign of Ned. At ten-thirty Benny breezed in to announce that Brian had awakened with a bad sore throat, and so thought he'd better hang around home. At first Shelley hoped that he hadn't somehow caught Caroline's throat infection. It was a while before it occurred to her that if that were to have happened it already would have happened. But even then she didn't become suspicious as to what Brian might really be up to.

* * *

With Christmas so close, it began to appear that most people—at least those interested in purchasing VCRs, or even cassettes—had already done their shopping. Ned, who had arrived in the early afternoon, left at seven, then nearly turned back.

He and Shelley just weren't communicating well, something he blamed on himself. He had told her she knew him. And he had been speaking the truth...but, he now admitted to himself, only to a point. It would be more correct to say that Shelley had come to know him, in a relatively short space of time, far better than anyone else had in years. But even that acknowledgement left a lot of gaps.

He pulled the hood of his parka over his head as he struck out from the mall. It was cold, and the knife-edged winter wind was back again, slashing at his jeans. He thought about stopping for a pizza and some coffee, or maybe dropping by the pub for a drink. But he wasn't hungry, and for reasons he couldn't entirely define he didn't want to drink alone tonight.

One of the reasons, he supposed, was that it was a season of the year when even loners often joined forces with each other, to forge a temporary camaraderie. It was supposedly the time to be jolly. The season when the hope for peace on earth plus an honest sense of goodwill toward one's fellow man took—or were supposed to take—top priority.

Well, he was all for peace on earth, Ned thought wryly, but try though he had for almost exactly four years, now, he had yet to achieve peace for himself. That driving, intangible need to move on, to sidestep entanglements, was still a main propelling force with him. But he was beginning to realize that the terrible restlessness that possessed him so frequently was no closer to being satisfied than it had been when he had turned his back on everything and everyone, four Christmases ago.

Just what did that mean? The lesson to be learned, he supposed, was fairly obvious. Problems were not solved by running away from them.

Ned corrected himself. He had not been running away from a problem. Nothing that simple. He had been running away from caring, involvement, life.

These past four years, he thought ruefully, *I could have been a zombie.*

Wherever he'd gone and whatever he'd done he essentially had been moving around in a self-created vacuum.

Shelley had stirred him back to life. Not because that's what he had wanted to have happen, but because he had been unable to negate his response to her. She was lovely, and he wasn't thinking only of physical loveliness. Shelley was beautiful, but he had known a lot of beautiful women. Much more important, she was warm and wonderful, caring and giving. And, certainly, she didn't deserve to cast her lot with anyone like him.

Ned gritted his teeth. It could be, of course, that he was too sensitive. That was one character trait he hadn't been able to rid himself of entirely.

He corrected that. Until he met Shelley, his sensitivity had not really been tested for a long time. No one had touched him deeply, for a long time. Which, he admitted wryly, was a hell of a lot safer way to live.

Still, when on the spur of an especially impetuous moment he had broached the idea of her taking off with him when he left the Cape and going south for the pure escape of a tropical holiday, she had looked shocked, startled, uncomfortable. A combination of a lot of things, none of which was very positive as far as he was concerned. Then they had been interrupted by the twins. And, as if by mutual design, neither of them had returned to the subject since.

Ned suspected Shelley didn't want to return to it, because she would never contemplate leaving Devon to wander off with a man who still, essentially, was a stranger in so many ways. For his part, he had avoided the issue because he regretted having issued the invitation in the first place. Not regretted it, exactly. He could think of nothing more wonderful than sharing with Shelley the kind of brief escape he had envisioned. But he should have known better than to think an interlude like that would be possible between the two of them. If he were able to whisk out a magic carpet and they were transported to an island paradise for a finite time—a couple of weeks at the most, probably—he knew in his soul it would be impossibly difficult to let her go. He wouldn't be able to turn his back on her and go off in another direction while she returned to Devon and her work.

For Shelley, there would undeniably be trauma as well as pleasure to such an interval. Emotions went very deep with Shelley. She already had made a commitment to him he was sure she would never forget . . . for he knew, if he knew anything, that Shelley was not a woman to give herself lightly, and she had given herself so completely to him. Something he was not apt to forget either, he reminded himself grimly.

Frustrated, Ned swerved into the pub entrance, needing a spate of warmth and noise and companionship. He looked around as he settled down at the bar. He'd come to know quite a few people around town, but there weren't that many people at the bar tonight, and no familiar faces among them.

Almost Christmas, he thought. Most people who have homes are home with the people they love.

Ned downed the bourbon he ordered, nearly ordered a second drink, then decided against it. He paid his tab and went back out into the cold night.

A few minutes later he turned out of the mall and headed down the road that led to the lane where he lived. The moon, he noticed, was trying to press its way out from behind the clouds. He saw a slivered edge of it glint, and he saw a planet—Venus, perhaps—suddenly command center stage in the sky. The planet looked oversized and incredibly brilliant, and he stopped for a moment to study it. And became aware of a sound behind him. A crunch that could have been made only by a human foot. A foot that had paused at exactly the same time he had paused, and evidently wasn't going anywhere until he started up again.

Ned fought the desire to look back over his shoulder. Could it have been the wind rustling a branch?

He started to walk again, this time a bit more cautiously, his ears strained. He came to a driveway leading up to someone's house and stopped abruptly. Again he heard a telltale sound. It was hard to walk on a combination of ice, gravel and frozen ground and still be soundless. Unless someone were very experienced.

Ned grinned. Whoever was following him was an amateur. Of that much, he was relatively certain.

Beyond that, he was not certain of much. Maybe this was some kid out to mug him and grab his wallet, maybe only for the sake of getting some last-minute Christmas spending money. Stranger crimes had happened. Maybe it was some kid not quite so pure in motive, who wanted money for a drug buy. Whatever, Ned was on the alert, ready and prepared for what might happen next.

He was also ready to admit, at any given second, that the whole bit was a product of his imagination. Hoped, in fact, that it was a product of his imagination. He was in no particular mood to take on any would-be assailant tonight, whether amateur or pro.

He came to that point in the road where the lane on which he lived branched off to the right. He started down the lane, his senses finely tuned at this point, because sounds might not be so easy to hear on the frozen dirt surface. He came to the Carlsons' house and moved on toward the garage and the staircase that led to his cottage. The moon had disappeared again. Except for Venus, it was a very dark night.

Ned took advantage of the darkness to bypass the staircase, and go around the corner of the garage where he crouched against the eaves, waiting.

The Carlsons' house was now decorated with red and white and green lights around the rim of the roof. Ned's vision adjusted to the rainbow-pricked darkness and he saw the man who had been following him approach stealthily, come toward the garage, pause for a moment at the foot of the steps.

Ned went into action.

Everything he had learned years ago when he was boxing in college came back to him in a rush. Added to that technical knowledge was practical knowledge, such as fully appreciating the element of surprise.

He flung himself upon the intruder, grabbing with a hold that actually was a lot more related to wrestling than it was to boxing. He pinned the man to the ground, held him down with a knee and a hand, drew back his clenched fist and was about to put all his strength behind the blow he planned to deliver when he heard an agonized wail and the plea, "Ned! Hey, man, it's me."

Ned released his hold, and watched Brian Summers struggle to his feet. He saw Brian stagger slightly, then clutch his jaw as if Ned's contemplated blow actually had been delivered. "Wow!" Brian mumbled, then repeated himself. "Wow," he said again.

Ned was watching Brian closely, striving at the same time to hold back his simmering anger. Brian had been following him, deliberately following him. There was no doubt about it, and the idea was so infuriating that Ned slowly clenched and unclenched both fists, almost wishing he'd followed through and landed his blow on Brian's jaw.

He commanded, "Go on up the stairs."

"Hey," Brian protested, "that's okay, Ned. There's no need."

"There's a hell of a lot of need," Ned corrected. "Get up the stairs, Brian."

He spoke in a low voice. It was doubtful the Carlsons could hear anything, with all the house windows and doors closed. Even so, he didn't want to risk it. This matter between Brian and himself was something that needed to be settled without any outside interference.

Brian still hesitated. Ned reached out and gave him a slight shove. Brian reacted as if he'd been assaulted. "Hey, look," he protested.

"Get up the stairs, Brian," Ned demanded. He heard his own voice, and became aware that the low, even tone made him sound dangerous, even menacing. It was an amusing thought, or would have been under other circumstances. He hated violence. Yet his reaction to Brian's uninvited presence was enough to make him realize, not for the first time, that the capability for violence was something always present in the human psyche.

Once before in his life, Ned remembered vividly, he had discovered his own capability for violence. And had hated enough to kill.

Brian was still standing at the bottom of the first step. Ned reached out and pushed him, only slightly, but it was enough to make Brian recoil and then to start climbing. Ned followed close behind. By the time they reached the top, Ned had his key ready. He reached around Brian to turn it in the lock and shoved the door open. Then he rasped, "Go on in."

Brian stumbled as he crossed the threshold and, briefly, Ned almost felt sorry for him. Then the anger surged again. In his opinion, what Brian had done was despicable. Tight-lipped, Ned switched on a lamp and yellow light streamed across the floor.

It was a wooden floor, centered with a braided rug. The furnishings in the one-room studio were sparse, but more than sufficient to meet Ned's needs. A table piled with books and magazines. A comfortable armchair with a good reading lamp nearby. A studio couch that served as his bed. Another table, strong enough to hold a television set, plus the VCR he had rented from Shelley. Beyond the room there was a small kitchen area, and there was a small bathroom to one side. More than enough for a man by himself. A man who wanted to be by himself.

Brian, Ned saw, was looking at him apprehensively. Nevertheless, he was standing very straight, his chin held high, his expression defiant.

The kid has guts. The assessment came involuntarily, nevertheless it took the edge off Ned's anger. In a slightly calmer voice, he said, "Sit down."

Brian complied, his eyes still wary.

Ned sat down himself, pulling a chair into a position where it would be impossible for Brian to get to the door without being intercepted. "All right," he said. "Why?"

"Why what?" Brian asked. The words began to tumble out of him. "Why the hell are you acting like this, Ned?" Brian complained. "You'd think I'd committed some kind of crime."

"In my book, you have," Ned said levelly.

"Come on," Brian protested. "All I did was track you home."

"All?"

"Yeah, all. Is that such a big deal?"

"To me it is."

"What's so wrong with wanting to know where you live?" Brian asked.

"I think a better question is why it was so important to know where I live," Ned countered.

"It wasn't me," Brian said, "it was Shelley." He blurted the words then sat back, plainly horrified by his own admission. Hastily he began, "Look, Ned, that isn't like what it sounds."

"What is it like?" Ned asked, his tone cold, his eyes considerably colder. He saw Brian flinch beneath his stare, but didn't know why.

"There was no harm intended," Brian said. "That's what's important, isn't it? It isn't like someone set out to rip you off."

Ned's laugh was very short. "Look around," he invited. "I think you'll see I don't have anything to rip off. Except, maybe, Shelley's VCR."

"Look," Brian said, "Shelley only wanted..."

"I'm listening to you," Ned nodded, when Brian broke off.

"I can't tell you what it is Shelley wanted," Brian admitted miserably, looking like someone who has let a whole family of cats out of a bag.

"Then perhaps we'd better ask Shelley what it is she wanted," Ned suggested.

"No!" Brian exclaimed.

"Why not? If Shelley wanted something and sent you to get it, why shouldn't we ask her about it?"

"It's not like that," Brian said. "What I'm saying is, Shelley changed her mind . . ."

"Oh, come off it," Ned retorted impatiently. "Either Shelley persuaded you to follow me or she didn't. Which is it?"

"Both," Brian said, after a moment.

Ned's glance was scathing. "You can't have it both ways," he advised.

"But it is both ways," Brian insisted. "Look, what I want to say is—" He broke off again. "Oh, hell, hell, hell," he muttered unhappily.

Ned stood. "Where's your car?" he demanded.

"My car." Obviously, Brian's thoughts were on other matters.

"Yes," Ned said, restraining his anger again. If Shelley had actually used Brian, who was so plainly infatuated with her, to spy, he was being introduced to a side of Shelley he would not have believed existed and which he disliked . . . violently.

"Benny's got the car," Brian said.

"How did you expect to get home once you completed your detective assignment?" Ned didn't bother to spare the sarcasm.

"Hitch, I guess," Brian muttered.

"Well, we're not going to hitch to Shelley's place if I can help it," Ned announced.

Brian looked at him in alarm. "Hey, wait a minute," he protested. "I am not about to go to Shelley's place with you."

"I disagree," Ned told him. "Come along with me. I advise you to stay with me, that's all, and to keep your mouth shut. Understand?"

For a moment, anger took over in Brian, too. "I am not some sheep," he said. "I'm not about to have you order me around, Ned. I—"

Ned cut him off. "Great, Brian," he said. "But you might stop to think you were behaving pretty much like a sheep when you agreed to do Shelley's dirty work for her. Now, come on."

Ned strode out of the studio and down the stairs. After a moment, Brian followed him. With Brian a step behind, they crossed to the Carlsons' house, and Ned knocked on the back door. A moment later, Jim Carlson came to the door, his face creasing in a wide smile when he saw his tenant.

"Hey, come on in," he invited. "You're just in time for a little pre-Christmas nog."

"Thanks, but I'll take a rain check, Jim," Ned said. "I have a favor to ask of you, as a matter of fact."

"Sure," Jim said agreeably. "Anything I can do."

"I'd like to borrow your car for an hour or so, if that wouldn't inconvenience you."

"No problem," Carlson decided swiftly. "Hang on and I'll get you the keys."

He returned shortly and handed the car keys to Ned. "She may balk a little getting started, but once she's warmed up she runs good. No hurry about bringing her back. Freda and I aren't going anywhere tonight."

"Thanks," Ned said, and reflected that sometimes real friendship showed up in unexpected places.

The car did balk, but soon steadied. When they reached Main Street, Ned asked Brian, "Where do you live?"

"About a quarter mile past Shelley's on the way to the beach," Brian said.

"Okay. I'm going to take you home."

Ned caught a glimpse of Brian's anxious face out of the corner of his eye. "Then what are you going to do?" Brian asked apprehensively.

"Pay Shelley a visit, and please don't try to phone her to warn her I'm coming. I wouldn't appreciate that, Brian." Glancing again at Brian's stricken face, Ned relented slightly. "I think you'll agree I need to talk to Shelley," he said more mildly. "I don't know what this is all about, and I think it's up to her to make an explanation. But I've been doing a bit of thinking and I see no reason for you to be present when she makes it. It'd be better, in fact, if you're not."

"I think maybe I should be present," Brian decided suddenly.

"Why?"

"Maybe to protect Shelley," Brian said. "The way you looked a while back I wouldn't want to be in her shoes when you walk in. You looked like you could beat the tar out of her. I'm not about to let that happen, Ned."

Ned had to feel some admiration for Brian, especially after the way he'd floored him earlier. He said softly, "I can assure you, Brian, I won't beat Shelley up."

That was true enough. The thought of physically abusing a woman was anathema to him. But that didn't mean he had any qualms about beating her up verbally. That was something, in fact, to which he was definitely looking forward.

Chapter Thirteen

Ned was tight-lipped, his eyes were blazing. He towered over Shelley, and she backed away from him. Although he was a menacing figure, she was more appalled than frightened. Horrified. Dismayed. And hopelessly confused.

She had been soaking in a warm, gardenia-scented bubble bath. Like a ridiculous, star-struck fool—so she told herself now—she had been pretending that she and Ned had really embarked on that tropical idyll he'd talked about. He was waiting for her, and she would go to him with a hibiscus blossom tucked into her dark hair, wearing a creamy white satin robe, ready to journey with him to the far reaches of paradise...

Well, he had been waiting for her all right. He had kept one finger on her doorbell while he pounded on the door with his fist. Hastily, Shelley had climbed out of the tub, putting on not white satin but a well-worn terry robe with a sash she tied tightly around her waist.

She'd gone down the stairs barefooted, her heart pounding. She was sure something terrible must have happened and although she normally scoffed at so-called feminine intuition her intuition was telling her the "something" involved Ned. Her hands were trembling by the time she neared the door and her fingers fumbled with the lock then slipped on the knob and it seemed an eternity before she got the door open. To find Ned on her threshold, almost literally breathing fire.

He stomped past her, went to stand in the center of the living-room rug and laced her with the most scathing glance she'd ever seen.

Instinctively, Shelley stopped short. Though she could not believe that Ned would ever physically hurt her, a primitive sense of terror began to take over her logic and to sweep away her dismay, leaving only basic, momentarily ungovernable fear in its wake.

Ned saw the fear, and was appalled himself. This was Shelley, he reminded himself, and was shaken to realize that, in his mind, she had taken on the shape of another woman. Clare. He actually had been looking at Shelley, feeling about Shelley, as if she were Clare.

Blindly he turned away, an even more profound consternation mixing with his rage. Behind him, he heard Shelley finally speak in a voice that didn't sound like Shelley at all. "Ned," she implored hoarsely. "For God's sake...what is it?"

It was the wrong question to ask him. Though he steadied himself, anger predominated again as he swung around to face her. "I think you know precisely what it is," he said coldly.

Shelley looked wretched. It took a little effort for Ned to totally steel his heart against her. Her voice quavered as she said, "I have absolutely no idea what you're talking about."

He imagined, for a moment, that she sounded like Clare—which was preposterous, because there was no way Shelley ever could sound like Clare, who had been mean and vindictive. Nevertheless, he reacted. "You are lying through your teeth."

He saw the change that came over Shelley. Saw the fright go out of her, to be replaced by a gritty courage he had to admire. She snapped defiantly, "I am not lying. And I would like to know exactly what the hell you think you're doing, pounding down my door and then storming into my house as if you want to blow it up and me with it."

Ned looked at her and some of his anger began to ebb away. As if he were analyzing himself aloud, he said, "I suppose a lot of what I'm feeling is plain damned resentment. Like a fool I had faith in you, when God knows I should have known only a fool trusts any woman..."

Shelley started to speak, then decided to wait. She wanted to give Ned the chance to pour the words out, no matter what those words might be. He needed that kind of a catharsis. The heat of his pent-up anger had shown her graphically how much he had been holding in.

All the stumbling blocks between us, she found herself thinking. *He's been hoarding all of them, building block upon block...*

Suddenly he sighed, a long sigh that sagged his shoulders and made his cheeks look pinched. He asked abruptly, "Do you have any whiskey around?"

"Yes," she nodded. "Both bourbon and Scotch, I think."

"Could I have some bourbon?"

Ned looked unutterably weary, as if the fire in him had suddenly been extinguished. Perplexed, Shelley said, "Yes, of course."

He ran a hand through his hair, rumpling the usually smooth surface. "We need to talk," he said.

A moment ago she wouldn't have thought he was in a state to be able to talk clearly about much of anything. Because of that, she frowned slightly. "Tonight?" she asked.

"Yes, tonight," he said, an edge of the anger showing again. "Any objection?"

Shelley squared her chin. "No, I have no objection, Ned." She hesitated. "It's cold in here," she said then. "Would you make a fire in the living room while I get the drinks?"

He nodded, and went ahead into the living room. Shelley, keeping a tight grip on her nerves, headed for the kitchen. She made two hefty drinks, light on the water and heavy on the bourbon.

When she got back into the living room, Ned was kneeling in front of the fireplace, coaxing the kindling to start burning. She watched him, still perplexed and not at all sure that she was up to hearing whatever was coming.

The fire started to burn. Ned got up and accepted the bourbon she handed him, then sank down in an armchair to one side of the fireplace and stared moodily at the gold-orange flames.

Shelley sat down on the couch and put her drink on the coffee table. She had a feeling she'd probably be needing it later on. She didn't want it yet.

She noted that Ned, on the other hand, quaffed half his drink before setting his glass down on a small maple end table. The moody expression on his face was deepening, if anything. She felt as if a cloud were being formed between them and Ned was about to hide himself in it. She had the feeling that if she didn't manage to dissipate the cloud it was going to solidify, and there'd be a barrier between Ned and herself that would last forever.

She clutched at courage and said, "I think you should explain why you came in here as you did."

"Because I was so furious I couldn't see straight," Ned said, after a moment. "After I let Brian out at his house..."

"After you let *Brian* out..."

"Yes, Brian," he said, giving her a withering glance. "You know. Brian Summers. One of the twins who work for you."

"Please, Ned," she protested.

"Brian, your fellow conspirator," Ned persisted. "Your willing dupe. I damn near beat his brains out, if that's any consolation to you. Fortunately I found out first who he was. Just a kid sent to do your dirty work."

She sat up straighter. "Exactly what are you talking about?" she demanded.

"Your setting Brian up to spy on me. To find out where I live. If it was that damned important to you, Shelley, why didn't you just ask me?"

It was Shelley's turn to flare. "Because you wouldn't have told me."

"What makes you so sure of that?"

"Because I *have* asked you. If you'll remember, the very first time you came into the store you refused to give your address. Subsequently, when I've offered to drive you home, or the twins have, you've refused. It's been pretty obvious that you didn't want anyone to find out where you live. For reasons I can't imagine, but I suppose you're going to tell me that's none of my business."

When Ned didn't answer, Shelley continued, "In any event, I did not set Brian to spy on you."

"Please, Shelley," Ned protested wearily. "He told me himself the reason he followed me was because you asked him to."

"Yes, I asked him to and then I told him definitely I didn't want him to. I said if your privacy meant so much to you then you were entitled to it. He must have decided to go ahead on his own..."

"Are you saying he wouldn't have reported his great discovery back to you?" Ned inquired cynically.

"No, I'm not saying that. I suppose he would have told me. He knew why I wanted to know and—"

"And why did you want to know, Shelley?" Ned asked, when she broke off.

There was bitterness in his eyes as he looked at her, and cynicism still laced his voice. He was completely unprepared for her answer when she said, "I wanted to surprise you on Christmas Eve with a birthday cake and a few little gifts. A—a small pre-birthday celebration, I guess you could call it. The twins were in on the idea, and we were going to bring Caroline if she felt strong enough. But we couldn't very well surprise you if we didn't know where you lived. So..."

Finally, Shelley reached for her drink. "Oh, skip it," she advised Ned, feeling her self-control slipping and tears threatening once again.

Ned felt as if his heart was actually turning over. The pain was intense. At the same time, a feeling of the most intense shame washed over him. He got to his feet and focused only on Shelley, who was still clasping the glass of untouched bourbon and looked as stricken as if her entire world had suddenly slipped out from under her. He stood, and quickly crossed to the couch and sank down at Shelley's side.

"Please," he said. "Oh, please, *please*. Look at me, will you, Shelley?"

She kept her eyes averted.

"Look at me," Ned pleaded. "I feel like the worst kind of a damned fool. I don't know what to say to you, how to make this up to you, but I do know that I have to say a hell of a lot. The problem is where to begin, and it's not going to be easy for me to say anything at all. You have to understand that, Shelley."

She still didn't look at him, and her voice was muffled as she said, "I think I understand."

"Do you?"

"I know," Shelley said slowly, "that there's been a lot of misery in your life. I know that at some point it must simply have gotten too much for you, and so you walked out."

"Oh, God," Ned said, "that is such a simplification."

"I imagine," Shelley went on, "that it had something to do with your being a doctor. I imagine—or I have imagined—that maybe a patient died, and you felt to blame for it. And so..."

Ned reached out and touched her chin with his fingers, gently forcing her to turn her face toward him. His voice was tight as he said, "It wasn't a patient, Shelley. It was my daughter."

She couldn't answer him.

"Lucy was three years old," he said. "She had coppery hair and big, topaz eyes...so much like your eyes, Shelley. We lived in Scarsdale at that time...up in

Westchester County. I practiced in Manhattan... That's to say I was on the surgical staff of a large hospital in Manhattan. My work was...extremely demanding. It wasn't always possible for me to make the commute back and forth from home to hospital. Finally, I rented an efficiency apartment for times when it was so late when I got through in the operating room, I was too damned tired to head for a commuter train. Then it got so a lot of the time it was easier to head for the apartment than it was to go home. Home, Shelley, was not the happiest place to go to. My wife, you see, was an alcoholic.''

Shelley stared at him bleakly, still unable to speak.

"At that time," Ned went on, "I didn't see it...didn't realize she was an alcoholic, that is. Pretty unobservant for a highly trained doctor, wasn't I? I also didn't realize, for quite a while, that in the absence of me and my affections she was turning elsewhere. Until someone told me they'd seen her coming out of a New York hotel at an odd hour with a doctor who also happened to be a med school classmate and a personal friend of mine. Even then, I didn't immediately think 'affair.' But there was, indeed, an affair. One in a series of affairs that Clare had been carrying on.

"By then, what Clare did or didn't do wasn't of too much concern to me. I know now that there had never been real love between us in the first place. Attraction, fascination, in the beginning a certain amount of passion. Nothing more. So, you see, what mattered wasn't Clare. What mattered was Lucy.''

Ned stopped. "Would you mind if I get myself some more bourbon?''

Shelley shook her head, knowing that the worst of what he had to tell her was still to come, and dreading it. "No, of course not," she said.

"Want me to freshen up your drink for you?"

"No, thanks, it's fine."

She tried not to think while Ned went out to the kitchen to make himself another drink. She tried not to think about anything at all, to make her mind a blank. Like a big black hole, swimming out in space. But intruders kept poking their way into the hole.

Clare. What had Clare been like?

Lucy. What had happened to Lucy?

Shelley discovered she was afraid to hear the answer to that question.

Ned came back, and sat down in the armchair again. He looked across at Shelley and said, "I'd better get it out quickly. Then...well, we'll see what happens then. Two days after Lucy's third birthday, Clare left her at home with a maid. The maid was out in the garden with Lucy, she heard the phone ringing, she went in the house to answer it. She was not, I might say, the brightest of girls. Yet, in all honesty, I suppose you can't say she should be blamed for what happened. It was Clare who should have had the common sense not to go off and leave Lucy with that kind of person.

"Lucy was a very curious, very fun-loving little girl. Obviously, something beyond the garden gate attracted her, and she went after it. We'll never know what it was, because she ran out into the street and was hit by a car. She was killed instantly."

"Oh my God, Ned!" The cry was wrung from Shelley.

"Let me finish or I won't be able to. Even after all this time it's...it's very difficult..."

Ned changed position, crossed his legs. Staring at the fire, he said, "I was in the OR and no one could get through to me for a while. Not that it would have mat-

tered. When the word did come, I went directly to Scarsdale. Clare was home by then. Drunk. She blamed me for
Lucy's death and everything else...she accused me of
neglecting her for years because of my profession. Neglecting Lucy, as well. She said I'd been a hell of a father. And you see, the bad part of it was that she was
right,'' Ned finished quietly.

"No," Shelley said sharply. "No, I don't believe that.
You could never have been a bad father, Ned."

Ned went on, as if he hadn't heard her. "I couldn't stay
in the house that night," he said. "I couldn't bring myself to go back to the apartment, either. I got in my car
and drove around until daylight. My sorrow was overwhelming. I...loved Lucy so much. And the sorrow was
all weighed down with guilt. It was a load so heavy I felt
I would almost surely break under it.

"Time always passes, that's one thing. The next few
days passed. At the funeral, Clare and I sat next to each
other. She didn't look at me, didn't speak to me. I began
to hate her; I can't tell you how much I hated her. I began to understand how it's possible to get to the point of
wanting only to kill someone..."

Shelley's voice was very small. "What did you do,
Ned?"

He looked up, and smiled very faintly. "I didn't kill
her, Shelley, if that's what you are asking me," he said.
"I'm not a fugitive from justice. And, as far as my practice was concerned, there were no tragic mistakes leading to my being expelled from medicine.

"I went back to New York. To the hospital. To my
work. All I wanted to do was work. To try to make sick
people well again. I guess you could say it was a desire for
atonement. As if anything could have atoned for what
happened to Lucy.

"Then, late in the fall, I got another phone call one night. Clare was dead. She'd been driving down the Saw Mill River Parkway and she crashed, went into another car. She was drunk, she probably never knew what happened to her. The especially sad part is that the two perfectly innocent people in the car she hit were gravely injured. Both will bear scars of that accident for the rest of their lives.

"I sat in the front pew in church at another funeral, and accepted condolences. People, naturally enough, treated me as a bereaved widower who had suffered two terrible losses in such a short space of time. I felt like a fraud where Clare was concerned. I think I accepted the condolences for Lucy...

"I didn't go out to the house in Scarsdale for over three weeks. As a matter of fact, it was Christmas Eve when finally I went out there. I can't tell you what motivated me, all of a sudden I had to go. I went upstairs to Lucy's room, and all her toy animals were still on their shelves. Her little bed was made up, and her favorite teddy bear was sitting in the middle of a pile of pillows. The music box she loved was on her dresser, and I started playing it. And something broke inside me, Shelley.

"I stayed in the house all night, but I never went to bed. That next morning, it was both Christmas and my birthday. And that's when I decided to give myself the birthday present. There was nothing to hold me any longer. And there had been so much, for so long. Way before Clare ever got into my life."

Confused once again, Shelley stared across at him. "I don't think I understand . . ." she began.

"Let it go for now," Ned said. She saw the marks of strain etched on his face, the lines grooved on either side of his mouth. She could imagine how he would look years from now if he kept wandering, and the bitterness kept on growing inside him. Because the bitterness *had* kept growing, these past four years. She would have sworn to that. Maybe Ned had given himself the gift of freedom for his thirty-fifth birthday, but she also would have sworn that freedom had not given him the release he was looking for.

"You can't run away from life," she said suddenly.

Ned looked startled. "What?" he asked.

"I was just thinking out loud, Ned," she said.

"No. If my ears were hearing correctly, you made quite a profound statement. I'd just like to be sure that I heard it right."

"You can't run away from life," Shelley repeated, rather reluctantly.

She saw Ned's eyes flicker, saw him flinch ever so slightly. Then he said, "No, you can't, can you?" He stirred restlessly. "God knows I've tried. Tried all kinds of places, all kinds of odd jobs. I worked in a lumber camp out in Washington State. I dug potatoes in Maine. I learned how they burn the sugar cane crop in Hawaii. I even tried my hand at selling condos, down on the west coast of Florida." For just a second, a slight glint of humor surfaced. "I was a lousy salesman," he confessed.

"Sometimes," he went on, "I didn't do anything. I suppose you could say in one sense I'm one of the lucky ones. I don't have to worry about money. I have a lawyer in New York, he's the one person who knows where I am, at any given time. He sends me bank checks on a regular basis, easily converted into cash. Oh, what the hell," Ned said, exasperated. "The logistics don't really matter. The fact is, I think I freed myself as much as any individual ever could free himself. And I had the illusion that maybe I'd succeeded, until one November day I wound up on Cape Cod and walked into your store. And it began to catch up with me, all that life you just said one can't walk away from."

The implication was plain. Ned was as good as saying that she was the one who had made life catch up with him again. It was an implication that made her uncomfortable. She didn't want to have that kind of responsibility. Ned, she could see now, had left a place behind him...but the people she had assumed he might also have abandoned were dead by the time he walked away from Scarsdale.

One thing had been left to him, though. His career. She dared to ask one more question. "Don't you ever miss medicine?"

He answer with a question. "Would it really matter? I'm out of medicine, Shelley, by my own volition. Can you imagine how much ground a surgeon loses in four years away from his job? Modern medicine changes on a weekly, even a daily basis. You have to keep up. Even people right in the thick of practicing their profession find it inordinately difficult to keep up. Anyway..."

Ned suddenly stood and stretched. He looked down at her, but she couldn't read his expression. He said, "I need to get the Carlsons' car back to them."

"The Carlsons?"

"My landlords. I rent a studio apartment up over their garage. After Brian followed me home, I asked Jim if I could borrow his car for an hour. It's been more than that."

Shelley could not possibly have said how much time had passed since Ned had stormed into her life. All she knew was that she felt totally wrung out by the things he had told her during that interval. Drained. She was neither acting, nor reacting, at peak performance.

Ned said, "Look, I'll catch up with you tomorrow. Do you plan to open early and stay late?"

"I think I'll open at the usual time," she said, not having really given the matter any thought at all. "How late I stay open...depends."

"Will the twins be around to help you out?"

"As far as I know," Shelley said, wondering what he was leading up to.

She found out soon enough. "In that case," Ned said, "I think I may wait till afternoon to come in. By then you may need a little extra help."

Shelley had not expected him to come back to Video Vibes again, not tomorrow, not any time. God knew he had no obligation to her, and all she'd done for him was to open up wounds that maybe, finally, had started to heal, though she wasn't sure of that.

Ned started for the kitchen. Shelley followed slowly and watched him pick up the green parka, which he had tossed over a chair, and sling it on. He looked taut and exhausted and she'd never in her life felt at such a loss as she did watching him, and wondering what to say or do next.

Ned wasted no time in his leave-taking. There was no such thing as taking her in his arms at the last minute, to let passion resurface and take over between them. No move toward so much as a good-night kiss. He opened the kitchen door and said, "I'll see you tomorrow," and then he was gone.

Shelley stared at the blank surface of the door he had closed behind him, and never before in her life had she felt such a failure.

Chapter Fourteen

In a desperate attempt to put some holiday cheer both into Video Vibes and her own life, Shelley set out for the store, the morning before Christmas Eve, with two heirloom punch bowls brought down from her grandmother's attic. Then she stopped at a candle shop and bought a supply both of Christmas candles and holiday cocktail napkins.

At noon, she left the twins minding the store and went out for bourbon, eggnog, nutmeg and cookies. Once back in the store, she asked the twins to set up the folding table for her, then filled the punch bowls with "with" and "without" eggnogs and, in a reckless mood, sampled a cup of the "with" herself.

She decided that from now till she closed for the holidays she was going to hold open house for her customers, having given up the thought of having an eggnog party in her own home this particular Christmas season.

It was shortly after two when Ned walked into the store. Shelley saw Brian glance rather apprehensively at Ned, but Ned greeted him casually and made his way to the table, where she was replenishing the cookie supply.

"Well," he said. "I thought the big party had already been held, Saturday before last."

"I decided that at this point everyone could use a small transfusion of holiday spirit and energy," Shelley said. She stole a glance at Ned. He looked a lot better than she would have expected him to. Evidently he'd slept better than she had. His eyes were clear, he was freshly shaven, his hair combed carefully. He was wearing a bright red sweater that looked terrific on him, and very well-tailored gray slacks. Shelley swallowed hard. Why did he have to be so damned attractive?

They were busy that afternoon, but not too busy. There were free time spaces when, ordinarily, Shelley would have welcomed a chance to lead Ned into some conversation. But not today. Today she was the one who didn't want to talk. Ever since he'd left her house last night, she'd felt depressed, dispirited. Right now, she didn't want to talk to anyone about anything.

She thought about putting some Christmas music on the stereo to liven things up a bit more and was about to pick out a cassette when she heard the screams, the sound of brakes screeching and the hideous crash of a car careering into a plate-glass window.

She raced toward the door, but Ned was there ahead of her. She saw him dash out into the parking lot, saw people gathering around something—someone—lying out on the grimy, sand-sprinkled concrete. Heard a woman moan, "Oh my God, it's a little girl!" And suddenly felt so sick it was all she could do not to retch.

The twins already had gone out to join the crowd. Shelley hung back, overcome by a terrible dread. From her doorway, she could see that a car had leaped the sidewalk in front of the pharmacy, which was across the mall to her right, and gone into the huge window. Shattered glass lay everywhere.

The sound of sirens grew louder. Two Devon police cruisers careered into the parking lot. A moment later the rescue squad and a fire engine followed. Her heart in her throat, Shelley watched paramedics make their way through the crowd and then she slowly worked her way to the edge of the crowd. When a momentary gap opened up she saw the little girl lying on the ground, Ned bent over her.

Ned drew back briefly, and Shelley was able to see the child more clearly. Her eyes were closed, and she looked more like a wax doll than a human child. For a terrible moment Shelley was sure she was dead. But then she became aware that Ned was talking to the little girl in low, steady tones, and she saw one small, chubby hand move ever so slightly.

Ned, she saw, was very carefully keeping the crowd away from the child. Only when the paramedics came up to him did he stand and speak quickly, with an air of authority that Shelley suspected was unconscious with him.

She knew one of the paramedics—he'd been in high school with her. She recognized the other man, but he was a relative newcomer to Devon. She saw Ned speak to one of the police officers, and the officer instructed the crowd to move back. Then a stretcher was brought out of the rescue squad ambulance and the child was gently and carefully placed upon it. At that moment, the little girl's hand fluttered, as if she were seeking something. Shelley couldn't see if she'd opened her eyes or not. But she did see Ned reach down and very gently take hold of the small hand, and tears filled her eyes as she thought of what this must be doing to him.

The ambulance departed. Shelley saw the two police officers talking to Ned. Then they got into their cruiser and drove off.

Shelley retreated to her doorway and waited for Ned. But his progress back to the store was intercepted by a number of people, evidently asking him questions about the accident. Even from the relative distance of her vantage point, Shelley was aware of his politeness and his patience.

It seemed an eternity before he was standing by her side. Then she was afraid to meet his eyes. Afraid the pain she'd see in them—the ghosts of haunting memories—would be more than she could deal with.

Finally, Ned said sharply, "Shelley," and she had to look up at him. He was frowning as he asked, "What is it?"

Shelley tried to find the right words to say, and couldn't. She shook her head, faltered, then asked, "Is the little girl badly hurt?"

"Injured, yes, but she's going to be okay," Ned said. "For a moment, I thought I'd have to do an emergency tracheotomy, but it wasn't necessary. I'd say she has a concussion, I suspect a collar bone fracture and also, maybe, a fracture of the right ankle. Plus assorted contusions and abrasions... But over all, nothing really life-threatening. She's going to hurt for a while but before too long she should be fine again. Also, fortunately, the driver of the car that hit her is unhurt, except for an understandable bad case of nerves."

Ned spoke levelly, with no overriding emotion, and Shelley suddenly became sharply aware that she was speaking to a physician, a very competent surgeon, rather than to the bereaved father of another little girl who had not been as lucky as this little girl today.

Ned said, "Hey, there," and Shelley also became aware that she was not only staring at him, but had become lost in an entirely new train of thought. "Hey," he said again, and smiled at her. He took her arm. "How about letting the kids mind the store for half an hour and we'll cut over to Nonnie's for some coffee?"

Just then, Shelley would have taken off for the moon with him, if he'd asked her to go.

She spoke briefly to the twins, and then she and Ned walked out of the mall onto Main Street, and turned up Main Street toward Nonnie's.

Ned was silent. Now and then, she stole a glance at him, and saw that at this point he'd become lost in thought. Not for the first time, she wished she had the power to read his mind.

In Nonnie's, people were talking about the accident. Several of those people immediately recognized Ned who, it developed, was getting credit for having saved the life of the small accident victim.

Ned was self-deprecating and charming as he parried both praise and questions. Finally he and Shelley were allowed to progress to a corner table, and Nonnie brought their coffee personally.

When Nonnie had departed, Shelley said, "You've become a hero."

"For an hour, maybe," Ned conceded. He stirred sugar into his coffee, making a bigger action of the stirring than he usually did. He said evasively, "This too will pass, Shelley. Don't take it so seriously."

"I don't think it will pass," Shelley contradicted him. "People in Devon are going to remember you." She at first bit back the rest of the words she'd started to say, then decided to say them, regardless. "Long after you've gone," she finished.

She saw Ned's eyelashes flicker, but he didn't look up at her. He concentrated on the coffee, this time stirring some cream into it. Finally he said, "Look, I happened to be there today when I was needed. I had the skill to do what needed to be done, immediately. It was important to clear an air passage so the child could breathe normally. Also, to make sure she wasn't moved suddenly or abruptly. You saw how the paramedics handled her when they got to the scene."

Shelley realized suddenly that she'd been so intent on Ned himself that most of the questions people had been asking him and the answers he'd given had only dimly registered with her. Now she was timid about asking questions herself, because this was getting into an area that must be very painful to Ned. This little girl, after all, evidently had run out in the path of a car just as Lucy had...

Ned was watching Shelley closely. He saw the play of emotions on her lovely face, and was sure he was close to reading her thoughts accurately. He felt a slight annoyance with her, then chastised himself for feeling any annoyance at all since, obviously, Shelley was trying to repress her natural curiosity because she didn't want to hurt him.

Suddenly an awareness of how much he had come to love this woman sitting opposite him swept over Ned, and for a couple of seconds he was speechless himself. Then he said, gently, "Shelley, it's okay to talk about it."

She looked up at him, startled. Ned went on, "About the comparison between today and what happened to Lucy. No, don't look at me like that. I *want* to talk about it, Shelley. Because today, traumatic as it was, brought home a truth to me I've never fully recognized before. Accidents *do* happen . . . and they are exactly that. Accidents. Unexpected. Traumatic. Sometimes catastrophic. But, frequently, something that can't be prevented. I, who've spent God knows how many hours in hospital emergency rooms, should have known that. Accepted it. But I never did. It was much easier, far more of a consolation, to put the blame for Lucy's death on my wife's shoulders.

"But you see," Ned continued, "what happened today was an accident that nearly paralleled what happened to Lucy. The little girl today—her mother works as a receptionist in a lawyer's office here in town. She was at work, and the little girl was with the baby-sitter. The baby-sitter had some Christmas shopping to do, and took the girl with her. This girl—the baby-sitter—met someone she knew and they stopped to talk. The little girl was looking at some coloring books in the toy section of the shop one minute. The next minute she was gone, then the baby-sitter heard a scream . . ."

Shelley watched Ned's carefully controlled expression, and wanted to scream herself. She couldn't believe that telling her this wasn't tearing him apart.

"This little girl was four," Ned said. "Evidently something attracted her attention and she wandered off, out of the shop, and was into the parking lot in a flash. Fortunately, the driver who hit her was looking for a place to park, so was moving very slowly." Ned drew a deep breath. "All the way around," he said, "it was an accident. You could say the baby-sitter was careless, I'd say she was acting as anyone might have acted. As the child's mother might have acted. As you or I might have acted. In other words, no one is really to blame. Do you understand what I'm saying?''

"I think so," Shelley murmured. "There's no reason for anyone to feel guilt.''

"Yes," Ned said, "that's exactly it. For the first time since Lucy died, it is beginning to occur to me that there's no reason why I should go around for the rest of my life carrying a burden of guilt that has been so heavy, much of the time, I've nearly fallen from the weight of it.''

He broke off. "I guess we'd better get back to the store," he said, closing off the subject.

Shelley left questions she wanted to ask die unspoken. It was not the time for them. But as they walked back to Video Vibes, she did say, "How did you find out so many details about what happened today?''

"The cops told me," Ned said. "While the paramedics worked with the child the cops were doing some preliminary investigating, and that's what they came up with. I think I may go talk to both the mother and the baby-sitter. I think it might help them if I shared my experience with them. On the other hand, I suppose they might feel I was butting in...''

"They wouldn't feel you were butting in," Shelley said softly. And her love for this tall, wonderful man walking at her side overflowed.

Early in the evening Ned sought out Shelley and said, "The twins told me I could borrow their car. I'm going to drive over to Hyannis, to the hospital. I checked, and it looks like the little girl is going to be fine, just as I thought. Both the mother and the baby-sitter are there at the hospital and the more I think of it the more I feel I should talk to them.''

Shelley nodded agreement, but she couldn't keep herself from saying rather bitterly, "You could have borrowed my car, you know."

She didn't add that, had he suggested it, she would have closed up the store early and gone to Hyannis with him.

Ned, looking surprised, said, "It just didn't occur to me. When the thought hit me, Brian and Benny were standing right there, so..."

He grinned unexpectedly. "Anyway," he said, "I'd say Brian owes me one."

Watching Ned leave the store, Shelley felt pretty sure that she still hadn't heard the last of Brian's having played sleuth. She'd made one rather halting explanation which happened to be the truth. Well...partly the truth. She had wanted to have a birthday surprise party for Ned, just as she'd said. But actually that could have been arranged either right here in the store, or at her home. The whole truth was that she'd wanted to know where Ned lived simply because...because she wanted to know where he lived.

Her curiosity about Ned still was far from satisfied. There were times when she felt she knew him very well, as he himself had said she did. There were other times when she felt she didn't know him at all. This afternoon she'd had a clear glimpse of Edward Alexander, the doctor...and it had been a glimpse of a stranger.

Edward Alexander?

It was a shock to realize that she still didn't even know Ned Alexander Question Mark's full name!

Time passed. Shelley sent Benny out for pizza, and she and the twins took turns going back to the kitchenette to snatch a few bites of food. There were more last-minute Christmas shoppers than Shelley had expected there would be, with just a single day to go between now and the holiday itself.

Around eight, Brian summoned her to the phone. She had the sudden hope that it was Ned, calling her from Hyannis, but it wasn't. Rather, it was Caroline who said, "Shelley, Brian said you've really been rushed tonight so I'll be brief. I wanted to ask you to do a favor for me."

"Of course, Caroline," Shelley said swiftly.

"I want to get something for Ned . . . Christmas is also his birthday, you know."

"Yes," Shelley said ruefully. "I know."

"I still can't get out myself, so I wondered if you'd do this bit of shopping for me. Wally offered, which I appreciate, but I'd really like your advice."

Caroline was speaking of a particular "bit of shopping" that Shelley had yet to accomplish for herself. She still hadn't been able to make up her mind about what to get Ned for his Christmas birthday.

"What do you want to get him?" she asked Caroline.

"A mini camera," Caroline announced promptly. "Something small enough so he can easily carry it around with him. But something good enough so that it will be reasonably guaranteed he can produce good pictures with it.

"He was saying the other day," Caroline elaborated, "that he wished he'd taken pictures of every place he's been. But he said he's never carried a camera with him. That's what gave me the idea."

Shelley felt a slight stab of envy. It was a great idea, she only wished she had thought of it herself.

A new camera shop had opened only recently in the mall, and passing by the window Shelley had admired both the display technique and the merchandise itself.

Now she said to Caroline, "Look, I'll go right over to Shutters and Such and see what they have."

"Dear, there's no need for you to do that right now, when you're so busy," Caroline protested. "I thought maybe if you could steal just a few minutes tomorrow..."

"All right," Shelley compromised. "I'll take a mid-morning coffee break tomorrow, get the camera and bring it over to you. Okay?"

"Fabulous," Caroline said. "Oh, Shelley..."

"Yes?"

"One more thing. I don't know what everyone's plans are for Christmas Day, so I wondered if maybe you and the twins and Wally and I could stage a little surprise party for Ned tomorrow night, here at my place..."

Shelley didn't know whether to laugh or to cry when she heard that. She wondered how many people, in the course of Ned's travels, had gotten on the same wavelength about him and wanted to do something for him...especially at Christmas.

"We can talk about it tomorrow," she told Caroline, and escaped back into work.

It was late when Ned walked out of Cape Cod Hospital. The wintry breeze sweeping in from Lewis Bay had the tang of salt to it, and in the distance he heard the moan of a foghorn. Sometimes, especially in Devon's shopping mall, he forgot the closeness of the Cape to the sea, the affinity that came in this meeting of slender land and vast, open water. In the mall, one could almost be anywhere. Malls, like condominiums, like cinema complexes, were everywhere, and basically unidentifiable. But so much in the Cape Cod area still remained unique, despite the so-called path of progress.

He had gotten sand in his shoes, Ned realized, as he slowly walked across the wide parking lot to the twins' car. Then cautiously, reflectively, his mind turned to review the six weeks on the winter Cape, and how much his life had been turned upside down.

Shelley. He had fallen in love with her, which scared the hell out of him.

Lucy. Finally he could think of his little girl and experience the kind of natural grief that would mellow in time, so that she would become a sweet memory.

Himself. Today as he bent over another little girl— Marla—he had, somehow, switched mental gears and almost without being aware of it slipped back into a long-familiar pattern. He had become a doctor again.

Again? No, Ned corrected himself, he had never stopped being a doctor. A long time ago he had taken the Oath of Hippocrates, and that oath had become a vital part of his reason for being.

The Oath of Hippocrates. He smiled as he got into the car, remembering the day that oath had been administered to him. His med school class had participated in the main university graduation ceremonies, then had progressed to a special ceremony held on the lawn in back of the university president's mansion, where the coveted degree itself had been bestowed.

One hundred and forty-two brand-new doctors, assembled, had been instructed to speak the Oath of Hippocrates, and they had fumbled collectively on the very first line.

The dean of the med school, Ned remembered, had peered at them over his rimless glasses and in a tone he might have used to a bunch of kindergarten kids had admonished, "Very well, ladies and gentlemen, shall we start again? Now, follow me. 'I swear by Apollo...'"

A long time ago, Ned thought. Thirteen years ago, next May. So much had happened over those thirteen years. But even before he'd spoken those words, "I swear by Apollo," he had been a doctor, in heart and mind. And though he had turned his back on his profession, there was no way he could write it off.

No way he wanted to write it off, he realized suddenly. And was staggered.

Traffic was light, at this hour on a just-before-Christmas night. Ned drove slowly, and he was thinking profoundly every inch of the way.

He couldn't escape the feeling that tonight, there in the hospital, he'd gone home again. He had talked to Marla's mother, frantic when he had arrived, much calmer when he had left. He had talked to the baby-sitter, who was still crying her eyes out when he arrived, but had stopped crying when he left. He had been made to realize that he hadn't lost the touch. Had never lost the touch to communicate with people in great need of him, and his skill.

Had he lost the skill? In all honesty, he doubted it.

Could he go back? Could he catch up if he did go back?

Questions stabbed, but the answers to most of them were not that difficult. If he went back, yes, he could catch up. He knew himself, he knew his capacity to absorb knowledge. He could go back, he could catch up. Yet he would never want it to be the way it was before.

Wandering had given him a freedom he'd never had before. He had learned the vastness, the tempo, the infinite variety of the world beyond hospital walls. Each place he'd been, each thing he'd done, had brought a wealth of new experiences and a greater understanding of people and life. He knew so much more now about compassion, about tolerance and, yes, about love than he had before.

Today, Ned knew, he would be a far better doctor than he had been then. Blended with skill would be soul.

He pulled up at the twins' house, his mind racing. Conflicting emotions tore at him. He was positive, on the one hand. On the other... plagued with doubts.

There was so much to be resolved.

Brian came to the door, and was shrugging on a parka as he opened it. He said somewhat defiantly, "I'll run you home. Okay?"

Ned grinned. "Okay," he said. "Since you know the way."

Brian shot a suspicious glance at him, and Ned chuckled.

Brian took the wheel this time, and almost immediately said, "It's all over town that you saved that little girl's life today."

"People exaggerate," Ned said calmly.

"They're saying you're a famous doctor," Brian persisted.

"Well," Ned smiled, "I think maybe you could strike the famous."

Brian ignored that. But after a moment he said, "Ned..."

Ned caught the urgency in his tone. "What?" he asked quickly.

"About Shelley. Look, I followed you on my own last night."

"Are you saying it wasn't Shelley's idea? Initially, anyway?"

Brian hesitated. Ned could see that fibs didn't come easily to him and finally Brian groaned slightly and admitted, "Yeah, it was her idea at first. But then, just like

I told you, she said to bag it. Like I told you, she said you
had a right to your privacy. I went ahead and followed
you anyway, and I shouldn't have. Shelley was right, I
mean if you don't want people to know where you live
that's your business.''

Ned said slowly, ''I didn't want people to know where
I live. Now it really doesn't seem all that important.''

''Well, all I'm saying is, it would be wrong to blame
Shelley. I guess I was thinking she'd chickened out and it
would please her if I went ahead anyway. But she was
mad as a hornet at me....''

Ned smiled. ''She'll get over it, Brian. I'm sure she's
probably gotten over it already.''

''Yeah,'' Brian said. ''I guess maybe.''

They lapsed into silence. But Ned imagined Brian was
thinking about Shelley even as he was. The kid had a
crush on Shelley, there was little doubt of that. But he'll
outgrow his feeling for her, Ned thought wryly. I won't.

Again, he remembered asking Shelley to go off to a
tropical paradise with him. It had been a genuine invitation, though he doubted it had come across as such. And,
from her instinctive, visible reaction, he was sure that she
would have turned him down, if he'd persisted.

Shelley was not a wanderer at heart, he knew that.
Maybe he wasn't totally a wanderer at heart himself, but
he'd had a taste of that kind of freedom and he knew
there would always be moments when he'd have to indulge the desire to escape.

Shelley, on the other hand, wanted something entirely
different from life. Stability, mostly, from what he'd
gathered from her. He could understand why. Her family life had been shot to hell when she'd been at a very
vulnerable age. She'd discovered that the father she
adored was an idol with clay feet, as she had put it, and

although she had come to terms with her father's weakness and even felt compassion for him she wanted her own feet on very firm ground. That much was clear to Ned.

Shelley wanted a husband who would be a solid citizen, work a nine-to-five job and offer her devotion but no surprises. She'd had her share of surprises. Shelley would want kids, a couple of kids, anyway. And she would want them to be brought up in an environment where that nine-to-five father would have plenty of time to spend with them.

If he went back to medicine, Ned reminded himself, that was a kind of environment he couldn't possibly offer Shelley. True, he would never again let himself become the captive to his profession he'd been before. A good part of the reason he'd become so captive was a different kind of need to escape, because he had been so bitterly unhappy. Nevertheless, a surgeon's life was incredibly demanding. A surgeon's time could not be called his own. Though that time could be managed far better than he'd ever managed it, Ned conceded. If...

It was an enormous if.

Brian brought the car to a stop at the foot of the garage steps. Ned blinked. He'd been so lost in reverie he'd not even realized it when Brian turned off the side road onto the lane where he lived.

"Thanks," he told Brian. And added, "Look...don't worry. I don't blame Shelley, I don't blame you. Okay?"

"Okay," Brian said, plainly relieved.

Ned nodded, and started up the stairs. If only everything were so easy to resolve!

Was he wrong about Shelley? he asked himself, as he let himself in the apartment and for a moment stood staring into darkness. Was she maybe more of a gambler than he thought she was?

There was one way to find out, of course. To ask her. But he wasn't sure he was enough of a gambler himself to put so much on the line.

Chapter Fifteen

Shelley couldn't get to sleep. She tossed and turned, punched her pillow in the effort to make a comfortable nest for her weary head, turned the pillow over, opened the window and let the cold air stream across her face, then closed the window again. Nothing worked.

Muttering to herself, she got up, put on her old terry robe, thrust her feet into well-worn scuffs and went downstairs. She had turned the thermostat down when she went to bed, so it was chilly in the house. Shivering, she went out to the kitchen and put a kettle of water on the stove. Tea? Coffee? Hot chocolate? She didn't know what she wanted.

On the contrary, she knew exactly what she wanted. She wanted Ned.

The longing that came over her was like a summer wave, swelling and cresting, then crashing into foam against the shore, little puffs of spindrift breaking off to race along the glistening sand.

Shelley turned off the heat under the kettle, poured herself a glass of sherry and took it with her into the living room. She turned on a single, dim light and settled down on the couch, staring at the blackness of a hearth in which no fire burned.

She felt so very mixed up. Today's happenings had only confused her all the more. Now Ned, in some ways, seemed more of a stranger than ever to her. And yet in other ways she truly did know him. And she loved him. She had no doubt about the depth and veracity of her love. There never in her life had been anyone like Ned; there never would be again. Of that much, she was certain.

She wasn't certain of many other things. She'd felt a stronger than usual sense of strain, as she'd walked back to the mall with Ned after their short time at Nonnie's. Ned, on the other hand, merely had seemed preoccupied. Preoccupied, but in control. Outwardly, she supposed she also had seemed to be in control. Inwardly, she'd been splintering off in so many directions.

She wished she had said yes the other day, when Ned had talked about going off to a tropical island. A fervent yes, an unqualified yes. She could only imagine the emotional chaos that would have descended for her when their idyll ended. But she was beginning to believe that there was truth to that old saw about it being better to love and lose than never to love at all.

Better to live than never to live at all, Shelley paraphrased.

She couldn't be a wanderer forever. It wasn't in her. On the other hand ... what was security, if there was no one you cared about to share it with? Shelley suddenly could picture herself years from now, safe and secure and alone. Or maybe not alone, she conceded. But with someone who never had been able to capture her heart to even the slightest extent Ned had. The love between them seemed to have sprung as naturally and inevitably as trees leaf out in spring and flowers bloom in summer, Shelley thought, rather incoherently.

The love between them. It *was* a shared love, damn it. That conviction swept over Shelley and she suddenly got to her feet and decided that for once in her life she was going to follow her heart. Do what she wanted to do, had to do right now, without stopping to think about the possible consequences, the later hurt, that might follow.

Ned was sitting in his comfortable armchair, pretending to read. He had read the same paragraph five times, and still had absolutely no idea as to what the words were saying.

He had fixed himself a bourbon-and-branch-water nightcap. The glass sat on the table by his side, its contents still untouched. He wanted a drink; he didn't want a drink. He wanted to read; he didn't want to read. In every area he could think of, he was finding it exceedingly difficult to put his act together and make much sense out of anything.

Earlier he had switched on the television, then turned it off. Then turned on the radio, and switched it off. The radio had been playing Christmas carols, and tonight he didn't want to hear Christmas carols. The familiar old refrains were evocative of a time that was supposed to be the best time of the year, replete with love and joy and kindness. As he well knew, it could also be the loneliest time of the year.

He stood, feeling restless as a caged tiger, and knew he needed to move, needed action. He put on his boots, his parka, thrust a wool scarf around his neck for good measure and started out for the nearest beach along Cape Cod Bay.

It was a bright and sparkling night. The winter moon was riding high. Venus reigned supreme in her segment of the sky. Smaller stars glittered, sprinkling their brilliance across the vast, black panoply that stretched above the earth.

From the shoreline, white ice floes stretched as far as the eyes could see. Ned looked from earth to sky, focused on a star, and found himself repeating, aloud, the old rhyme, "Star light, star bright . . ."

I wish I may, I wish I might, have the wish I wish tonight. The words echoed. He wondered how many thousands of people must have voiced them over the years? And how many of those people had had their wish come true?

What did he wish, for that matter? If he could concentrate on one, single wish, what would it be?

Shelley? Would he wish for Shelley?

He would always wish for Shelley, Ned thought bleakly. But right now she seemed as out of reach to him as the star he'd just focused upon.

Slowly, he turned and started back along the road toward his studio and climbed the stairs up. At the top, he found Shelley waiting for him.

Shelley had been knocking on Ned's door, not loud enough to wake his landlord but loud enough so she was sure she'd wake him, if he were asleep.

Soon she decided he wasn't asleep. He was out. Somewhere.

Disappointed, chagrined, she turned and was about to start down the stairs when she saw him slowly trudging up them. Huddled in the shadows on the landing, wearing a dark coat, she realized he hadn't seen her. As he came closer, she saw that his head was down and he was moving slowly, heavily, as if he were both very tired and very preoccupied.

Then he looked up and, as if it had been programmed, a shaft of silvery moonlight slanted down to earth, bathing both their faces with its radiance.

Ned spoke her name disbelievingly. She didn't answer him. She didn't have to. For, quickly, impulsively, he took her in his arms and kissed her with all the force of a man who has been starving and has just found manna in a desert.

Then, tenderly, he drew her into his studio, holding her with one arm while he reached out with the other to switch on a light. Only then did he release her, to stand back and devour her with his eyes while he said something he'd never said before.

"Oh, God," Ned murmured hoarsely, "I love you."

Shelley let out a little cry and hurled herself at him, clasping his shoulders with frantic fingers, pulling him close to her, unable to get him close enough. She wanted him and she made no secret of it. Every gesture became eloquent. Her body spoke its own kind of language and Ned succumbed.

Time went into a new dimension as they made love—wonderful, feverish love at first, then the tempo slowing after passion's initial slaking, slow, languorous love that took desire to the apex only to reveal the knowledge that there are higher points still beyond the highest point.

Replete, eventually, Shelley drifted to sleep in Ned's arms, and he watched her sleep, feeling an inexpressible tenderness toward her. He was intensely aware of the scope of her giving tonight. She had cast all of her private cautions to the wind in coming here, he knew that. She had come prepared to offer herself to him as completely, as totally as she could. He felt humble, thinking of the magnitude of her gift. Hoping she knew, or that he could show her, what her gesture had meant to him.

After a time he slipped away from her, tucking the coverlet firmly around her. He went to stand at the window, watching the first gray light of dawn creep across the land, blotting out the moon and the stars.

With the coming of daylight, reality intruded. Ned sat down in the armchair and tried to put his thoughts in order. Tried to think logically about where he and Shelley could hope to go from here.

Shelley stirred, sat up, rubbed her eyes. She glanced toward the window and said, appalled, "Daylight."

Ned crossed to her, smiled down at her. "Darkness doesn't last forever," he reminded her gently.

"I know, but I had no intention...I mean I had no—"

"No thought of spending the night here?" he suggested.

"Yes." She was rattled, he saw. Disconcerted. It occurred to him that maybe Shelley was even more conventional than he had thought she was.

"Shelley," he pointed out, "you're a big girl."

"What is that supposed to mean?"

"It's no big deal if you drive back to your house in broad daylight and your tenants see you," he pointed out to her.

Shelley looked uncomfortable. Ned knew he had scored. He said, "Seriously, why should you be that concerned about conclusions people may jump to?"

"What makes you think I'm concerned?" she snapped back.

"It's showing, Shelley."

Irritated, Shelley said, "Ned, if you don't mind. I mean, if I could have just a little privacy? I need to get dressed and . . ."

"Okay," Ned said. "I'll be enormously gallant. I'll go stand at the window with my back to you until you're fully clad."

Shelley didn't answer him. Ned stalked across the room, looking out into the woodland back of this property where there was mostly scrub pine and a few struggling oak trees. He, too, was irritated, annoyed with Shelley because it seemed to him she was, by her attitude, cheapening what had been between them. He resented that. On the other hand, he reminded himself, this was a small town they were both living in. A place loaded with curiosity bumps. Subject to gossip, some of which could become malicious. Also, it was Shelley's place, not his. She had her reputation to maintain, whereas he didn't give a damn about what his reputation might or might not be in Devon.

But even so, he thought resentfully, she didn't have to be quite so narrow-minded.

She suddenly loomed up at his elbow to say, "Ned, I know I'm being silly."

He looked down at her, and tried not to let himself be affected by the anxiety showing plain upon her face. "Do you?" he asked her. "Know you're being silly, that is?"

"Yes. But I do feel funny about driving back home at this hour. I mean, maybe my tenants will see me, maybe they won't. But chances are they will and . . ."

"And they'll know you've been out all night?"

"Yes. I mean, what else could they think?"

"If they're friends of yours, maybe they won't think anything," Ned suggested. "Maybe they'll just accept the fact that you have a perfect right to lead your own life, Shelley, without becoming subjected to a lot of judgments, most of which would be false."

"People aren't like that, Ned."

"No," he conceded, "I suppose they're not."

"But it doesn't matter to you, does it?"

"Should it matter to me?"

"It would, at least it might, if you lived here," Shelley said. "Really lived here, that is. As it happens, in a couple of days you'll be moving on..."

He stared down at her curiously. "Why do you say that?"

"It seems to me you mentioned you always move on, by the start of any new year, and New Year's Eve is not that far away, Ned."

"True."

"Why don't you come out and say it?" Shelley challenged. "Why don't you tell me you'll be leaving here by New Year's Eve, if not sooner. Maybe today. Maybe tomorrow."

"Maybe," Ned said evenly, "because I don't know myself."

Shelley stepped back, one emotion after another crossing her face. Finally she said, "I don't think I understand what you're saying."

"I'm not sure I understand what I'm saying myself," Ned admitted. "Look, Shelley... I'm not just trying to change the subject, but you'd have more chance of getting into your cottage unobserved now than you will have if you wait here much longer. That's to say, your tenants may still be sleeping."

"Dale's an early riser," Shelley said.

"Even so." Ned sighed. "Okay, then," he suggested, "why don't I fix some breakfast for both of us while you shower and fix up your hair or whatever. Then you can go straight to the store from here."

"My clothes are much too rumpled," Shelley said.

Ned smiled slightly. "Sorry," he told her, "but I don't have an iron."

He watched her go over to the chair upon which she'd tossed her coat last night, pick up the coat and slip it on. She was upset, he could see that, and he knew he shouldn't be so impatient with her.

Suddenly he said, "I'm sorry."

Shelley swung around. "About what?" she asked him.

"I guess I should have sent you home under cover of darkness. Or never let you come in here in the first place, last night."

"Are you teasing?" she asked suspiciously.

"No, I'm quite serious," Ned said. "I didn't know that preserving the amenities meant quite so much to you. As far as I'm concerned, I wouldn't change a second of what happened between us last night . . ."

"And you think I would?"

"I don't know what to think, Shelley," he admitted. "I'd say you've overreacted . . ."

"And you've never overreacted?"

"Oh, hell," Ned said wearily, "there's no one alive who hasn't overreacted to something, at some time. I suppose it's just that conventionality, per se, doesn't mean as much to me as it evidently does to you."

"Because you're a wanderer," Shelley told him. "A loner. The rolling stone that hates moss. You go your own way. When you're through with one place and the people in it you simply move on. Freedom, I think you called it once. Well, I guess that's freedom, all right. No responsibilities. No obligations. No encumbrances. So it really doesn't matter a damn what anyone anywhere thinks of you. No one really knows you. I don't think I really know you, regardless of what you may say about that.''

Shelley's hand was on the doorknob as she said this. She stood on the threshold, facing him defiantly. "Do you realize," she told him, "I don't even know your *name*?''

Shelley left the twins in charge of the store at noon and went to the camera shop. She didn't know too much about cameras herself, but the salesman who waited on her was extremely knowledgeable. She left the shop, sure she'd gotten exactly what Caroline would want for Ned, though it had cost a fair bit more than she'd thought it would.

She skipped lunch and drove over to Caroline's condo.

Caroline was delighted with the camera. And also, it developed, with the plans she had been making.

"Ned stopped by this morning to see how I was doing," she said. "I told him if he didn't have anything special on I wished he'd stop by tonight and have a Christmas Eve drink with me. Without coming out and saying so, I think I gave him the message I was feeling lonely and would really welcome his company. So he said he'd come by. I suggested around eight o'clock or so would be a good time."

When Shelley didn't respond to this, Caroline said, "Shelley... you do remember what we were discussing, don't you? About having a little birthday surprise party for Ned?''

"Yes," Shelley admitted reluctantly.

"You haven't made other plans, have you?''

"No."

"Why do I sense a problem?" Caroline asked the world at large.

"There isn't a problem, Caroline," Shelley said. "It's just..."

"Just what?"

"What makes you think Ned would welcome having a surprise party?"

"It's a risk I'm prepared to take," Caroline said. "You know, Shelley..."

"Yes?"

"I'm old enough to be your mother," Caroline said. "Matter of fact, I'd love to have you as a daughter. But...well, maybe because you aren't my daughter I'll rush in where a mother might fear to tread. You are a beautiful and wonderful girl, Shelley. I'd say you have just about everything going for you. But sometimes your caution is like a yellow warning flag. I have the impression you suddenly make up your mind to get out of the race, if you know what I'm saying. To retreat to the sidelines. And, blast it, you don't belong on the sidelines, Shelley.

"I admit," Caroline continued, with a long look at Shelley, "that it's usually easier to stay on the sidelines. Safer. But life just isn't safe, Shelley. Not if you're going to live it. Savor it to the fullest. Which is what all of us should try to do."

Caroline paused, smiled. "Shelley," she counseled, "why don't you just take a chance that maybe Ned would really love to have a surprise birthday party?"

Shelley went back to Video Vibes, having promised Caroline that she would show up at the condo by seven o'clock and bring the twins with her. They'd probably want to be home with their family later; it was Christmas Eve, after all. But she was sure that they, too, would want to celebrate Ned's birthday.

As she entered the store, she already had a strong feeling that she wouldn't find Ned there, and she was right. But before she could even go back into the office and take her coat off Brian came over to her and said, "Ned stopped by. Funny, he asked for one of those forms we have for people to fill out. You know, when a customer first comes in and wants to sign up to rent videos?"

"Did you give him one?" Shelley asked.

"Yeah. He worked over it for a while and then asked for an envelope to put it in. And then he sealed up the envelope and asked me if I'd give it to you. So," Brian finished, handing out a long white envelope, "here it is, Shelley."

Shelley took the envelope, and felt an odd, prickling sensation. Whatever Ned had put down on the form was important, she was sure it was important. Probably so important, in fact, that she wasn't sure she wanted to find out about it.

Caroline's words suddenly rose to haunt her. The courage to take risks. That, essentially, was what Caroline had been saying.

Shelley went into her office, closed the door and sat down at the little round table.

She carefully removed the form from the envelope, spread it out and started reading.

"Edward Alexander Benton, M.D.," she read. "Address: 22 Chippendale Drive, Scarsdale, NY. Temporary address: c/o James Carlson, Wampanoag Lane, Devon, MA.

"Occupation: Surgeon and Professional Wanderer. Type of videos interested in: Just about everything."

Then, very neatly, the writing continued on the back of the form. "The videos are, for me, a valid way of catching up with a lot of lost time, years in which I immersed myself in my profession to an extent that went way beyond the necessary, and the necessary far transcends most ordinary obligations, as it is.

"But in my case, I was building my own ivory tower out of medicine. Very probably, it was not a career I initially would have chosen for myself. Only now, years later, can I see that it either was, or developed into, the right career for me. Originally, I was programmed to follow in my father's footsteps. My father was a famous surgeon, far better known than I will ever be. He was also a cold, hard man, a total autocrat. He had inherited a great deal of money from the maternal side of his family. My mother died when I was born. Maybe that was what helped make my father the kind of individual I remember him to be.

"By the time he suffered a fatal coronary, I was doing my internship. I went on from there. That same year I married the daughter of our family attorney. Although Clare's mother was alive when we married, I think she and Clare's father had 'separated' long before, in the true sense of that word and lived together only to preserve appearances—one reason why I'm not that much for keeping up appearances.

"I see now that it was family ties that brought Clare and me together in the first place and subtly pressured us toward marriage. We were never meant for each other. We came to despise each other. Enough said.

"I've already admitted it was wrong of me to blame Clare for Lucy's death as I did. She too suffered, and paid, in a terrible way. For the first time I feel genuine sorrow about that.

"I don't think I need to explain why I made the decision to wander, nor why I kept wandering. Also, I think it's fairly apparent that I also was hiding behind a form of camouflage—like the tinted glasses I sense you don't like, and clothes I picked up in bargain stores that don't fit me like the tweed coat. In a certain way, the wandering and the camouflage go together. Or did."

There was one more category to be filled out. References. Ned had written, "There is only one reference I want to give. I hope she'll be willing to act as my reference. Shelley Mitchell, whom I love absolutely, completely and forever."

Shelley Mitchell, whom I love absolutely, completely, and forever. The tears were streaming down Shelley's face by the time she read that statement twice. And for once in her life she made no attempt to staunch their flow.

At seven o'clock that night, Caroline let Shelley and the twins into her apartment. The twins looked like identical Santa Clauses, each carrying stacks of brightly wrapped presents. Shelley was carefully balancing the cake she'd made, having closed the store at four o'clock that afternoon so she'd have time to go home and make it.

"If people haven't finished their Christmas shopping by now that's their fault," she told the twins.

Shelley was wearing a Christmas-red dress. Rhinestone stars dangled from her ears. A white silk gardenia nestled against her jet hair. She had never looked lovelier, and she was so nervous she couldn't sit still.

Caroline, monitoring the situation, turned on the TV to cover the sound of their voices, but she still urged Shelley and the twins to speak in low tones. Wally, she explained, wouldn't be able to make it because he'd already promised a married son he'd spend Christmas Eve with his family.

Listening to Caroline proclaiming this in a hushed, sepulchral tone, Shelley found herself wanting to break into hysterical laughter, and she could imagine the lacing she'd get from Caroline if that happened. With an effort, she suppressed a fit of giggles.

Finally, the doorbell rang. Caroline, stunning in a gold brocade caftan, herded Shelley and the twins into the kitchen, then swept to the door and opened it. Shelley heard her say, "Ned, I'm so glad you've come. Christmas Eve is no time to be alone."

"No," Ned agreed. "It isn't."

Evidently he was bestowing something upon Caroline, for Shelley heard her say, "Honestly, Ned, you shouldn't have. Red roses! My dear, how lavish can you get? I can't remember when anyone last gave me red roses."

Suddenly, the twins could contain themselves no longer. In unison, they nudged Shelley and hissed, "Come on."

The trio burst into Caroline's living room. The twins' "Happy birthday" rang out over Shelley's. She croaked the two words, and her voice failed her entirely as she saw Ned turn, saw the stunned expression on his face, and suspected the three of them had thrown him a very real curve.

Then he said, "Hey." And, again, a broad smile developing, "Hey!" He turned to Caroline. "So this is what you've had up your sleeve," he accused.

"Well..." Caroline began. "Let's call it a team effort."

"Wait a minute," the twins put in, almost simultaneously.

Brian picked up the rest of their sentence. "This was Shelley's idea in the first place," he told Ned. "She wanted us all to bust into your place. That's why I . . ."

Brian's voice trailed off and he looked guilty. Ned chuckled, "Yes," he said. "I know."

Then his eyes met Shelley's, and he sobered. "It was your idea?" he asked her.

"Well . . . it was Caroline's idea, too," she said, suddenly embarrassed and feeling as if her cheeks had just been stung by a couple of bees.

Caroline said, "Boys, do you know how to open champagne?"

"Yeah," Brian and Benny said quickly.

"Then suppose you show me," Caroline said, and led them toward the kitchen.

Alone with Ned, Shelley said, "It was Caroline's idea, honestly it was."

"Don't protest so much," Ned said with a smile. "When an idea's a good one, you should take your share of credit for it."

Before Shelley could say anything, Ned leaned toward her, peering at her hair. "Is that mistletoe you have tucked in there?" he asked her.

"No," Shelley said. "It's a gardenia. A fake gardenia but . . ."

"Do tell," Ned observed, and Shelley looked up at him suspiciously. "Well," he decided. "It's white. And Christmassy. It'll do."

Chapter Sixteen

They drank champagne, Caroline permitting the twins to have half a glass each. Caroline insisted that Shelley bring in the birthday cake. She carried it, the candles glowing as she set it down in front of Ned. She saw a trace of moisture in his eyes.

Ned, with tears in his eyes? Shaken, Shelley resumed her place at the table and watched him blow out all the candles in a single puff.

Benny immediately announced, "Bet I could guess what you wished."

"Shut up," Brian admonished his twin, and Ned chuckled.

Ned opened presents, exclaiming over each as if he'd been given one of the world's greatest treasures. Shelley had bought him a book about Cape Cod after all, so he'd always remember Devon. A tin of imported cookies, because he always seemed to be hungry. And a small, silver

Santa Claus tie tack, to remind him of playing Santa at her store party. She had wanted to give him so much more. . . .

She recalled, now, how marvelous he'd been with the kids that day. She hadn't known, then, how difficult it must have been for him to deal with small children. Yet he had seemed to love being with the kids.

One day Ned should have another child of his own, she found herself thinking.

The twins had given him several boxes of film to go with Caroline's camera, plus some oversized candy bars and some shaving cream. Ned promptly put some of the film to use, taking pictures of all of them with his new camera.

It was Benny who suggested, "Hey, Ned, how about me taking a picture of you and Shelley?"

"Sure," Ned said easily. He drew Shelley close to his side, and she tried to smile as she looked into the camera. But it occurred to her that this was probably the one and only photograph she would ever have of Ned and herself.

Then the moment came to break up the small party. Ned looked around and said, "I walked over here, but do you suppose I could bum a ride home?"

The twins looked at each other, four eyebrows raised simultaneously, and discreetly remained silent. Shelley said, "Well, er, of course. I'd be glad to take you over to your place, Ned."

At her car, Ned said, "Want me to drive? That's to say, I was wondering if we could just drive around for a little while. I need to talk to you, Shelley. Not at your place or mine. On neutral territory."

Shelley nodded, not quite trusting her voice. Was this to be goodbye? He'd promised her he wouldn't leave without saying goodbye, hadn't he?

To her surprise, Ned drove across the Cape to the ocean side, and parked at a high spot atop dunes overlooking the shimmering North Atlantic.

He shut off the motor and, into the stillness, said quietly, "Looking at the sea is like looking at the stars. So much vastness, so much space. It puts things in perspective, at least it always has for me. Any time I've tended to get carried away with my own importance—and sometimes surgeons do, you know—all I've needed to do was look at the sky or the sea."

He turned, and in a quick switch that took Shelley by surprise asked, "Did you get the form I filled out?"

"Yes," she said.

"Any more questions?" he persisted.

"No," she said. She hesitated, then added, "I think you pretty much said it all."

"Did I? I wanted to. There were gaps to fill in. I wanted to fill them in as quickly, as succinctly as possible, Shelley. So that we can stop going in reverse and start moving forward. Do you agree with that?"

He was leaning back as he said this, keeping a deliberate distance between them. He knew that if he so much as touched Shelley, he couldn't trust himself to remain levelheaded. He said, "There's just one more thing."

"What's that?"

"I thought of taking a form for you to fill out," he told her. Then added, "But it was your store, after all."

"Are you saying that I was the one to make all the rules, Ned?"

"Not exactly, But, yes, in a sense. This is your place, you live by your rules. I think maybe we have a few differences of opinion where those rules are concerned. On the other hand, I'm willing to negotiate.''

Shelley said carefully, "I don't think you need to negotiate, Ned.''

"Oh?''

"What I mean," she said, "is that I've done my share of thinking and...I think I understand why you've done everything you've done and why you are the way you are and why you want to be free with the kind of freedom wandering gives you. And...''

"Whoa," Ned interrupted. "Wait a minute. I'm not sure I like the sound of that.''

"Why not?''

"I have the feeling you're dismissing me, Shelley. I don't want to be dismissed.''

"I'm not dismissing you," she said, shaking her head slightly so that the rhinestones dangling from her ears glittered with star-like brightness. "I just know that you don't want anything or anyone to hold you down again and I...I'll go along with that.''

Shelley drew a long breath. This wasn't easy for her. Slowly, she said, "The other day you asked me to...to go on a holiday with you. To the tropics. Paradise, I think you said. Well, Ned, I want to go to paradise with you.''

Ned stared at her. "Am I hearing what I'm hearing?'' he demanded.

"Yes," Shelley said steadily. "I love you...but I'll never try to hold you down. Personally, I think you have a God-given talent for medicine, but what you do about that has to be your decision. Meantime, I can't say how long I could wander with you, Ned. I know I could not be that kind of free spirit forever. But to go as far as paradise for a while...''

"Sweetheart," Ned said, "we're not going to paradise just for a while. We're going to paradise forever. Wherever we are, wherever we go, it'll be paradise. Some tropical oasis to begin with, yes. Soon . . . and for a honeymoon, I hope. But then . . . you're right, Shelley. Medicine is a big part of my life and though I blocked that out for a time it's come home to haunt me again. But being a doctor's wife can be difficult and demanding, I warn you. You may consider me a totally selfish bastard when I'm up to my forehead in my work and I don't seem to know anything or anyone else exists. But, I do swear one thing to you, Shelley. For me, you'll always be first. Life without you would be far blacker than the sky with no moon and no stars."

Shelley discovered she was holding her breath, and couldn't answer him.

Ned looked at her and said desperately, "Please. Say something, will you? Shelley, I wouldn't ask you to give up your own career. You could put Caroline in charge of Video Vibes and maybe open Video Vibes II in New York or wherever else we may be living. I'd like you to take your house back from your tenants when their lease is up, so we could have it for ourselves, a place where we could escape whenever we got the chance to do so. That, in its own way, is a form of wandering, sweetheart.

"Oh, God," Ned said helplessly when she still didn't answer him, "I never expected to feel like this again. I've never really felt like this before, for that matter. I have so many plans. So many plans. But you're at the core of all of them. Without you, they're just so much dust. Shelley, will you for God's sake say something?"

Shelley said softly, "I just found my own star."

"What?" Ned demanded.

"That star up there," Shelley said. "I have the feeling it's winking at me. So I made a wish."

It was uncanny, Ned thought. It was as if she'd been with him last night, standing on the beach looking up at the sky, making his own wish.

"What did you wish?" he asked her huskily.

"I think you know," Shelley told him.

Ned knew, but he made her speak her wish anyway. And it was everything he wanted to hear.

*   *   *   *   *

Silhouette Classics

COMING IN APRIL...

THORNE'S WAY by Joan Hohl

When *Thorne's Way* first burst upon the romance scene in 1982, readers couldn't help but fall in love with Jonas Thorne, a man of bewildering arrogance and stunning tenderness. This book quickly became one of Silhouette's most sought-after early titles.

Now, Silhouette Classics is pleased to present the reissue of *Thorne's Way*. Even if you read this book years ago, its depth of emotion and passion will stir your heart again and again.

And that's not all!

Silhouette Special Edition

COMING IN JULY...

THORNE'S WIFE by Joan Hohl

We're pleased to announce a truly unique event at Silhouette. Jonas Thorne is back, in *Thorne's Wife*, a sequel that will sweep you off your feet! Jonas and Valerie's story continues as life—and love—reach heights never before dreamed of.

Experience both these timeless classics—one from Silhouette Classics and one from Silhouette Special Edition—as master storyteller Joan Hohl weaves two passionate, dramatic tales of everlasting love!